G8

Also by Mike Brogan

Business to Kill For

Dead Air

Madison's Avenue

G8

A suspense thriller

Mike Brogan

Lighthouse

This book is a work of fiction. Names, characters, businesses, organizations, places, events and incidents either are the product of the author's imagination or are used fictitiously. Any resemblance to actual persons, living or dead, events or locales is entirely coincidental.

ISBN 978-0-9846173-0-2 (Hardcover)

Library of Congress Control Number 2013952635

Printed in the United States of America
Published in the United States by Lighthouse Publishing

Cover design: Vong Lee

First Edition

For Marcie, Brendan, Chloe, Jay,
and Ms. Brogan Dolata who's almost six.

ACKNOWLEDGMENTS

To all my European colleagues, all you Belgian, French, English, Dutch, Italian, Scandinavian and German folks... who provided me with the background and knowledge to make this story possible... and for teaching this naive American the mysterious ways of Europe.

To my writing pals: Four-time Shamus Award winner Loren D. Estleman, and distinguished writers like Pete Barlow, Phil Rosette, Len Charla, Jim O'Keefe, Annick Hivert Carthew, and gracious friends like John and Mary Ann Verdi-Hus – your helpful suggestions and guidance have made this story better. To Rebecca M. Lyles for her excellent, thoughtful editorial assistance and guidance.

And finally, to the late Elmore Leonard who advised me to spend a lot of time with the bad guys. I've tried to do that in *G8*.

ONE

BRUSSELS, BELGIUM

Katill hid behind a thick oak tree in the *Forêt de Soignes*. He watched the lights go out in the master bedroom upstairs. Donovan Rourke and his wife, Emma, were going to sleep for the night.

Only one would wake up.

Two hours later, Katill pulled down his mask and climbed a rope to the second floor balcony. The balcony doors, as expected, were unlocked. He checked his suppressed Glock, stepped inside and walked past an exquisite Louis XV desk and an antique mahogany china cabinet. The scent of lemon curry lingered in the air.

He walked down to the master bedroom and entered. Moonlight filtered through the lace curtains onto a human shape in the large bed. *One* shape. Female. Emma.

Where is Donovan Rourke? I was told he was here! Most unfortunate. So... Plan B.

He moved to the bed and stared down at the woman. Attractive face... inviting body.

Her eyes began to move beneath the lids. She seemed to sense his presence. He leaned closer. Her eyes opened, then her mouth. His hand muffled her scream.

Fighting back hard, she reached up and yanked his mask off and looked at his face. He was shocked! No one had ever seen him as he worked! Enraged, he slashed her neck with his knife. Her eyes widened as she realized what he'd done. He watched blood pump from her severed arteries.

And moments later, he watched life drain from her eyes.

Noise. Behind him.

Donovan Rourke?

Stahl spun around. No one. He hurried down the hall, accidentally knocking the Mickey Mouse nightlight from the socket. The nightlight was next to a door marked *TISH* in big sparkling letters. The door was open. He looked in.

Standing beside her bed, staring at him, was a young girl, maybe four. Old enough to remember.

She saw his face.

And maybe what he'd done.

TWO

MANHATTAN

"Who's Fuzz… ?" Donovan Rourke asked on his cell phone as he sat in *Heltberg's Bar*, sipping his second beer.

"BUZZ!" Tish said.

"Oh… "

"Buzz Lightyear!"

"Who's he?"

"He's a space ranger!"

"Wow!"

"And he's at Macy's. Can we please go get him?"

"Hmmmmmm… "

"Tonight, *please*?"

"Hmmmmmm… Well, okay."

Her squeal might have injured his eardrum.

After hanging up, Donovan admitted yet again that he was a pushover when it came to his beautiful, five-year-old daughter. Tish was the love of his life. He'd do almost anything to make her happy, *and* help make up for the loss of her mother.

Donovan looked around the bar. Some New York University students drinking pitchers of beer. A businessman nursing his third scotch. A fat guy sleeping on a barstool who hadn't moved a muscle in thirty minutes. The guy could be dead.

Dead like Benny Ahrens, Donovan thought. Benny, his friend, was killed because of a piece of paper. The same paper Donovan now held in his own hand.

A cute, green-haired waitress walked by and winked at him. He smiled back and figured he must not look too bad for a thirty-four-year-old guy who'd spent the last ten years of his life avoiding people trying to end it.

So far, no bullet scars above the neck. Four limbs that worked. The family jewels intact. And a six-foot-two inch frame that could still run five miles in thirty-six minutes, and even faster if he was being shot at, which was quite likely because of the paper in his hand.

Green Hair placed a bowl of roasted peanuts on his table.

"Peace," she said, winking and sashaying away.

And may Benny Ahrens rest in peace.

Yesterday, Benny, a Mossad agent, had discovered the deadly note. The message on it was written in some ancient cryptic symbols that meant absolutely nothing to Donovan.

But meant death to Benny. And Donovan feared it could mean death to Professor Sohan Singh who was meeting Donovan here in twenty-five minutes, unless Donovan phoned him and told him not to come.

But Donovan had strict orders – *Give the message to Singh. He's our best shot at translating it.* And orders must always be followed, right?

Wrong. There's a time to screw orders. Like when his gut told him to. Like now. He pulled out his phone, dialed Sohan's cell and was bounced into voice mail and left a message saying, "Sohan, everything worked out. We don't need your help now. But thanks anyway. I'll call you later."

It bothered Donovan that he lied so easily. But then his job paid him to lie.

As he hung up, the bar door opened. A strong blast of Manhattan bus fumes swept in... along with Professor Sohan Singh, twenty minutes early. Singh, a slender, well-dressed man in his early sixties looked around and smiled at Donovan.

Donovan waved his former NYU French professor over. They shook hands and sat at the table.

"So," Singh said, "you're going to beg me for another racquetball rematch?"

Donovan smiled. "I'm going to beg you to walk back out of this bar."

Singh stared back.

"This thing is too risky, Sohan."

"A translation thing?"

"Yeah."

Singh glanced down at the note in Rourke's hand.

"Would that be the translation thing?"

"It would."

Donovan scanned the bar and made sure no one was paying attention to them. No one was.

"Sohan... this note is deadly."

Green Hair appeared. Singh ordered a Heineken and seconds later she set a frosty bottle in front of him.

"Why so deadly?"

"We don't know yet. But my Mossad friend was just killed a mile from here because of it. He intercepted the message and told me it was very serious and very urgent. The NSA cryptographers are at a loss to translate it. They're convinced the symbols are some very ancient Middle Eastern language. They say you can translate it much faster than they ever will."

Singh sipped his beer.

"But Sohan, trust me, this note is – "

"Hazardous to my buns?"

"Very."

"And one's buns are still pro-choice, right?

Donovan nodded.

"And this note is important to our country's security?"

"Benny Ahrens said it was."

"So give me the damn message or I'll bore you again with amazing but true saga of how my poor dear mother scrubbed floors on a Calcutta steamer coming to this land of the unwashed masses yearning to be free."

As Donovan started to protest again, Singh snatched the paper from his hand and began studying it. Singh sipped some beer. A drop splashed onto the message, but he didn't seem to notice. Donovan studied his former professor. Still scholarly and relaxed. Maybe a bit more gray around the temples, another crinkle around the eyes, an extra liver spot on his hand. His brown tweed sports coat matched his turtleneck. And his pipe ashes, as usual, had sprinkled onto his Hush Puppies.

Donovan worried that Singh was helping.

But then the CIA paid Donovan to worry. And lie. And get shot at.

"The NSA is right," Singh said.

"Very old symbols?"

"Old as dirt. In fact, they were first written in dirt. I'm quite certain they're Sumarian, maybe Mesopotamian. Around 3,500 B.C. Each cuneiform pictogram, or mark and symbol represents a word."

Can you translate it?"

"Depends… "

"On what?"

"On whether certain symbols are in some old books at my apartment. Which reminds me, I have to get back there. My daughter, you remember Maccabee, she's coming in from Princeton tonight and I promised to cook dinner. I'll call you as soon as I have something."

Donovan nodded and remembered Singh's daughter. Singh had been incredibly proud of her when she followed his footsteps and became a professor of foreign languages.

"How is Maccabee?"

Singh smiled. "Beautiful, and smart like me."

* * *

"Dumb like you!" whispered Milan Slavitch, a thickset man, sitting in a dark blue Toyota van ten feet from *Heltberg's Bar*. He'd listened to Rourke's conversation with Singh through a laser eavesdropping device that picked up their voice vibrations from the bar's window.

Slavitch sipped absinthe from a silver flask, then rubbed the flask down his five-inch facial scar, the relic of a Serbian bayonet. The man who held the bayonet died quickly when Slavitch slit his neck with a razor-sharp Yemeni jambiya dagger.

He punched in a number on his cell phone, relayed what he'd overheard and hung up.

Moments later, Rourke and Singh stepped outside the bar and got in a taxi.

Slavitch followed in the van. Singh was dropped off in front of a five-story brownstone on 73rd Street and went inside. The taxi drove off with Rourke.

Slavitch parked, but as he started to get out, a woman and two small kids walked out and began playing in front of Singh's apartment. Slavitch decided to wait.

A half hour later they left.

Slavitch shoved a fifteen round magazine into his prized Croatian Army Beretta that he'd smuggled into the states years ago.

He got out of the van and strolled toward Singh's apartment building.

THREE

"It's Gramma Anna time!" Donovan said, closing his laptop in his small East 83rd Street apartment.

Smiling, Tish grabbed her new Buzz Lightyear and ran to the door. At times, her robin-egg blue eyes, thick brown hair and especially her smile reminded him of Emma so much it hurt.

Outside, they took a taxi. On the way, Tish played with her new Buzz Lightyear. He smiled as he watched her. Tish was the best part of his day. And his life. He marveled at how much better she was doing compared to the first weeks after Emma's death. Back then, she'd often stare at her mother's picture for minutes on end.

Sometimes she had nightmares that 'the mean man who hurt mommy, might come back for me.' And when she asked him, "Why did the mean man make mommy go to heaven?" Donovan could not tell her the real reason.

Because of me.

Still, each week she seemed a little better. And having Emma's wonderful mother, Anna, nearby was a godsend for Tish, and for him.

After dropping Tish off, he returned home and microwaved some not-so-lean-cuisine, a cheese-laden lasagna. He popped the lid on an icy Killian's Red and plunked down in his Laz-E-Boy to watch the Yankees-Tigers game. His phone rang. Caller ID flashed *Sohan Singh*.

"My favorite professor!"

"Lady Luck is with us," Singh said. "My books have most of the ancient Sumerian symbols and logograms in your cryptic message."

"You're amazing."

"No, the *Sumerians* were. Around 5,000 years ago, they were scratching these logograms and pictograms into mud tablets on the banks of the Tigris. They created the world's first known full-fledged written language. Fortunately, your message has only about thirty words. So give me a few more minutes and I'll phone the translation to you."

"Don't phone it."

"Why not?"

"The bad guys have very sophisticated listening devices."

"I'll e-mail it... ."

"The bad guys have too many sophisticated hackers."

"How about an unsophisticated fax?"

"Same bad guy problem. How about I pick it up in twenty minutes or so?"

"Works for me."

"Thanks, professor. What would we do without you?"

"Weep and gnash your teeth?"

"This is true."

Minutes later, Donovan stepped from his brownstone into warm, humid night air. Thick gray clouds, like wads of steel wool, were rolling in from the West. He heard the distant rumble of thunder and sensed rain coming. He liked how rain cleaned the city streets and left them smelling fresh. Too bad it didn't also clean the terrorists off Manhattan's streets.

He flagged down a taxi, gave Singh's address to the thin Haitian driver and they drove off.

Donovan's thoughts turned to Sohan. Over the last seven years, the man's translations had helped the CIA prevent two terrorist attacks in Germany, a Metro bombing in Paris, and a nerve gas release at a Los Angeles amusement park. He spoke twelve languages fluently, plus some obscure ones like South American Amerindian and Navajo. His linguistic gifts were a national treasure.

Minutes later, the cab stopped in front of Singh's brownstone building.

Donovan got out and waved to Ned, the friendly doorman, who buzzed him in. Donovan looked around the charming 1930s lobby, a pleasing blend of gleaming Italian marble, crystal chandeliers and Carpathian burled elm walls. He took the elevator up and walked down to Singh's fifth-floor apartment. He paused when he saw the door slightly ajar. Maybe Ned called Sohan and he left it open for him.

Donovan stepped inside.

"Sohan... it's Donovan."

Nothing.

He looked around.

"Sohan... ?"

Still no response. His pulse kicked up a notch as he walked through the foyer to Singh's study. He was surprised to see copies of *Translation Journal* scattered across the beige carpet. Singh was a very tidy man.

Then something else on the carpet caught Donovan's eye - specks of tobacco sprinkled like a column of ants over to Singh's pipe.

Donovan hurried over.

And saw a foot behind the sofa.

Heart pounding, he looked behind the sofa and saw his friend Sohan lying on his back in a pool of blood draining from the large bullet hole in his head.

Donovan yanked out his gun, swept the room. No one.

He felt Singh's neck, but couldn't detect a pulse. His skin was still warm. Donovan began pumping Singh's chest, praying for a heartbeat.

He jerked the phone off the desk and called 911.

"An ambulance is on the way," the operator promised. "Keep doing CPR and stay on the line."

He placed the receiver down nearby and continued CPR. He listened to Singh's chest, but the only heart he heard was his own.

As he pushed down, again and again, Donovan's anger rose. Anger at himself for involving Singh. Anger at his CIA bosses and the NSA for insisting that he ask for Singh's help. Anger at himself for not grabbing the note back after Singh grabbed it. And mostly anger at the shooter and whoever overheard them at the bar.

Outside, an ambulance siren wound to a stop. Seconds later, paramedics rattled the gurney into the apartment and over to Singh's body. Within seconds, they attached the defibrillator pads to his chest.

Donovan backed away, searching their faces for hope, seeing the opposite.

"Clear!" shouted a short muscular paramedic. "Hit it!"

Singh's body bolted up, then fell, but the monitor's green line remained flat. They tried again. And again. The line didn't budge. Donovan sensed it was too late.

But was it too late for his translation?

Donovan looked around for the ancient Sumerian language books Sohan had mentioned, but didn't see them. He checked the numerous bookshelves, then looked for notes, a clue, any hint of the translation. Nothing. The assassin had probably taken it and his books.

"Three sixty," said the attendant. "Clear!"

Singh's body jerked up and down again. The green line stayed flat.

Donovan walked behind the desk and looked at the computer.

The screen showed Singh's desktop page. He clicked on *Recent Documents*. The most recent was titled *DR*. My initials? He clicked on *DR* and a document flashed on the screen:

> *Donovan, here's the translation:*
> *"Medusa proceeds. Katill will deliver the*
> *heads of all eight serpents in the sixth moon*
> *(June) in the land of the Far Northwest.*

25 million received. 25 million more upon delivery."

> *P.S. Donovan, what the Sumerians called 'the land of the Far Northwest', we call Europe.*

The message had about thirty words. Just as Sohan said.

'Medusa proceeds?' Donovan's mind raced with questions. Wasn't Medusa a Greek monster? A female with snakes for hair? Yes. And wasn't her head cut off? Yes. But who is Katill? And whose heads is he cutting off?

Donovan reviewed the facts. Sohan Singh and Benny Ahrens were just killed by someone linked to someone named Katill... an assassin planning to kill eight people in Europe in June.

This is June.

What's going on in Europe in June? He recalled concerts in London, some jazz festivals in Holland, the Spring Festival in Munich, the *Tour de France*. But these events involved thousands of people. Who were the eight serpents targeted to be killed? Europeans? Israelis? Americans?

He started pacing. He racked his brain for what else was taking place this month in Europe? On the coffee table, he saw hardcover books. *Paris, City of Light... Irish Castles... Amsterdam, the City and Her History... and Brussels, The New Heart of Europe.*

Eight people... ?

He stopped and looked back at the Brussels book. He looked at the cover. A beautiful photo of the city's famous square, the *Grand Place*. Something was happening on the *Grand Place*, he recalled. What was it?

Then it hit him like a hockey puck in the throat. He slumped down into a chair.

The G8 Summit! Eight heads of state!

It was being held in Brussels in a few days, in the sixth month, June. *Eight* of the most powerful leaders in the world, would attend!

And so it seemed would an assassin named Katill.

Donovan checked the desk calendar and blinked. The G8 Summit started in three days!

He told himself to calm down. G8 assassination threats happen each year. He'd worked security on two G8 Summits before. Security is massive, virtually impossible to breach. Nearly a billion dollars are spent to build sophisticated walls of physical, electronic and human security around the G8 leaders. The inner wall was virtually impenetrable.

But was it?

Today, assassins like Katill and groups like Al Qaeda could choose from a candy store of advanced weapons: explosives, biological, chemical, and radiological.

The EMS paramedic walked over to him. "Sorry sir, there was nothing we could do."

Donovan nodded, then slumped into a chair as they put their defibrillator paddles back in the case. He felt nauseated as he looked at the ashen face of his good friend lying in a pool of blood.

Blood, I spilled.

Like I spilled the blood of Emma.

FOUR

D onovan stared down at his dead friend. *I should have grabbed the damn note back from you, Sohan! The NSA could have probably translated it - hopefully in time!*

Donovan's guilt grew faster than the pool of blood around his friend.

Using a safe phone, Donovan had just called in Singh's translation to Bob Rosiek, Director of the Counter Terrorism Center at CIA Headquarters in Langley, Virginia. Rosiek was devastated to hear of Sohan's death – *and* shocked to learn of the plot to assassinate the G8 world leaders in days.

After briefing Rosiek, Donovan called in the NYPD and minutes later a Lieutenant Clark arrived. Donovan presented his credentials and explained that Singh was most likely murdered for helping the Agency on national security. Donovan did not mention the translation. The fewer who knew about the G8 plot, the better.

The CSI team began working the crime scene. As they did, Donovan walked over to the fireplace mantle. He stared at a family photo of Sohan Singh, his deceased wife, Moira, and their daughter, Maccabee. They were standing outside Macy's at Christmas time, smiling, their arms filled with shopping bags. Maccabee's next Christmas would be difficult for her.

Donovan suddenly remembered that Sohan said Maccabee was arriving here tonight.

I can't let her walk in here.

Donovan hurried over to Singh's desk, flipped open a directory and found Maccabee's phone number. His hand trembling, he dialed. The phone clicked into voice mail and he hung up. This was not a subject for voice mail. He saw the number for Sohan's sister, Helen Singh, and dialed it.

She answered on the second ring.

"Hello."

"Helen… this is Donovan Rourke."

"Donovan, what a nice surprise. It's been far too long, young man. How are you?"

Devastated. "Not good, Helen… "

As he told her what happened, Helen began to weep. He whispered how sorry he was and listened to her cry as his own eyes teared up. After regaining some composure, she said she'd let him know about funeral arrangements. Then, to his great relief, she said she would tell Maccabee, expected at her apartment any minute.

He hung up and thought of Maccabee. The last time he'd seen her was at her mother's funeral a few years ago. The tall, attractive young woman was twenty-four-years old and had just earned her doctorate from Princeton. Now, she was a full professor of Indo-European languages and her father could not have been prouder. A few months later, Donovan recalled, she'd been devastated when her fiancé died mysteriously. Now, she would be very much alone, except for her Aunt Helen.

Donovan looked across Central Park at the skyscraper lights. Shimmering stalagmites poking up into the black sky. So many people behind the lights. *Living* people, some making plans, some making dinner, some making love…

… and some making innocent people dead.

Donovan looked back down at his friend's body and made him a promise: *Sohan, I will get the man who did this, and those behind the man.*

Outside, he got into a taxi. His Agency training made him check for anyone paying special attention to him. No one was.

Five turns later, someone was. Two men in a dark Toyota van had made the same six turns as the taxi.

"Turn left here," Donovan said.

"Sure thing."

The van turned left.

"The dark Toyota van behind us is following me."

The driver checked the rearview mirror. "You wan' I should lose 'em?"

"No, just act like we don't know he's following and head south toward Bryant Park."

Bryant Park was near Donovan's office, the CIA anti-terrorism Manhattan bureau. He flipped open his secure phone and dialed his office.

Special Agent Judy Kaufman answered. "Hi Donovan, what's up?"

"Judy, I've got a dark Toyota van following my taxi. We're on Columbus Avenue heading south. I'm going to draw them down toward the bureau. Can you get someone on - ?"

"Hang on - Bart just walked in. What color's the van?"

"Dark *blue*, I think. Two men in front."

"License?"

"It's doctored. Can't read it."

All of a sudden, the Toyota van raced up close behind the Donovan's taxi. The passenger stuck a gun out the window and fired. Two bullets ripped into the taxi's trunk.

"Son of a bitch!" the driver shouted, flooring the gas pedal.

Donovan hated shooting in crowds, but he hand no choice. He pulled out his Glock, leaned out the window and fired back at the van's passenger.

The bullet shot off the van's passenger-side mirror.

The van slowed to a stop, paused a few seconds, then turned and raced down a side street.

"Judy, the guy in the van just shot at us! I shot back, knocked off the passenger-side mirror. The van bolted west on 45th. Bart in his car yet?"

"He's just driving out of the garage!"

Rourke pressed his badge and eight twenties on the taxi's partition glass. "The money's yours if you can track that van!"

The driver looked at the money, nodded, then hung a fast u-turn and sped off after the van. They raced past two city busses and a Budweiser truck and shot down 45th.

Donovan saw no blue Toyota vans.

He glanced down side streets. No blue vans.

They headed down another street, then another.

No luck.

"Turn right."

The taxi careened around the corner and he saw only cars, trucks and busses.

They searched for three more minutes without success.

"Bastard's gone!" the taxi driver said. "Probably shot through the Lincoln Tunnel or pulled into a garage."

Donovan nodded, then stuffed the eight twenties into the pay slot. The driver earned it, considering he had risked his life and broken most city traffic violations at least twice.

"Hey, thanks mister!"

"Sure." He picked up his phone. "Judy… ?"

"Bart's heading down 45th. He's got two other cars searching. We'll let you know."

"Okay."

As they drove back toward his apartment, Donovan realized he was now locked in the crosshairs of a major assassination plot.

Washington would go nuts trying to find out who was behind it.

———

A blur of briefings, meetings, committees, joint task forces from the National Intelligence Center, CIA, FBI, NSA, Homeland Security and Secret Service, each spinning their needs and perspectives as *the* priority. And in Brussels there would be the eight presidential secret service contingents adamant about the security of their leader, while the Belgian authorities would be adamant about maintaining overall G8 security responsibility.

On top of that there was Interpol and God knows how many others to coordinate and placate - one major police pissing contest in which many egos would get damp.

Thank God he was in the domestic division these days. The CIA and other agencies already had experienced operatives in Brussels assigned to the G8. And while he loved the city and its people, he had no desire to reignite painful memories of Emma's murder there.

That memory always reminded him that he hated certain consequences of his job. Consequences like death.

He hated that Sohan was dead because of him. Hated that Emma was dead because of him. Hated that Tish was growing up without her mother because of him. Hated that the Agency's strict secrecy requirements often destabilized marriages. Including his. Hated it enough that he was still considering whether to leave the Agency and join the normal world.

He thought back to when he'd missed Tish's second birthday party. When he hadn't phoned home, Emma became hysterical over not knowing where he was. He hadn't phoned her because he was chained to a pole in a garbage-strewn Teheran basement teeming with rats. When he'd escaped and returned home, she understood, but laid down the law. She said that with future assignments, he had to give her *some* idea of how to reach him or someone who could. He'd agreed.

She also asked him to try avoiding those assignments that were very likely to make her a widow with a young daughter. He'd promised to try, and he did.

But five months later, the job made *him* a widower with a young daughter.

Donovan's Company safe-phone buzzed and he answered.

"Rosiek."

"You brief the brass?" Donovan asked.

"Yeah. We're gathering info on this guy, Katill. We need you here in Washington tomorrow morning."

"You already know everything I know."

"But Director Madigan himself wants you to brief him."

Donovan wondered why Charles Michael Madigan, the Director of National Intelligence, whom he'd known when Madigan headed the CIA, wanted him there?

"I'll phone Madigan."

"He wants you here in person."

Donovan breathed out slowly. One didn't say no to Michael Madigan, unless one was brain damaged or independently wealthy.

"Donovan… ?"

"Yeah. I'll be there."

FIVE

B ob Rosiek hung up from Donovan Rourke. Rosiek was worried about his friend.

Donovan Rourke was the most capable candidate he'd ever trained at The Farm, the CIA's training facility in Virginia.

And maybe the most eager to join the Agency. After graduating with a Masters in foreign languages from the University of Michigan, Rourke had applied at the CIA. When Rosiek asked him why he wanted to join the clandestine service, Donovan said, 'To find the terrorists who killed my parents and eight other innocent people in a explosion near London's Victoria Station. And to help protect our country against future terrorist acts.'

Donovan's parents died when he was a senior in college, and according to friends, their death sent him into a deep and prolonged depression. His depression soon turned to a kind of vengeful anger that he channeled into his CIA work. Soon his Agency work gave him new meaning, new purpose in life. He focused less on his pain and more on those who caused it.

But today, Rosiek knew, Donovan carried a more recent pain. The loss of his wife, Emma. A deep, chronic malaise his colleagues said he couldn't shake. He didn't socialize much, didn't date, didn't form many close relationships outside the office.

Which is why Rosiek always asked him about little Tish. It was the only time Donovan's eyes lit up.

But tomorrow, Rosiek knew, Donovan's eyes would dim like a snuffed candle.

***

Donovan's driver dropped him at the entrance to the CIA Head-quarters in the wooded hills of Langley, Virginia. Donovan had arrived to brief Director of National Intelligence, Michael Madigan.

He stepped outside and watched the steamy summer air smooth the wrinkles from his grey suit.

He walked under the arched entrance and into the reception area. As always, he paused a moment to pay homage to the black stars on the memorial wall, each star dedicated to an unnamed CIA officer who'd given his or her life for the country. He felt stars should be added for Benny Ahrens and Sohan Singh even though they weren't official Company people.

Donovan cleared the security guards and electronic gates, and strolled along the familiar, gleaming marble floor.

One minute later, a young trainee escorted him toward the visiting office of Michael Madigan, Director of National Intelligence, a cabinet level post.

Madigan's main office was in the nearby NIC building, but he regularly visited all his intelligence fiefdoms: the CIA, NSA, Pentagon's DIA, FBI and all his other groups. He liked to remind everyone to share information, and butt-kick when they didn't. Normally, Dono-van's immediate boss, CIA Director Anthony Breen, would attend this meeting, but Breen was already in Brussels preparing for the G8.

Madigan's long-time assistant, Greta, smiled at Donovan and gestured for him to enter the Director's office. Donovan walked in and plowed his way though cumulus clouds of cigar smoke toward Madigan who'd justified his smoking by installing at his own cost a ceiling exhaust fan that managed to suck up maybe half of his cigar smoke.

Madigan, on the phone, waved Donovan to a chair opposite him. The Director, an ex all-Big-Ten defensive linebacker, was fifty-eight, six-feet-four, two hundred-forty pounds and still looked like he could suit up for a game. A handsome man, his dark blue eyes were framed by ruddy skin and thick black-grey hair combed straight back.

Madigan hung up and looked at him.

"Sit back, Donovan. Relax! Lost a little weight?"

Same old Madigan. Two directives and a question in one breath.

"Lost a few pounds, sir."

Madigan nodded, then his eyes saddened. "Our good friend Sohan lost everything!"

"Benny Ahrens, too," Donovan said.

"We are deeply indebted to both men. Jesus, I can't believe they're dead!"

Donovan said nothing.

Madigan puffed out another shaft of cigar smoke and watched most of it head up toward the ventilation fan. "NSA agrees with Sohan's translation. This asshole, Katill, plans to wipe out the G8 leaders in Brussels in the next few days."

"Any background on this assassin, Katill?"

"Not yet. But we're coordinating with the Belgian Security people and the national security teams protecting each leader. Plus Interpol, MI6, DGSE, BND, all the national spook groups. Gonna be a real bitch-slappin' hand-holding assignment with everyone claiming he's suckin' hind tit!"

"A delicate balancing act."

"And that's why we need you over there!"

Donovan felt like he'd been punched in the chest. *Over there meant…* Brussels… and the most painful memory in his life.

"I know it might be difficult for you, but you worked and lived there. Know how to get things done. You know the secret service security people from each country. You know the Belgian Security people. And you're friends with the Belgian director of their Security Intelligence Division, the counter-terrorism group. What's his name, Johnnie WaWa... ."

"Jean de Waha."

"Yeah, him."

"But I'm not up to speed on this Summit."

"The enemy's up to speed on *you!* Tried to shoot your ass dead in that taxi last night!"

Word travelled fast.

"But you already have qualified operatives in Brussels."

"Yeah, but your boss, Director Breen, wants you. And I want you, Donovan. So does Jean de Waha. He says you're the only guy he trusts to work with him on this."

"I'm flattered, but – "

Madigan's phone rang. He picked up, listened a few moments, then nodded. "Be happy to."

Madigan covered the phone with bratwurst-sized fingers. "White House Chief of Staff says the President wants to talk with you."

The President?

Donovan realized he'd been *Madiganned*. The Director had arranged for the President to phone at this time. William Colasanti, first Italian-American president, was a highly-successful straight-talking former CEO who'd terrified Washington fat cats with his frightening new strategy: *cut government fat.* A day after his election, slimy bureaucrats and silk-suited lobbyists were seen slithering under the nearest rocks. Donovan liked the man and his no-nonsense policies.

Madigan punched the speaker button.

"Mr. Rourke, it's a pleasure to talk with you," President Colasanti said.

"Thank you, Mr. President."

"I've read your file. You've served our country with great distinction. And for that I'd like to thank you on behalf of our citizens. Let me also commend you for uncovering this G8 plot."

"Actually, Mr. President, my friends uncovered the plot. And they were both killed because of it."

"Yes, I just heard. Most unfortunate. Our country will honor them soon."

"Thank you, sir."

"The President cleared his throat. "Now, Director Madigan tells me that he and your boss, and the Belgian G8 security director all feel that you are right man to head up our security for the Summit." The President paused a moment. "But I also learned that you lost your wife in Brussels a while back."

Donovan was shocked that the President knew this detail. "Yes, sir... ."

"Please accept my belated condolences."

"Thank you, sir."

"And if you feel that returning to Brussels would prove too difficult for you, please feel free to decline this assignment."

Donovan wanted to decline the assignment, but he sensed the President's grave concern about the G8 plot. "Mr. President, this threat is serious. My two good friends just died because of it. I'd like to help make sure they didn't die in vain."

"I understand."

"And I'm honored you've asked me. I'll do my best, sir."

"Thank you, Mr. Rourke. The President paused. "Gentlemen, this G8 Summit is critical. Our nations face serious problems: terrorism, trade wars, banking failures, global economic recessions, pandemic diseases, racial genocide, famine in Africa and more. This G8 is more than a photo op. We need to find solutions!"

"I understand, sir."

"But, if you and your security colleagues feel the threat from this plot is simply too great, let us know. We might be able to curtail the itinerary, or change some venues, or possibly even postpone."

"I'll let you know, sir."

"Thank you. And good luck, Mr. Rourke."

"Thank you, Mr. President," Madigan said, as they hung up.

Director Madigan walked over to a small bar, poured two tumblers of Glenfiddich and handed one to Donovan.

They clicked glasses and sipped some.

The single malt scotch tasted great and Donovan realized that if he were alone, he'd knock back another big scotch or maybe four. He knew he'd been drinking too much since Emma's death. He also knew he had to get control of the situation.

The intercom buzzed. "Mr. Jean de Waha from Brussels is on the line," Greta said.

"Interesting timing," Donovan said with a smile.

Madigan smiled back and punched a speaker button.

"Director de Waha, this is Mike Madigan with Donovan Rourke. Donovan will be arriving in Brussels tomorrow."

"That's good to hear Director Madigan. Hello, Donovan?"

"Hey, Jean. And thanks for roping me into this thing."

De Waha chuckled. "You're welcome."

Donovan paused. "This Katill, ever heard of him?"

De Waha went silent for several seconds, too long, like maybe he was stalling to frame his answer.

"Katill's a codename," de Waha said softly. "Katill means 'assassin' or 'killer' in Arabic. His birth name is Valek Stahl, but he uses several aliases, like Axel Braun and others."

Donovan sensed that de Waha was still holding something back. "Jean... ?"

"Yeah?"

"What else?"

De Waha took a breath. "Donovan... I'm sorry to tell you, but we've just learned that Katill was identified as being in the *Forêt de Soignes* behind your apartment the night Emma... " His voice grew faint. "We have video of him in a hardware buying the rope he used to climb to your balcony. Katill murdered Emma."

Donovan felt like ice had been pumped into his veins.

———

32

He squeezed his whiskey glass hard enough to break it.

Director Madigan, clearly as surprised by the news as Donovan, turned and locked his eyes locked on Donovan. No one spoke for several seconds.

"You're absolutely certain?"

"Yes."

Donovan's heart slammed against his chest. He stood and paced. "Why didn't you tell me sooner?"

"I just found out a few days ago, and I wanted to tell you we'd captured him. But we can't locate him. No one can. Ari Levine of Mossad says Katill's a ghost, and the most terrifying assassin Mossad's ever faced. He might never be caught."

"Jean... ."

"Yeah?"

"They're wrong."

SIX

" Five minutes to Reagan National," said Donovan's driver, an attractive young brunette CIA agent, as she sped along the George Washington Memorial Parkway.

"No rush. My plane will wait for me."

"And for me."

"Why?"

"I'm your pilot."

"Oh... "

Donovan smiled as he thought about how the CIA had changed from the "good old boys" club where women were secretaries - to an agency where a growing number of women held key executive positions. Some women had even given their lives defending our country.

He also thought about what had just been dumped in his lap. The President and the Director of National Intelligence had just asked him to protect the world's eight most powerful leaders in a city where he couldn't even protect his wife. A city where every location would rekindle a warm memory of her - followed by the nauseating flashback to their blood-drenched bed where he found her body.

Donovan looked down at his two-day list of things to do. It was at least a six-day list. No way he could do everything. He'd need help from all Agency operatives in Brussels.

His cell phone rang.

"Hello… ."

"Donovan… it's Maccabee Singh."

Guilt hit him like a barn door. "Hi, Maccabee." He swallowed a dry throat. "How are you doing?"

A long pause. "About the same. It's still so… unreal… so hard to accept."

She sounded almost as anguished as when he'd spoken with her and her Aunt Helen earlier.

"For me too, Maccabee. If I can help in any way, please just ask."

She paused. "Actually, you can help."

"Just name it."

"I've been thinking about my father's translation."

"Yes… "

"You said there might be similar messages out there."

"Well, yes."

Pause. "I'd like to continue dad's work."

Donovan closed his eyes and felt his chest tighten.

"So his death was not in vain," she said.

Donovan squeezed the armrest hard, searching for a way to talk her out of this. He signaled his driver that he needed a private conversation. The young woman put on her MP3 earphones.

"But the killer took your father's ancient Sumerian book."

"No. I found it on dad's bookshelf. And two years ago, I wrote a paper on Sumerian logograms. I compared their SOV order, you know, subject, object, verb structure to the SOV of Akkadian. I know most Sumerian logograms and pictographs and the sentence context should probably indicate those I don't. So if you find more Sumerian messages, I think I can translate them."

Donovan felt his gut constrict. If those behind this knew she could translate their messages, they'd come after her.

"Maccabee, please understand how risky this could be."

She paused for several moments. "I do. But I'm willing to take that risk."

He paused. "Please think more about this." He couldn't believe he was repeating the same warning he'd given her father.

"I have, Donovan, and continuing dad's work means absolutely everything to me now."

Donovan knew it did. He also knew that the NSA had just intercepted a short message written in what looked like Sumerian logograms. Translating them might provide an important clue.

But he was torn between her need to help and his need to keep her safe. She'd be safe for the next few hours, since the enemy wouldn't know she was translating. But after that, they might find out and she'd need heavy security.

He tried to think what was best for everyone and everything concerned. He decided that saving the eight most powerful leaders in the world was worth the brief potential risk to one individual.

"Donovan… I *really* need to do this."

He paused. "And we need you. We just intercepted what looks like a short message. Do you have a fax machine?"

"Yes." She gave him the number.

Donovan put her on hold and called Director Madigan's secretary who put him through to the Director. Madigan agreed to fax the message to her. Donovan clicked back to Maccabee.

"The fax should arrive any minute."

"Thank you, Donovan."

"You're welcome. If you translate it, call Director Madigan immediately. Tell *only* him." He gave her Madigan's direct office line. "And Maccabee… ?"

"Yes… ?"

"Tell absolutely no one that you're helping us. Not even your Aunt Helen."

"Okay."

"Promise?"

"Yes."

They hung up and Donovan slumped back in the seat as they pulled into Reagan National Airport. His gut was churning.

Had he done the right thing?

Or had he just signed her death warrant?

Like he'd signed her father's...

SEVEN

Maccabee sat in *his* chair.

The mauve, tufted, executive chair in her father's study where he'd worked, read, told stories, laughed, and wept the night her mother had died of cancer. Maccabee rubbed her hand over the supple leather... leather that still held the pleasant scent of his Dunhill pipe tobacco, his scent.

She looked down at the frayed pages of his ancient Sumerian book. It had helped her translate the brief message Director Madigan had just faxed over. She dialed Madigan's office and got his secretary, who put her through to the Director.

"You're fast, Miss Singh."

"The message was only a few words, Director."

"Really? What are they?"

"TO NORTH COUNTRY I TRAVEL.
ALL 8 HEADS WILL I DELIVER. 25

MILLION RECEIVED. 25 MORE UPON
COMPLETION.

                                            KATILL"

She heard Madigan sigh with obvious concern.

"The 'north country' is Europe," he said. "You've confirmed Katill
is heading to Brussels, or is there and plans to assassinate the G8 leaders. Fifty million probably refers to dollars or euros. That much money
proves this is a very serious threat. So Katill is backed by a *very* well
financed group, perhaps even a rogue government. This is most helpful,
Ms. Singh. Thank you."

"You're welcome, Director. And if you get another message, I'd like
to help."

"That's very kind. I'll let you know. But please tell absolutely no
one you're helping us."

"I won't."

They hung up.

* * *

And so did Milan Slavitch, a barrel-chested man in the basement
of a building four blocks from Maccabee's apartment. He stood up and
stretched his linebacker shoulders, and rolled his neck, straining his
twenty-one-inch collar. Hours earlier, posing as a Verizon repairman,
he'd installed a button-sized listening bug in her apartment phone.
And now it had paid off. The woman was making the same mistake as
her father. Translating the ancient language. Bad decision.

Behind him, Milan heard his sidekick, Nikko chuckling and slapping his knee.

"Hey Milan, look at this!" Nikko said, pointing to the television.

Slavitch turned to Nikko who was riveted to the *Jerry Springer
Show.*

"Look at what?"

"This guy's pecker stayed hard for six weeks!"

"Who cares! Singh's daughter can translate that Sumeria shit!"

Nikko Nikolin spun around fast, his eyes bulging like frog eyes, which always made Milan suspect that Nikko's mother had fallen into a pond and somehow swooped toad semen into her crotch... and Nikko was the result.

"What'd you say?"

"Maccabee, the daughter, can translate that Sumerian stuff. She just figured out another message. Then she told some guy in Washington! Guy named Matten... Maddingly, no Madigan."

"Did you say *Madigan?*" Nikko said, jumping to his feet.

"Yeah, Madigan."

"Shit! We gotta tell Bennett."

"But he's in Curacao."

"So's his cell phone, moron!" Nikko paced back and forth.

Milan Slavitch didn't like being called moron. He'd warned Nikko many times. *One day, Nikko, you're gonna go too far and I'll snap your fucking neck like a toothpick.*

Nikko dialed Bennett and hit the speakerphone.

Simon Bennett picked up. Nikko explained and Bennett ranted and cursed for a full minute. "There are other messages out there. She could expose everything!"

"Whaddya want we – "

"Have Slavitch handle her and grab that goddammed Sumerian book!"

"Right!"

Nikko hung up and looked at Slavitch who nodded back.

Slavitch liked assignments from Simon Bennett. The guy paid top dollar. Slavitch spun a suppressor onto his 9mm Beretta and left.

Outside the building, he put on his wraparound sunglasses and walked toward Maccabee's apartment just blocks away. A few steps later, the two crows, right on cue, swooped down toward his head and flew away. He hated the black bastards. They reminded him of the crows at the orphanage in Sarajevo.

Even though he was only ten when he was left there, he knew he'd been dumped in a pile of *govno yedno! Horseshit,* as the Americans call it! On the other hand, the orphanage taught him life's big lesson early - from the day you're born, scud missiles are honing in on you. You may not see them, but they're coming, and you had to watch for them and then destroy them before they destroyed you.

His parents failed to see their scud – the Serbian sniper who assumed they were Muslims and shot them in the back. Sixteen years later, Milan found the bastard, a fat drunk named Branko, who also didn't see his scud – Slavitch's machete - that sent Branko's head rolling down an alley like a bowling ball.

And today Maccabee Singh won't see her scud.

Me.

He reached inside his coat and fingered the Beretta. He loved the power it gave him, how it leveled out life's unfair stuff.

At her apartment building, he ducked into the alley and walked up to the rear service door. He looked at the new tumbler lock and chuckled. The same brand and type he and Nikko popped open when they greased her father. Some people never learn.

He put on his gloves, reached into his small satchel and pulled out his selection of skeleton keys. The sixth key popped the lock like a Dollar Store trinket.

He stepped inside the swanky apartment building and smiled.

The elevator was just ahead, its door open, waiting just for him.

EIGHT

Donovan sat in the lap of luxury. He was surrounded by thirteen, plush, *empty* Gulfstream II seats – all empty because he had to get to Brussels fast. The CIA didn't sweat seats when sweating a major terrorist attack.

The Gulfstream, racing across the Atlantic at 40,000 feet, was branded *MedPharms Inc.* In fact, it was a Company aircraft, part of a CIA fleet that many around Washington referred to as Spook Air.

This same Gulfstream had flown rendition flights of terrorist prisoners to countries where interrogators were unencumbered by things like laws and the Geneva Convention.

In Brussels, Donovan and his friend, Jean de Waha, had to finalize the security details for each G8 event.

He sipped his second scotch as his agency safe phone rang.

"Rourke."

"Madigan. You en route to Brussels?"

"Yes."

"Maccabee Singh just gave me her translation."

"Great. What'd it say?"

"It confirms that Katill is heading to Brussels or is already there, and is being paid fifty million dollars or euros to kill the G8 leaders. This is a credible, major threat."

"Funded by *big* money. Rogue state money maybe."

"Very possibly. Hang on, Donovan, I have an urgent call."

As the director put him on hold, Donovan thought about how little they knew about Katill. The terrorist-assassin had left scores of bodies throughout Europe for years, but no trace of himself. No fingerprints, no voiceprints, no DNA, and only one grainy photo several years old.

Director Madigan came back on. "Bob in Munich just intercepted another message with what looks like Sumerian pictographs."

"Where'd he intercept it?"

"Dusseldorf. When he heard we're interested in pictographs, he faxed it over. I'll get it to Maccabee Singh."

"Good idea."

"But we're damned lucky, Donovan!"

"I know. She can translate *Sumerian!*"

"Yeah that, but we're also lucky because the Verizon guy fixed her phones this morning."

Donovan spilled his scotch. "Did you say *Verizon?*"

"Yeah, why?"

"I saw a *Comcast* phone bill on Singh's desk!"

Director Madigan paused, cleared his throat. "You think the Verizon guy's dirty?"

"I think he probably bugged her phone!"

Madigan cleared his throat. "So they know she just translated the message."

Donovan's heart pounded. "She's in danger!"

"I'll call her – "

"No, They'll hear! I'll call her cell phone."

"Do it!" Director Madigan said. "You have any agents near her?"

43

Donovan had to think. "One guy maybe six minutes away."

"Send him. I'll send people too."

They hung up. Donovan pulled out a scrap of paper with Macca-bee's cell phone number and dialed.

The phone rang and he was bounced into voice mail. He left her a 'get out of the apartment fast' message. Then he called Special Agent Pete Carvell, a smart, tough, case officer at the Plaza Hotel. No answer. He tried Pete's pager and waited, gulping more scotch as he stared down at the Atlantic waves.

Seconds later, Carvell phoned him back. Donovan explained and Carvell raced off toward her apartment.

As Donovan hung up, the Gulfstream dipped, then hit heavy tur-bulence. Some of his second double scotch spilled on his tray. He wiped it up and started to ask the steward for a refill. Then he paused and stared at his glass.

He'd been drinking too damn much. His nasty little secret. The heavy drinking started right after Emma's murder and tended to get heavier when things came down hard on him. Things like the death of Benny Ahrens, and the death of Sohan Singh, and the lack of time he was spending with Tish, and now, the concern he had for Maccabee. He had to ease up on the sauce. Especially in the next few days.

He pushed the glass away.

The phone rang. He checked Caller ID. Director Madigan.

"Verizon sent no one to her apartment building today or this month."

Donovan tried to swallow, but couldn't.

"Where's your case officer?"

"Maybe... four minutes away."

They hung up. Donovan turned and stared down at the waves curl-ing atop the ocean seven miles below. He realized he had one more option. The apartment phone. Even though it was probably tapped, he could tell her to leave immediately. Maybe she could get out before they got to her.

He dialed the number. No one answered.

* * *

Maccabee wiped perspiration from her eyes as she jogged on the treadmill in the exercise room off her father's bedroom. She thought of the many hours her father had jogged on this treadmill, how his doctor told him he was in excellent shape, had no serious health problems, and would probably live into his nineties.

Then came the bullet.

She hoped the running would ease her stress a bit. She cranked up her pace and the volume on her iPod earphones and listened to *Addicted to Love.* She liked the song, even though it always reminded her that she'd once been addicted to love.

Love lost!

His name was Andrew. Four weeks before their wedding, he disappeared from her life.

Like her father just disappeared. She still couldn't believe he was dead. She would miss him terribly. Her daily chats with him. His guidance, his encouragement, his suggestions, his warnings. He was the kindest man she'd ever known. He would want her to help Donovan, but also to be safe.

She was helping Donovan. And she *was* safe, since only Director Madigan and Donovan knew she was translating.

She thought she heard the apartment phone ringing. But then she always thought the phone was ringing when iPod music was pounding in her ears.

* * *

Milan Slavitch stepped into the empty hall of the fifth floor. Classy building. Thick, plush carpeting. Oil paintings in gold frames. Fancy chandeliers. The place *smelled* rich.

Sometimes he wondered how he would have turned out if he'd grown up in fancy joint like this… instead of the Orphanage From

Hell in Sarajevo.

Slavitch remembered that cesspool every day, the sewer smells, the rats crawling into his bed at night, the same rats who'd eaten some toes off screaming two-year-old Josif while the fat supervisor, Gernisa, drank his vodka in the next room. The same Gernisa who'd raped eleven-year-old Anna until she committed suicide five years later.

But Slavitch helped Gernisa pay for his sins. Slavitch remembered fondly the night he swung the crowbar into Gernisa's fat head over and over until it looked like a steamroller ran over it.

The elevator dinged open and Slavitch ducked into a small alcove. A man got off and walked the opposite direction. But then he stopped in the hall and talked on his cell phone. Finally, two minutes later the guy entered an apartment.

Slavitch walked down to Singh's door. He smiled when he saw the lock had not been changed. Quickly, he inserted the same key he'd used the other night. He pulled out his silenced Beretta, opened the door and stepped inside. He looked toward the study where he'd greased her old man. No one there. No TV on. Maybe she'd gone out. If so, he'd just wait for her.

Then he heard something. A machine running, shoes hitting a hard surface. A treadmill maybe.

He turned and walked toward the sound. He looked into the master bedroom and heard someone in an adjoining room, running. He glimpsed the shadow of a female jogger. Young and curvaceous. Just the way he liked them.

* * *

Agent Pete Carvell slammed on his Chevy brakes and blasted his horn at the stalled Allied Van Lines semi-trailer blocking all traffic at Columbus Circle. Carvell drove his Impala up onto the sidewalk and raced ahead. Two hundred yards later, he was blocked again, this time by construction scaffolding.

"*SHIT!*" he shouted as he jumped out and sprinted down Central

Park West.

He heard a traffic cop shouting for him to come back and move his car.

He kept running. Her apartment was still several blocks ahead.

* * *

Milan Slavitch stepped into the bedroom, walked over and peeked through the door of the exercise room. A wall mirror gave him a partial view of her. Nice, long legs, gleaming with perspiration. Real wraparounds. Nice melons, too. Nice everything. Her smooth, tawny skin reminded him of Hala, a seventeen-year-old hooker he had his way with one night in Kosovo.

Slavitch's gaze crept slowly down Maccabee Singh's firm, glistening body.

He felt himself getting aroused.

Hey, nobody said he couldn't have some fun.

* * *

Pete Carvell sprinted into the lobby of the apartment building and flashed his ID badge at the confused concierge.

"*Singh* apartment?"

"Fifth floor, 502."

Carvell hurried to the elevator, pushed the button and saw the car was up on Eleven.

Cursing his luck, he ran to the stairwell.

He took out his Glock, ran up the steps two at a time, and moments later, gasping for breath, yanked open the door to the fifth floor. He dashed down to 502 and turned the knob. Unlocked. Bad sign.

He moved into the foyer and looked around. No one.

Then he saw it. A large shoe imprint on a plush carpet. To the left, he heard a machine running. He moved silently toward the sound, trying to hush his breathing. He peered through the crack in the bedroom door.

No one.

Then a long thin shadow inched across the wall.

The shadow of a *handgun with suppressor.*

Carvell spun into the bedroom, surprising a large, thick-shouldered man standing beside the door to the exercise room. The man swung his gun around toward Carvell.

"Drop it *NOW!*" Carvell shouted.

"Yeah, yeah, okay!"

Then, with amazing speed, the big man leapt sideways and fired off two shots as Carvell dove beside the bed. The bullets missed Carvell by inches and split off chunks of the wooden bedpost.

Carvell crawled to the far end of the bed, leaned out and fired twice. The first bullet entered the man's left eye, the second, his heart area. The big man froze, swayed a bit, then collapsed to the floor.

Keeping his gun on the man, Carvell reached down and yanked the Beretta from his fingers and then a small pistol from an ankle holster. The man's remaining eye was locked open. Carvell couldn't detect a pulse. He was gone. And so was any chance of learning who sent him here, or who was behind this attempt.

Carvell stepped over the large pool of blood and moved to the door of the exercise room. The treadmill was still running, but there was no sight of Maccabee.

"Ms. Singh?"

Silence.

"Ma'am, if you're in there, you're safe now. I'm Agent Pete Carvell. I work with Donovan Rourke. He realized your phones were tapped and you were in danger right after you phoned Director Madigan. Are you okay?"

No response.

"Ma'am… ?"

Then a faint whisper, "Yes."

"It's safe now."

She stepped tentatively from the exercise room, glanced down at the bloody body and turned away.

Carvell could see she was frightened and shaky. He eased her from the bedroom to a chair in the foyer.

"Is he the Verizon man you saw this morning?"

She nodded.

"We should leave. Others may show up when he fails to report in."

"Give me a minute... ."

* * *

Maccabee shut her bedroom door and leaned against it, her body trembling faster than her pulse. A man had been seconds from murdering her... and would have if Donovan hadn't put it all together.

Donovan was right. She was in a game of life and death. A game she was not prepared for. Should she get out now? Leave this to the professionals?

Or should she help with the translations her father gave his life for?

She sat on the side of the bed as her eyes filled with tears.

NINE

This jerkwad actually thinks he's turning into a Dutch elm! Nikko Nikolin thought. *Is he nuts?*

Nikko loved the *Jerry Springer Show.* He probably watched it too much, but hey, the guests were so weird they made him feel normal.

What wasn't normal was that Milan had not returned from Maccabee Singh's apartment. He'd been gone for over an hour and hadn't phoned in. Milan always phoned in.

I better go check things out.

Minutes later, as he approached the Singh apartment building, he saw the flashing lights of an ambulance and two cop cars. He relaxed, realizing Milan had nailed her and was probably lying low until the cops left.

The apartment building entrance opened and attendants rolled out a gurney with a covered body. *Mission accomplished!* As the gurney bounced down the steps, an arm flopped out.

A thick, muscular arm tattooed with a Slovakian flag!

Milan! Dead!

Jesus! This is in-fucking-credible!

Nikko felt like he'd been whacked upside the head. He must be hallucinating. He leaned against a street pole and sucked air into his lungs.

Milan dead! No way this could happen! Milan was a pro. Always delivered. For seven years, time after time, he'd delivered dead bodies like the US Mail delivered junk mail. Nikko couldn't believe it.

More EMS people walked inside. Maybe Milan killed her. Maybe a second gurney would roll out.

He hurried over to the ambulance attendant, a fat blond guy with silver ear studs and a nasty harelip.

"My sister lives here. Any more bodies up there?"

"No. Just this man. That your sister over there?" The attendant pointed at a police car. Nikko turned and saw Maccabee Singh in the back seat talking with a cop and another guy wearing a suit.

She's alive! Simon Bennett would go ape-shit! Nikko walked into a nearby alley, flipped open his cell phone and dialed Bennett's private number.

"I told you not to call this number!"

"Milan's dead and Maccabee's alive!"

Bennett cursed for several seconds.

"Where is she?"

"Here."

"Handle her. Fast!" The line went dead.

TEN

DUSSELDORF, GERMANY

Katill scraped Anna's fresh blood from beneath his fingernails.
She'd bled from her mouth just seconds after he gave her a whiff
of Novichok, a delightfully lethal nerve gas. Just one quick inhale and
her eyes shot wide open in fear, then, as expected, she began to shake,
gasp and bleed out, and then eighteen seconds later, she died.

He wiped the blood off his X-ACTO blade and put it back in its
sheath.

Of course, Anna would have died soon anyway. From starvation,
just like the seven other stray alley cats he'd tested Novichok on.

Novichok was the little known, *instant death* Russian chemical
weapon that could be inhaled or absorbed through the skin. It even
passed through most masks and human protective gear. The perfect
weapon. Just one of many in his arsenal.

Valek Stahl, born Valek Stahl, but also known as Axel Braun, Horst
Speerman and other aliases, walked to his window and looked down at

the Rhine River meandering past his penthouse in Dusseldorf's posh Carlstadt area.

Beside him, a cell phone rang. An untraceable phone. Only one person had the number. Stahl answered.

"Herr Braun?"

"Yes," Stahl said.

"*Medusa* has received its final go-ahead."

"Excellent."

"Yes indeed."

"Upon completion, I'll expect the additional fifty percent of my fee immediately."

"Of course. Wired to the Nevis bank?"

"No. To my Belize account."

"As you wish."

Stahl hung up and looked back at the Rhine… flowing as smoothly as *Medusa*. Stahl was pleased. Not just for the twenty-five million dollars already earning interest in his protected Nevis account, or the additional twenty-five million that would be deposited in a numbered Belize account. Fifty million was appropriate, considering the significance of *Medusa*.

The irony was that even if they decided to call off *Medusa* at the last second, he would complete it anyway. He would even complete it for free. He had his reasons. And money was just one. Besides, he already had more than enough money to live very comfortably for the rest of his life.

As Stahl stretched his powerful six-foot-three frame, he caught his reflection in the window. He realized the face looking back at him would no longer exist in a few days.

He checked his watch. It was time to visit his favorite antique dealer. He pulled out a phone directory, found the number for *Wolfgang Rutten*, and dialed.

"*Antiquitäten Cologne*," Herr Rutten wheezed.

"How's the antique business?"

"Ah, Herr Braun, it's always better after talking to you."

"Can we talk in a couple of hours?"

"I'll be waiting." Herr Rutten sputtered into a coughing fit.

Stahl hung up, walked over and punched in the combination to his large walk-in wall vault. He stepped inside the safe and took a large black briefcase. He opened it and studied its contents for a few moments, then carried the briefcase from the vault.

An hour later, with the briefcase on his passenger seat, Stahl drove his BMW 760 onto the autobahn and headed toward Cologne twenty-five kilometers away. He listened to Wagner's *Tannhauser* swirl around him. He loved Wagner's operas, as did one of Stahl's heroes, Adolph Hitler.

Stahl hummed the melody.

His thoughts turned to *Medusa*. The most significant jihad in history. Armageddon for the eight major infidel democracies. The world's most powerful leaders would die horrifically and deservedly for their crimes against Muslims.

He, Valek Stahl, would exact vengeance against those governments whose immoral occupying armies have desecrated and continued to defile sacred Islamic land. And he would exact revenge against the Israelis who slaughtered his family many years ago.

In Cologne, he drove toward the gigantic twin spires of the 12th century Cathedral, the *Kolner Dom*. The Cathedral, despite taking seventy-one hits by Allied bombing in World War II, had remained standing, while every building around it was flattened. He parked down the street from the Cathedral and got out with the black briefcase.

Stahl walked past the popular *Café Reichard,* then entered Rutten's antique shop, tinkling the doorbell. Stale, moldy air filled his nostrils as he looked around the dimly lit room. He strolled down an aisle of dusty antiques that some idiots would pay outrageous amounts of money for.

Along a back wall he saw a row of antique porcelain dolls. Beside them, World War II German toy soldiers stood next to three Zyklon B canisters, cherished keepsakes of Herr Rutten's days as a teenage guard at Sobibor.

In the back of the shop, a door opened, and yellow light spilled out, silhouetting the hunched-over shape of Wolfgang Rutten. He looked even more bent over and decrepit than four months ago. His black cigar drooped from lips that looked like aged veal.

"Herr Braun, how nice to see you."

"Good to see you too, Herr Rutten."

Rutten rubbed his bushy eyebrows, then coughed serious phlegm into a blood-smeared handkerchief.

Stahl opened his suitcase and showed him the contents and the photos. He explained in detail what he wanted.

"So, can you make this?"

The old man used a magnifying glass to study the contents and photo more closely.

"Yes."

"*Exactly* like this?"

"No problem."

"It cannot fail!"

The old man's grin revealed flakes of tobacco between his yellowed teeth. "Have I ever let you down before?"

"No. But I want a failsafe backup system."

"I'll include two."

Stahl nodded. "One hundred thousand euros is acceptable?"

The huge fee caused Rutten to hack more phlegm into his handkerchief.

"Most satisfactory, Herr Braun."

"Fifty thousand tonight, and fifty thousand when it performs."

Rutten's eyebrows shot up. "Most satisfactory indeed."

"One last point."

"What's that?"

"I need this tomorrow at this time." Stahl wanted a fast turnaround to diminish any chance of discovery.

Rutten looked back at the contents and photos a moment. "No problem, Herr Stahl. As you may know, almost everything I need is in my lab."

Stahl handed Rutten a large grey envelope stuffed with fifty thousand euros. The old man's rheumy eyes moistened as he fanned the bills.

"Until tomorrow evening, Herr Braun."

Stahl nodded, stepped outside the shop and looked around. He saw two old women chatting in front of the *Kolner Dom* Cathedral. The taller one glanced at him and continued to stare. Something about the way she looked at him gave him concern. He turned quickly, walked to his car, got in and drove off.

Herr Rutten would deliver, Stahl knew. The old man's handiwork - some would call them body parts – were imbedded into the crumbled walls of Europe's train stations, offices, and cafés. Rutten was a master...

... a master making his final masterpiece.

ELEVEN

S omewhere over the Atlantic, Donovan crawled inside Valek Stahl's head. You know the detailed itinerary for all G8 events, don't you, Stahl? You know our security procedures for each event.

You know we've spent nearly one billion dollars to protect the G8 leaders. You know that thousands of police, military and security personnel will be watching for you and other terrorists. But especially for you. You know that the walls of protection surrounding the leaders will be virtually impenetrable and that you'll need special IDs to get past each wall. And finally, you know that access to the leaders' innermost circle will be virtually impossible to acquire.

Unless you get inside help.

The problem, Donovan knew, was that Stahl could get inside help. All it took was money and the right contacts. Stahl had money, enough to produce the right contacts.

The CIA Gulfstream II hit some turbulence at 30,000 feet near the British Isles. Donovan tightened his seatbelt. He didn't like turbulence.

His life had enough.

A minute later, the flight smoothed out.

Donovan was on his laptop, reading through the top secret *G8 Security Plan*. He'd read the strengths and weaknesses of each G8 event, and studied the photos and bios of all attendees and all security personnel, many of whom he knew from his years as a CIA senior operations officer stationed in Brussels.

He noticed the photo of a young Canadian security agent, an attractive woman with black silken hair. She reminded him of Maccabee.

His thoughts turned to Maccabee. After Agent Carvell killed the assassin in her apartment, Carvell had a CIA agent drive her to her friend's home and remain on guard. But the more Donovan thought about it, the more concerned he became that those behind this plot could find out where she was. Once they knew, they'd come after her again, perhaps send a hit team to overwhelm the guard and eliminate her.

She'd be much safer in Brussels, surrounded by the virtually impenetrable walls of G8 security.

He phoned Maccabee's friend, a young woman named Marilyn Gardner, who picked up. He introduced himself.

"Is Maccabee nearby?"

"She's right here, Donovan. Hang on... ."

"Hi, Donovan. I'm glad you called. We're just making a list of dad's things for charity. Is there anything of his you'd like?"

Donovan smiled. "His racquetball paddle. It possesses demonic powers. Your father pummeled me with that thing for years."

"It's yours!"

He felt relieved to hear a smile in her voice.

"Where are you now?"

"Five miles above the Atlantic."

"Heading toward Brussels?"

"Yes, and... well... I'm thinking you should too."

"Me?"

He paused. "You'll be safer there, Maccabee. We've got massive security in place. Can you spare a couple of days?"

"I can spare a week. I'm on leave. But are you sure it's necessary?"

"I'm sure it's safer."

"Because they know I can translate Sumerian?"

"Yes."

She paused a moment. "Well, all right."

"We'll handle your hotel and flight. You'll stay with us at the Amigo Hotel in Brussels. But don't tell anyone where you're going."

"I won't. Which flight?"

Donovan looked at his watch. "There's a JFK United flight to London in three hours."

"London?"

"Yeah. It's a precaution. They'll be watching US-to-Brussels direct flights."

"The people who attacked me?"

"Yes."

She paused. "I can make that London flight."

"Good. Our people will handle your tickets, drive you to the JFK, and escort you in London and Brussels."

"Oh, wait. My passport is back at Princeton."

Donovan paused. "Don't worry about it. We'll issue a special temporary passport. It'll be waiting for you at the airport."

"Okay."

"So I'll see you at the Amigo hotel. And, again, Maccabee, thanks for your help."

"Donovan... ?"

"Yeah?"

"I *need* to help."

He paused. "I understand."

"Dad despised terrorists. Especially those who kill innocent men, women and children. He called them... 'gutless chickenshit asshole bastards!'"

"He had a way with words!" Donovan said, laughing.

He heard her laugh and felt good that she did.

Then something occurred to him. "Maccabee, it might be a good idea if your friend Marilyn stayed with someone for a couple of days. Just in case they come looking for you there."

"She's flying to Miami tonight."

"That works."

Moments later, they hung up.

The Gulfstream II banked hard right. He looked out and saw the emerald west coast of Ireland.

His thoughts turned back to the task ahead. He had to stop Katill, or Valek Stahl, or whatever the hell his name was, from killing the G8 leaders – or *I'll live in infamy as the inept agent who failed to stop the assassination attempt I knew was coming.*

Should he, as the President suggested, recommend postponing the Summit if the chances of an assassination appeared too great? Or should he, as the DNI Director Madigan suggested, avoid caving into the terrorists unless absolutely convinced the assassination would succeed?

He weighed the pros and cons of both positions for several minutes, finally deciding he would recommend postponement *only* if he, Jean de Waha and a majority of other national security chiefs felt circumstances absolutely warranted it. Postponed leaders are better than dead leaders.

As the steward served Donovan coffee and rolls, he looked out at the white cliffs of Dover and the English Channel. He would be landing in Brussels very soon. Once there, he and de Waha had to work fast. Diplomatic protocols would need to take a back seat.

So would some personal memories. While he loved Brussels, a spectacular, beautiful, fun city where he'd enjoyed many terrific times with smart, friendly, interesting people, the city was also where Emma was brutally ripped from his life.

He could not let that memory cloud his judgment during this assignment.

On his laptop, he pulled up *Le Soir,* a leading Belgian French-language newspaper. G8 headlines dominated the front page, but an article about the *Forêt de Soignes,* a sprawling forest, south of Brussels caught his attention.

The *forêt* was 27,000 acres of towering oak and beech trees, spectacular vistas, old chateaus and abbeys and meandering footpaths down which the armies of Caesar, Napoleon and Hitler had walked.

And so had Valek Stahl the night he killed Emma. The forest abutted the home where Emma and he had lived.

Donovan's mind swept back to that night, the most horrific in his life. He'd been in nearby Antwerp, getting critical information from a contact about a secret Iranian uranium enrichment plant. He'd arrived home about 3 a.m. and the moment he saw Tish's Mickey Mouse nightlight in pieces on the hall floor, he knew something was wrong.

Quickly, he looked into his daughter's bedroom and saw she was sleeping. He ran to the master bedroom, grabbed the doorknob and felt something sticky. And then he smelled the coppery scent of blood. He hurried inside, flicked on the light and saw Emma's face, sheet-white, her nightgown drenched with blood, her eyes locked open.

He ran over, felt for her pulse, got none. Her cold fingers already stiffening.

Crazed, he slammed his fist down hard on the bed table, shattering its glass cover and cutting his palm wide open. Blood poured from the wound. *Well-deserved* blood... in the room where Emma had bled to death.

Because of him!

That night and every night since, he reminded himself that *he'd* caused her death, because he'd been the target – payback, he knew, for killing three terrorists about to bomb a girls' grade school in Kandahar. One dead terrorist it turned out was the son of a wealthy Syrian arms dealer who immediately swore a personal *jihad* against Donovan and hired Valek Stahl as his jihadist.

Every day since, Donovan had blamed himself for not taking the *jihad* against him more seriously. He should have insisted on more protection for Emma and Tish when he was traveling. Insisted on moving them to a safe house. But he hadn't.

And he knew why. His arrogance. Foolishly, he'd believed he could protect them. And his arrogance, his failure, took Emma's life... and with it a huge part of his.

Even today, nearly two years later, her death still haunted him, still gnawed at his core, still made him question whether he'd ever be able to muster the courage to risk loving someone again.

Deep down, he knew he probably wouldn't. And probably *shouldn't*. His job was simply too unpredictable and secretive and dangerous for normal family life, too unfair for a wife and family.

But it was the only job he knew.

TWELVE

CURACAO

The black Mercedes limousine hugged the narrow mountain cliff road like a stripe of paint as it drove along North Point on the Caribbean island of Curacao. A thousand feet below, the turquoise sea crashed against the rocky cliff, leaving a frothy white carpet in its wake.

In the back seat, Simon Bennett, a thin, hawk-faced man with dark eyes, flicked lint from the sleeve of his black Savile Row suit. He added up a column of numbers in his leather folder and smiled. He took his gold Mont Blanc and underlined the bottom line: sixty-eight million dollars. All *his*... very soon.

But peanuts compared to what he was about to show the boss.

The chauffeur turned onto a private road, drove up through a tropical forest and soon stopped at a tall, wrought iron gate. He whispered the day's password into his cell phone and the gate screeched open. Two minutes later, the limo drove onto a circular drive in front of a massive, white, 1880s Dutch mansion basking in the tropic sun. In front, shirtless men, glistening like ebony statues, bent over gardens of white roses and orchids.

The limousine crunched to a stop on the pea-gravel driveway. Simon Bennett stepped out into and felt a humid breeze sweep off the ocean. The salt air smelled fresh and clean. The mansion door opened and the ancient butler, Karl, as always, nodded at him. Bennett nodded back and followed him inside to the icy foyer.

As they walked down a long hallway, Bennett passed several Picassos and Chagalls, and two Rodin sculptures. The artwork's owner, the person Bennett came to meet, could afford a warehouse of Picassos. After all, only three people in the world had more money.

Bennett entered the familiar anteroom and nodded at young Fritz, the stern-faced secretary with twitchy eyebrows, diamond stud earrings and dagger tattoos jutting from beneath his white cuffs.

"Good afternoon, Fritz."

Fritz nodded, as usual, with all the warmth of a pit bull, mostly because he'd never learned the reason for Bennett's numerous visits. Only two people knew: Bennett and the person in the adjoining office.

Fritz ushered him into the massive office.

"Your visitor has arrived," Fritz whispered, twitching his way back out and closing the door.

Bennett walked in, his feet gently sinking into the supple floor tiles made from soft Nigerian alligator leather. He sat opposite the massive desk, whose occupant remained hidden behind the salmon-hued pages of the *Financial Times*. The office was ice cold and dark except where the desk lamp cast pale yellow light on the newspaper. The usual sour musty odor hung in the air.

The person behind the newspaper continued reading, despite knowing Bennett had just traveled two thousand miles. Moments later, as the newspaper was lowered a bit, Bennett stared into the jaundiced eyes of Karlottah Z. Wickstrom.

Now in her late-seventies, Wickstrom's face was even grayer than two months ago. Her eyes seemed to have been sucked further back into her skull. Beads of sweat dotted her forehead despite the wall thermostat that Bennett noticed was set at fifty-nine.

A drop of blood had dried on her cracked, grey lips. As always, she wore a black pinstriped suit, diamond earrings, a gold necklace with dozens of carat-sized diamonds, and a custom-made Rolex, also diamond-studded. People could retire on the jewelry she was wearing.

Wickstrom was number three among the five richest people in the world, thanks to family money, global real estate, oil tanker fleets and decades of massive profits from insider trading information given to her by a now disgraced, disbarred and deceased U.S. Senator. Conservative estimates put her wealth at fifty-eight billion dollars. *Fortune* magazine said sixty-four billion. In reality, she had billions more she kept hidden from the IRS.

She had everything she ever wanted in life, except one. She wanted to be the wealthiest person in the world.

And now that Carlos Slim of Mexico has split his seventy plus billion among his family members, Wickstrom had a chance to pass Bill Gates and others and become the richest in the world.

But she needed a few billion more. And she needed it fast.

Karlottah Wickstrom had seven months to live. Incurable amyotrophic lateral sclerosis, Lou Gehrig's disease, was chewing away at her muscles and nerve endings every second. And two months ago, she'd been diagnosed with stage-four pancreatic cancer.

Couldn't happen to a more deserving person, Bennett thought.

Finally, she put down the paper and stared at him. "Well… ?" Her eyelids drooped as though she was drugged.

"*Medusa* goes well," Bennett said, deciding not to tell her about Milan Slovitch's failure to eliminate Maccabee Singh in the apartment.

"And our *Medusa* network?"

"They've completed all financial arrangements, all futures contracts, options, both calls and puts, derivatives, all margin buying, everything's functioning."

"And the shell corporations?"

"Working perfectly."

"For *all* buying groups in *all* countries?"

He nodded.

"The SEC?"

"Clueless."

"Says who?"

"My people on the inside."

"You trust them?"

"Yes."

"Why?"

"Because I pay them much more than the SEC."

She blinked real slow, like a lizard.

"Besides," Bennett continued, "our global process is far too dispersed and fragmented to be detected. Too many buyers from too many countries over too many months. SEC computers haven't red-flagged anything! And if they do, our IT insiders will quickly de-flag it!"

She coughed, dabbed her lips with a handkerchief stained with phlegm. "Anticipated profits... ?"

"Very good news! Much higher than I anticipated." He handed her a piece of paper with the terrific profit picture.

Bennett watched her eyes scan down the long column of numbers to the bottom line, a figure much higher than she was expecting. She stared at the number, lizard-blinked again, then bent her lips in a rare smile. But the smile split her cracked lip and spilled a fresh drop of blood onto the paper. She looked down at the blood as though Bennett had somehow caused it and shoved the paper back to him.

What a bitch! No 'job well done, Simon.' Just take your bloody paper back!

"Everything depends on Brussels," she whispered, holding her handkerchief to her lip.

"I understand."

"And this man, Katill?"

"The best in the world. He's eluded the police for fifteen years. They have no idea where he is, *who* he is, or what he looks like. He's never failed."

"He better not for what I'm paying him."

Bennett nodded.

Karlottah Wickstrom turned and stared out the window at the blue Caribbean. "So, I won't hear from you until after Brussels."

"No. Not unless something — "

"Nothing will go wrong, will it, Mr. Bennett?" she said, her voice surprisingly hard.

"No."

"My investments with your financial institutions amount to over twelve billion, do they not?"

He nodded, sensing her usual threat coming.

"If *Medusa* fails," Wickstrom continued, "I will remove the entire amount. Do you understand, Mr. Bennett?"

"Yes." He hated groveling to the old bitch. But for his sixty-eight million dollar payday he could grovel like a politician on Election Day.

"One last thing," Wickstrom whispered.

"Yes?"

"When this Katill completes his Brussels assignment – terminate him!"

"I'm not sure anyone can find - "

"Terminate him!"

"But he only communicates through untraceable e-mail drafts. And he's disappearing after this assignment."

She paused. "That's my point. Your job is to make sure he disappears. Permanently."

"But - "

"Your problem!" She pushed a button beneath her desk and the office door clicked open. Wickstrom's eyes looked back at the *Financial Times*, letting Bennett know he was dismissed.

At the door, Fritz stood twitching like a rabid animal, ready to pounce if Bennett didn't leave immediately.

Bennett stood and walked out. At least he was comforted with the knowledge that very soon he'd have more money than he could count.

———

He was also comforted with the knowledge that Karlottah Wickstrom was dying.

Slowly and painfully.

THIRTEEN

B ob Rosiek was worried. Donovan Rourke, his protégé, faced a horrific assignment in a city where he faced a horrific memory. The man's thoughts and work would be interrupted with visions of his wife, Emma.

Rosiek had not been in favor of the decision to send him to Brussels, but had been overruled.

He phoned Donovan on the CIA Gulfstream.

Donovan picked up on the first ring. "What's up Bob?"

"We've just got Maccabee Singh set up for her flight to Europe. She's well protected, Donovan."

"Good."

"Also, NSA thinks there may be a couple more messages in Sumerian pictograms."

"Where?"

"In Europe. They're gathering them now."

"She told me she feels she can translate them."

"Good. All the more reason to have her in Brussels under better protection with all of you"

"Agreed."

"How you doing?"

"Fine."

"You going to be okay over there, Donovan?"

"Yeah. I'll be okay."

"You sure?"

"Yeah. I've got a lot to keep me focused."

"Like the assignment."

"Yeah, that and revenge."

"I understand. But, don't let revenge screw up the job."

"I hear you."

"Be careful, Donovan."

"I will."

They hung up.

Rosiek sat back and looked out his office window. He was still worried about Donovan. The man was returning to the location of his wife's brutal murder. His need for revenge could make him less attentive to protecting the eight most powerful leaders in the world.

On the other hand, he knew Rourke had an ability to compartmentalize his grief and focus on the job at hand. He'd seen him do it before.

Rosiek remembered back at the CIA Farm. Early on, he'd known that Donovan had the right stuff: brains and guts. He remembered one night during paramilitary training when Donovan had trudged through a freezing sleet storm, crawled through icy slush, and navigated himself to the team's pre-assigned map coordinates forty minutes before the other candidates.

Another time, he won the obstacle course race by cutting through a snake-infested swamp and then used a cigarette lighter to remove several leaches and ticks from his legs and chest.

Since The Farm, Donovan's real world experience gave him the all-around tradecraft abilities second to none. His skill had earned him the

Top Secret/SCI All-Access Clearances to virtually everything in the Agency.

But his skill had cost him big. An assassin was hired to kill him, but when Donovan wasn't home, murdered his wife.

Devastated, he and his young daughter, Tish, had flown back to the states where he tendered his resignation. But, Michael Madigan, then CIA Director, persuaded him to stay in the Company and assigned him to their Manhattan anti-terrorism bureau. Donovan buried his loss in eighteen-hour workdays.

But today, Rosiek knew, he still carried the pain of losing Emma.

And in Brussels, Rosiek knew Donovan would be reminded of that pain everywhere he looked.

FOURTEEN

Donovan's face was on fire. He opened his eyes to blinding sunshine pouring through the Gulfstream window. He'd slept for a whopping twenty minutes.

In the next three days, sleep would be a dereliction of duty. He had too much to do and too little time. Even though he'd be working with his friend, Jean de Waha, they still had a lot to do.

He looked out the window and saw the orange tile roofs of a familiar Brussels suburb. He recognized an ancient church steeple and a cobblestone road where a blur of red-jerseyed bicyclists raced around a tight curve. He was back home, his second home. Just as he left it. Charming. Rustic. Peaceful.

Life-changing for him.

Life-ending for Emma.

The Gulfstream touched down at Brussels International Airport and taxied to a private hangar. Donovan deplaned and was met by a colleague, Special Agent Perkins, who whisked him through diplomatic G8 customs and into a black Chevy Suburban.

Twenty-five minutes later, in the center of Brussels, which many people considered the capital of the European Union, they steered into the small circular drive of the Amigo Hotel. The Amigo was always Donovan's first choice, mainly because it was just a block from the *Grand Place*, the eleventh century square that was Donovan's favorite ancient site in Europe.

"Welcome to the Amigo," said a young red-haired bellhop opening Donovan's door.

Donovan thanked him, went inside and was escorted upstairs to his room. He looked around at the hand-painted antique armchairs and sofa, and the Louis XV desk that probably cost more than the housekeeper's annual wages.

At the window he gazed down at the little shops on the street below. One shop window was filled with small statues of the Manneken Pis, the legendary three-year-old boy who saved Brussels when he put out a major fire by urinating on it. Donovan smiled at the hundreds of little boys aiming their diminutive dorks at a group of giggling schoolgirls walking by.

He looked further down the street toward the *Grand Place* Square and his gut tightened. The G8 leaders would soon sit there - *in the open* - for windy speeches, surrounded by thousands of people and hundreds of windows from which Katill could strike.

His phone rang and he picked up.

"It's alive!" Jean de Waha said.

"SuperSpook never sleeps."

"Does he still imbibe?"

"More than he should at times." *Like every night.* Donovan reminded himself to control his drinking during the G8.

"Amigo Bar in ten minutes?"

"See you there," Donovan said, hanging up. It would be terrific to see Jean again. He hadn't kept in touch much simply because talking to Jean in Brussels usually conjured up memories of Emma.

Donovan grabbed his phone and called Tish in Manhattan. He

listened to her yammer on about the red clay bunny she'd made in preschool. He promised to bring her a new movie DVD about a young Belgian boy named *Tintin*. She screamed with delight. Hanging up, he realized that listening to Tish was better than booze.

He headed down to the Amigo Bar and sat in a private corner booth. Seconds later, Jean de Waha strolled in, the familiar spring in his walk.

De Waha looked about the same. A slender, distinguished, sixty-four-year old with thick brown-gray hair and a friendly, handsome face. His brow maybe had a few more lines, his suit a few more wrinkles, his tie a few more pipe tobacco crumbs. But his dark eyes, as always, were intelligent and focused.

They shook hands, ordered Stella Artois and seconds later the waiter placed the cold beers in front of him.

De Waha placed a small electronic device on the table and turned it on. Donovan recognized the new voice barrier machine that prevented electronic devices from eavesdropping on their conversation.

"So how's D. C.?" de Waha asked.

"It's *panic* on the Potomac!"

"Same here, and in Paris, London, Tokyo, Moscow, Rome, you name it."

Donovan nodded. "Some congressmen want our President to cancel his trip for fear he may get killed. Others want him to come here in the hopes he does."

De Waha smiled. "Nice people, politicians!"

"Mark Twain said it best."

"Said what?"

"'Politicians are like babies.'"

"How so?"

"Both need to be changed often."

De Waha cackled and sipped his beer. Then, he reached in his pocket and handed Donovan a folded piece of paper. "This new intercept appears to have Sumerian symbols similar to the message Professor Singh translated."

"Where'd you get this?"

"Dusseldorf. Three hours ago. We sent it to Rosenquist at NSA."

"Maccabee Singh can translate it faster. She's coming to Brussels." Donovan called Rosenquist who agreed to scan and e-mail the message to Maccabee immediately.

Donovan hung up. "Anything more on this Katill, Valek Stahl?"

"Nothing," de Waha said. "Interpol is updating his profile. The man's a ghost. Possible sightings in Germany near Cologne, a few in Riyadh, Paris, Yemen and New York. At least twelve aliases. Most recently, Horst Speerman, Ernst Fleischer, Phillippe DuMaurier, Axel Braun."

"Bio?" Donovan asked.

"German father, Arab mother. They were killed along with his young sister in an Israeli air raid on a terrorist bomb-making enclave in southern Lebanon. Stahl was nine, saw it happen. Damaged him forever. His father was a PLO bomb-maker, but Stahl still blamed Israel and is extremely motivated against it and those who support it."

"Like the G8 leaders," Donovan said.

"Like them."

They sipped their beers.

"And he speaks six languages fluently."

"Any more good news?"

"He never fails."

"He failed to kill me," Donovan said, then thought, but *killed Emma* instead. "What's he look like?"

"You name it. A crippled beggar in a London subway, a ski instructor in Norway, an old woman in a Tangiers souk. He's used latex noses, theatrical makeup, collagen injections, plastic cheek inserts, colored contact lenses. Basically, if it walks, hobbles or rolls in a chair, it could be him."

"And when he's not in disguise?"

"Thirty-five, six-three, blond-brown hair, medium tone complexion. Very strong. Serious weightlifter. He once dropped a three hundred pound Kawasaki motorcycle on a German intelligence agent, crushing the man to death."

"Jesus! Any photos?"

"Seven years old and fuzzy. We're enhancing them."

Donovan sipped more beer. "So, the bottom line is, Stahl's personally and financially motivated to kill the G8 leaders."

"Yeah, but who's paying him the fifty million?"

"A lot of willing donors out there," Donovan said.

"Yeah. And a lot of motives."

"Maybe Al Qaeda's payback for Bin Laden's death."

"Or the angry dethroned Arab Spring dictators? Fifty million dollars or euros is chickenfeed for them."

"Or maybe Hamas, Hezbollah, Jihadists, Taliban. "

"In brief, all the usual suspects."

Donovan nodded. "But imagine the implications of killing all leaders."

"Panic worldwide."

"Right. Al Qaeda would love that. Throw the world into chaos. That may be their goal."

"True. But eventually things will return to normal."

"I agree. These eight countries are not banana republics. They will replace their assassinated leaders through their legislative processes. The transfer of power should be fairly orderly in most cases."

"But maybe not so orderly," de Waha said, toying with his 'beer blotter.

"One thing won't be orderly," Donovan said.

"What?"

"The financial markets. The stock markets of the world will crash like asteroids. People will sell at any price. End of the world selling!"

"And financial experts who know exactly *when* the crash will happen could make a bundle."

Donovan nodded. "Money could be behind this."

They sipped their beer.

"Whatever is behind it Jean, our motivation is clear. Stopping the bastard!"

"But the bastard holds all the aces."

"Yeah. Stahl's methodically planned each detail. He's studied the Summit agenda. He probably knows *where* the leaders will be, at what time. He's chosen his location and learned our security procedures for it. He's convinced he's found a way around them."

"No wonder I can't sleep nights," de Waha said.

Over the next two hours, he and Jean reviewed security measures for each event. They then looked for ways to circumvent their own security, found a couple of remote possibilities and fixed them. One hour later both men came to a conclusion neither wanted to verbalize: there were a few narrow opportunities where Stahl might have a chance to penetrate their defenses, but only *if* he had certain inside information.

Information could always be bought. Especially by someone with money, like Stahl.

Donovan didn't like the uneasy feeling in his gut.

He also didn't like the phone call he received from the boss, the Director of National Intelligence, Michael Madigan, minutes before walking into the bar.

Madigan told him that all eight leaders had decided to proceed with the G8 Summit at all costs and regardless of the threat. They needed to reach agreements and find solutions to global problems. Too much was riding on the Summit.

It would not be cancelled or relocated.

And it began in hours.

FIFTEEN

DUSSELDORF

CNN's high-angle camera showed the caravan of eight black-velvet-draped coffins rattling down the cobblestone street. He watched blood drip from each coffin, and was delighted to see more blood dripping from the casket of the American President. Delirious crowds threw rocks at the caskets that had been smeared with yellow Christian crosses and Stars of David. People wept with joy.

Wolf Blitzer said, "Let's shift to Kabul, and then to Islamabad and Teheran where you'll see even bigger crowds celebrating."

In each city, the camera showed thousands of people rejoicing in the righteous deaths of the G8 Summit leaders. All eight of them...

Valek Stahl's eyes shot open. He stared at the ceiling above his bed and smiled.

Today's dream is tomorrow's reality.

He got up, stretched, and began his morning workout. After thirty minutes of heavy weightlifting, one hundred pushups and fifty chin-ups, he ran four six-minute miles on his new NordicTrack treadmill, checking world news on the treadmill's built-in Internet screen.

He showered, ate breakfast and turned on his laptop. He logged onto *Le Soir*, a Belgian French language newspaper, then *De Standaard*, a Flemish language paper, then the major international newswires and web browsers.

He was looking for any last-second modifications in the G8 Summit itinerary. There were none.

To confirm his findings, he phoned Wassif Aziz, a local police officer assigned to G8 security. Wassif, Stahl's Summit insider, lost his wife, three children, and parents from bombs in Baghdad years ago. Wassif detested the G8 countries. Although Al Qaeda had actually detonated the bombs, Wassif blamed the presence of allied troops, mostly Americans, for forcing Al Qaeda to detonate the bombs.

And, as a Muslim male, Wassif was committed to his moral duty: to avenge the death of his family. He accepted his duty. He also accepted Stahl's fifty thousand euros.

Wassif answered on the first ring.

"How's the weather today?" Stahl said in French.

"No clouds."

"If you see clouds, even small clouds, phone me or use our other venue."

"Of course."

Stahl hung up and realized it was time to go brief his team. He left his Dusseldorf apartment and stepped outside into a crisp breeze blowing off the Rhine River. He looked around and saw no one watching him.

Seven blocks later, he entered *Die Sahara*, a small middle-eastern restaurant. He smelled the rich aromas of garlic and basil and Chicken Shawarma. In the far corner, several wrinkle-faced old men with sunken eyes sipped fragrant Arabic coffee and argued politics.

Opposite the men, in a small alcove, sat a group of black-clad middle-aged women riveted to an Egyptian soap opera on television.

Stahl walked through to the kitchen where two women prepared lamb and rice dishes, while another poured chickpeas into a blender, making hummus. At a butcher-block, a tall, muscular, dark-haired young man chopped lamb shanks with a bloody cleaver.

Stahl spoke to him. "Yusef... ."

Yusef turned and seeing Stahl, smiled, then rushed over and kissed him on both cheeks.

"It is time," Stahl said. "Get your brothers."

Yusef nodded, then hurried up the back stairs. Stahl watched him go, noticing once again how physically similar Yusef and he were. Like Stahl, Yusef stood about six-three and weighed about two hundred ten pounds. Yusef also had a German father and Arab mother. And his parents, like Stahl's, were killed by Israeli raids in southern Lebanon. The only difference was that Yusef's hair was black while Stahl's was a brownish-blond.

Moments later, Yusef brought his two half-brothers, Ahmed and Iram, into the kitchen. The two younger brothers, shorter and darker, embraced Stahl warmly, clearly in awe of his reputation.

Yusef led them all to a basement storage room where they sat at an old wooden table. Iram locked the door and turned on a water faucet to prevent anyone from overhearing.

Stahl stared at them several seconds, letting the gravity of his visit sink in.

"Allah's sacred mission is at hand," Stahl said.

They leaned forward, anxious.

"And he has chosen us!"

Their dark, eager eyes widened.

"We shall retaliate against the godless infidels. We will avenge their evil occupation of our sacred Muslim lands... and the slaughter of thousands of our innocent men, women and children."

"*Allahu Akbar!*" The brothers said.

Ahmed leaned forward. "Tell us Katill - how shall we achieve Allah's glorious jihad?"

"We will avenge the murder of Osama Bin Laden and our other Al Qaeda leaders!"

Stahl paused, letting the suspense build.

"We shall assassinate *their* leaders!"

"Which leaders?"

"The G8 leaders at the Summit in Brussels."

Their mouths fell open.

"But a Saudi minister is attending," Yusef said.

"The man is a traitor to Islam!" Stahl said. "Has he not helped the great Satan – America?"

The brothers nodded.

"Has he not often refused to contribute funds to our sacred jihadist causes?"

They nodded again.

"Does he not deserve death?"

"Yes!" the brothers said with anger.

"Where shall we strike?" Ahmed asked.

Stahl spread a map out and pointed to a spot. "Here."

Again, their eyes widened in shock.

For the next twenty minutes Stahl explained his plan. He showed them how in the highly unlikely scenario that one attack was stopped, the backup plan, the second sword, would smite their archenemies.

When he finished, they stared at him. He could feel their admiration, perhaps adoration.

"It's brilliant," Yusef said. "But how did you learn about the – "

Stahl held up his hand. "Better if you don't know."

Yusef nodded. "But how will we escape? There will be thousands of police."

"We will escape as police. I will bring your uniforms to your Brussels apartment. After our attack, we'll drive to Montpellier, France. From there we'll be flown to Iran."

Stahl handed Yusef a thick envelope. "This will more than cover your expenses for the next two days."

Yusef fanned the twenty thousand euros inside and smiled. "You are too kind, Valek. We thank you."

Stahl nodded and stood. "Here are the keys to your Brussels apart-

---

ment. I will meet you there."

Stahl embraced them and left.

Outside, he walked back toward his apartment, knowing he could rely on the brothers. They were religious fanatics, who more than once had confessed their willingness to fight and die as martyrs for the cause.

As he walked down an alley, he heard scuffling behind him. Turning, he saw a building demolition site of partial walls and stacks of rubble.

Behind one wall, a large German construction worker with a tool belt slung over a large beer gut was kicking something on the ground. Stahl heard a gasp.

He walked closer and saw the worker was kicking a young, dark-skinned boy, maybe eleven. The boy was jackknifed in a defensive pre-natal curl.

"Arabische Scheiße! Verlassen Sie Deutschland! Arab shit… get out of Germany!" the big German shouted, kicking the young boy's face.

As the German prepared to kick the side of his head – Stahl moved with blinding speed, delivering a karate-kick to the back of the man's neck, smashing vertebrae. The big man collapsed, writhing in pain and gasping for breath.

Stahl lifted the bloody, stunned boy to his feet and told him to never return to the site. When Stahl saw his shabby clothes, he took out his wallet, and handed three hundred Euros to the young boy. The kid stared at the enormous amount of money, then weeping, kissed Stahl's hand and limped away, saying, *"Alhamdulillah! Praise Allah!"*

Stahl looked around and was satisfied that the rubble and walls had prevented anyone from seeing his attack.

"You bastard!" the fat German wheezed from the ground, his face contorted in pain. "I can't move my legs!"

"You won't need them."

Stahl reached down and snapped the man's neck like a stalk of celery. The racist pig would die from asphyxia within three minutes.

One less Arab hater, Stahl thought as he strolled away.

He'd learned about Arab haters early in life. His mother taught him. Even though she told him that Arab-hating Israelis had killed her parents, Stahl learned later that her parents had actually abandoned her when she was two.

She met Stahl's father, a teenage deserter from Rommel's *Afrika Korps*, in a Beirut brothel. She was looking for money. He was looking for sex. Soon, their mutual hatred of Israel and its supporters bound them together in ways love never could.

Young Valek simply accepted their hatred until one day when he was nine. On that day, their hatred became his. And it brought new meaning to his life. Hatred became his reason to live.

He'd been playing hide and seek with his young sister in the garden of their home in a southern Lebanese village. He'd walked up the hill in front of the house pretending to look for Bathshira, even though he knew she was hiding in the bushes near the house.

Then he heard something.

A deafening roar…

He looked up – something was streaking across the sky toward his house.

Bathshira, terrified, ran from the bushes toward him. One second later everything exploded in blinding white light. He was hurled backward, felt his body and head slam against the large boulders, felt warm blood trickle down his neck, felt his eyes close.

Seconds later, they opened and he sat up, disoriented.

Looking up, he saw two Israeli jets soaring south.

"Why?" he shouted at them.

He turned toward his house.

Gone!

Only parts of walls and stone remained. He ran toward the rubble, tripping over something.

A small bloody leg. His sister's. Just her leg.

He found the rest of her several feet away, saturated in more blood. Her eyes stared vacantly into the blazing sun. He bent down and took her hand. He begged her to wake up, but she would not.

He placed his ear on her bloody chest, but heard no heartbeat.

Screaming for his parents, he ran toward the house.

He squeezed between slabs of fallen walls and smoldering roof, looking for his mother.

Tears streamed from his eyes, strange cries roared from his throat. Then he saw her – pinned under massive chunks of concrete. The concrete had crushed her chest and head. Blood gushed from her mouth.

"Ummi, ehkee ya ummi... " Speak, momma...

She would not speak. She would not blink her eyes. She would not breathe. Flies crawled into her mouth. He hated the flies. He tried to lift the concrete off her but couldn't. He hated being small and weak. He saw her bloody amber prayer beads and pried them from her burned hand.

Who would take care of him?

Baba would! Where was Papa? He could wake momma. He ran toward the workshop rooms where his father had been. He was not there.

Papa escaped! He'd heard the planes and got away!

Stahl stepped over a slab of concrete and saw a bloody hand. On the wrist, his father's watch.

"Vater!"

The hand jerked.

He's alive!

Stahl bent down and tried to lift the heavy concrete, but couldn't. He scrambled to the other side of the slab and saw his father's eyes staring back at him. And *blinking!*

"Vater, vater!"

His father wheezed in German. *"Versprechen emir etwas, Valek."* *Promise me, something.*

"Ja, vater!"

"Töten Sie die, die dies gemacht haben!"

"Yes, papa, yes I will kill those who did this."

"Promise me, Valek."

Valek nodded as blood spilled from his father's mouth.

"Ich verspreche Sie, vater! I promise, papa. Please don't close your eyes like momma, please don't! I promise you, papa... just don't close..."

His father's eyes did not close... but they froze wide open... and then the light in them went away.

SIXTEEN

Maccabee settled into her plush, comfortable first class British Airways seat. She couldn't believe how spacious, roomy and luxurious it felt. Her usual tourist seat felt like a highchair.

The seat next to hers was empty, as were the seats across from her. Three rows ahead, a skinny middle-aged man worked on his laptop.

Then a large, muscular man with a heavy satchel walked on and sat down two rows behind her across the aisle. Earlier, in the departure lounge, she'd caught his dark eyes staring at her every few minutes. He'd made her feel uncomfortable.

Now, as he buckled his seat belt, he shot another glance at her.

Her suspicion cranked up a few notches.

"Something to drink?" the young, blonde stewardess asked.

"Sounds great," Maccabee said, still shaken from the attack in the apartment. "Vodka, please."

"How would you like that?"

"Enormous."

The stewardess smiled, and returned quickly with a large vodka. Maccabee thanked her, took a sip and leaned back. The alcohol tasted great. She took another sip.

Minutes later, the 747 hurled itself down the runway and soared into the sky.

No turning back now, she realized. She was in a cloak-and-dagger scenario, one she was ill prepared for. But Donovan had said she'd be safer in Brussels and she trusted his judgment. She hoped she wasn't a burden for him and could help with new Sumerian translations there. He'd said her translations could give them vital information. Her father, she knew, would want her to help.

She glanced back at the large man. Again, he was peering at her over his magazine. When she noticed the title of the magazine, she stopped breathing. *Soldier of Fortune.* An assassin's bible. Mandatory reading for hitmen.

She told herself to relax. Donovan had told her there was an armed air marshal on the flight. And each passenger had been frisked, X-rayed, semi-undressed and practically fondled by TSA Security personnel. Still, a Nigerian's underpants almost blew up a Detroit flight. And some guy recently breezed through TSA airport screening with a concealed weapon.

She looked back at the passenger. He was still reading. No way he could have brought a weapon aboard.

Unless... *he* was the air marshal.

But wait – what if he was a fake air marshal sent to kill her?

She was slipping into Paranoidville and knew she had to stop. She gulped down more vodka and told herself to relax. She remembered her friend, Marilyn, had given her an Ambien to help with jet lag. She took it from her purse and washed it down with more Vodka. Probably a bad combination, but hey, she needed to chill out and sleep now.

Moments later, she yawned and listened to the soft drone of the engines. Soon, her eyelids grew heavy, very heavy... and very closed.

A loud thud jolted her awake!

Bird strike? Terrorist?

She looked around. Everyone seemed calm. Then she realized she'd heard the landing gear lock into place.

Had she just slept over five hours?

She had, she realized, as she looked out the window saw London, a city she loved. The emerald grass and Serpentine Lake of Hyde Park slid by, then Big Ben and Parliament. It amazed her how much of America's values and culture emerged from this revered chunk of land.

She remembered the assassin, Mr. *Soldier of Fortune,* a few rows behind her. She turned and looked.

Sleeping, and drooling on his magazine.

They landed at Heathrow Airport where Donovan's friend, a British Intelligence agent named Nigel whisked her through VIP Customs and minutes later into the lobby of the airport Holiday Inn.

As Nigel registered her under his name, a tall young man in a business suit walked past her. She couldn't believe her eyes. She actually gasped out loud, leaned against the counter and whispered, *"Andrew!"*

The man's similarity was beyond shocking. The man was Andrew's *clone.*

Andrew Pierce. She flashed back to the graduate school party where they met. She couldn't take her eyes off him as he strummed folk songs on his scuffed-up Gibson guitar.

She spent the next few hours chatting with him, laughing with him, dancing with him. By the end of the party she was wondering about spending her life with him. They began dating, grew serious, and six months later were planning to marry after graduation. Everything was perfect.

Except the arterial walls in Andrew's brain. Over the years, a congenitally thin wall had slowly ballooned into a small aneurysm, then into a larger one.

Six months before their wedding, he was exercising in his apartment. Perhaps, he'd tried a few extra pushups, or lifted heavier weights. Whatever it was, the extra effort increased his blood pressure and sent blood pounding against the weakened arterial wall.

Pounding too hard... .

The aneurysm exploded, destroying brain tissue.

Late that night his roommate found him on the floor. Dead.

She had never known such pain, almost dropped out of school, but didn't because he wouldn't want her to. For weeks, she visited his grave and spent hours talking to him, thanking him for their brief, but cherished, memories together.

Over the next three years, she didn't socialize much. A few dates. Nice guys. Not going anywhere. Not Andrew. Even today, she didn't date much, still held back, afraid of committing to a serious relationship, knowing she couldn't withstand that kind of pain and loss again.

Sometimes she wondered if Andrew had been the one true love of her life.

Her thoughts shifted to Donovan Rourke, awaiting her in Brussels. His courage, honesty and intelligence reminded her in some ways of Andrew.

But Donovan also had an illness, a lingering sadness, a malaise that at times seem to drain all emotion from his eyes. And she knew why. The horrific murder of his wife had killed a part of him, and damaged him, perhaps forever.

* * *

The following morning at Brussels International Airport, Maccabee was met by an associate of Donovan's, a tall handsome man with thick, brown hair named Marcel de Paepe.

Twenty minutes later, Marcel escorted her into the luxurious lobby of the Amigo Hotel and over to the elevator. He explained that she was already checked in under a male alias, Mr. Antoine Charbonneau. The manager walked over, introduced himself and handed her a message.

Maccabee,

Welcome. Jean de Waha and I are out

for a while. If you need anything just ask the

hotel manager, or Marcel. A guard will be

outside your room at all times. If you feel up
to it, please join Jean and me in the Amigo
bar at 7 this evening, and then for dinner. If
not, just leave word at the desk.

I'm relieved you are here.

Donovan

I'm relieved I'm here, too.

Marcel escorted her upstairs to her room, where he introduced her
to her security guard, a large, powerfully built man named Theo, sitting outside her door.

"Nice to meet you, Mister Charbonneau," Theo said to her.

She laughed. "Nice to meet you, Theo."

She went inside, unpacked and began translating the new NSA
intercept she'd received via email from Donovan's colleague.

This message was longer and the Sumerian logograms looked much
more complicated.

Something clicked loudly behind her. She turned, saw nothing,
then continue working.

Seconds later, she heard the clicking again.

It came from the door connecting her room to the room next to
hers.

She noticed the locked dead bolt knob was slowly turning, unlock-
ing the door. Concerned, she stood and prepared to run out into the
hall and tell Theo.

Slowly, the connecting door opened.

"Oh... you in room already?" said a small woman housekeeper.
"Guard ask me to double-lock door. Is okay?"

"Yes," Maccabee said, breathing out.

SEVENTEEN

"**F**it for a King!" Jean de Waha said.

But is it safe for the King… and his guests, the world's most pow-erful leaders? Donovan wondered, as he gazed around the interior of the massive *Palais Royale,* the official palace of the King and Queen of Belgium. He'd always marveled at the massive neo-classical palace and considered it to be one of the most striking royal residences in Europe.

Now, Jean and he had to make it the safest residence in Europe.

"This is the Throne Room," said Georges Lafleur, de Waha's Dep-uty Director in the Security Intelligence Division. "We'll host the G8 leaders' state dinner here."

Donovan knew and liked Lafleur. The tall, muscular man with thick blond hair and blue eyes was an ex-soccer star who became a highly skilled anti-terrorist operative.

The Throne Room was enormous. It measured 150 feet by 87 feet with gleaming shades of parquet woods on the floor, Rubens on the walls, red drapes on the windows, and lavish gold leaf trim everywhere else. But what riveted Donovan's attention most hung from the ceiling

– eleven crystal chandeliers the size of lunar landing modules.

"In America we have a name for places like this," Donovan said.

"Motel 6?" Lafleur said.

Donovan laughed. "Museums."

De Waha smiled. "Hey, like Mel Brooks said, 'it's *good* to be the King!'"

"Mel's right," a deep voice said behind them.

Donovan turned and was shocked to see Albert II, the ex-King of Belgium, smiling and walking toward them with an entourage.

"Your Excellency," de Waha said, "what a pleasant surprise. Permit me to introduce my American colleague, Donovan Rourke."

King Albert smiled. "I've met Mr. Rourke before. In Bruges, a few years ago. A boring diplomatic function, as I recall."

"That's right, your Excellency. It's nice to see you again." He remembered him as a smart, friendly, respected and beloved monarch.

"And it's good to see you, Mr. Rourke."

They shook hands.

"So tell me, Donovan, is our humble abode here safe?"

"Safe as our Fort Knox, your Excellency."

King Albert smiled. "Minus the gold, of course."

"Well… yes."

"You know, the Nazis stole ours. Over $220 million worth of gold bars. Stamped little Swastikas on them. Used the gold to pay for their war."

"So I heard."

An aide whispered in the King's ear.

"I must go. Asparagus farmers are storming the palace gates! What's a king to do? If you need anything, let me know."

"We will, your Excellency," de Waha said.

As the King and his entourage left, Georges Lafleur led Donovan and de Waha down a long corridor to a steel door. Lafleur punched in a long code and the door slid open.

They entered the room and Donovan saw several security officers seated at computers beneath a huge wall of television screens.

"Our control room." Lafleur said. "Over two hundred screens monitor every palace opening: windows, doors, roof openings, garage doors, sewer openings, the chimneys. If even a bird invades an opening, a computer-guided camera will lock on it – and warn us with a buzzer and flashing light."

Donovan was impressed. "What about the ventilation systems?"

"We've installed the latest sniffers, the best biological and chemical detection devices."

"How often have the rooms been sniffed?"

"More than dogs in heat."

Donovan smiled. "And you've vetted the dinner guests and food service personnel, right?"

"Three separate times. Each person will be issued a photo ID with a hologram."

Donovan watched Lafleur sip water from a glass. "Georges, what about the water. You know, for drinking, ice cubes, cooking."

Lafleur nodded. "Any lethal agent introduced into the palace water system will be detected by our sophisticated sensors."

"And if the sophisticated sensors fail?"

"We have a low tech, back-up water sensor system." Lafleur signaled Donovan and de Waha into a nearby bathroom. He lifted the lid on the toilet tank and gestured for them to look.

Donovan looked and saw five gold fish swimming around.

"Fish are very sensitive to toxic water."

Minutes later, satisfied with palace security, Donovan and de Waha drove to the Congo Museum where thousands of animal displays, artworks, precious diamonds and gems from the Belgian Congo and other African countries were displayed. Security appeared excellent.

Finally, they were driven back to the Grand Place in the heart of the city.

This is where Stahl will strike, Donovan thought. *This is where I would strike.*

The reason was simple: the leaders would be sitting out in the open on the grandstand - like ducks on a pond - for *thirty-three* minutes of windy speeches.

Surrounded by thousands of people.

And hundreds of windows.

And even though all buildings would be cleared of all people, and all building doors locked and guarded, Donovan feared Stahl might somehow get inside one. Or was already inside, hiding, lying in wait.

Donovan looked around the *Grand Place*. The eleventh-century square, the size of two football fields side by side, had a long, glorious history. And more than its share of inglorious history.

Like in the 1500s when the Spanish conquerors beheaded Belgians on its cobblestones, and in 1695 when French cannons bombarded some of the buildings. And in 1941 when Nazi soldiers rounded up some of the 30,000 local Jews and sent them to die in the Holocaust camps. Donovan remembered his good friend, Maurice, who'd survived as a nine-year-old boy living day to day in alleys, eating handouts from Belgians who defied the Nazis and risked their lives to shelter and feed him.

Donovan looked up at the ancient buildings, their windows glimmering in the lights.

"The windows, Jean!"

De Waha nodded. "I tried to have them boarded up, but got overruled."

"By whom?"

"The Preservation of Antiquity Committee. They said boarding the windows is a desecration."

"But killing eight world leaders isn't?"

De Waha shrugged.

Donovan nodded, understood his friend's frustration.

The wind suddenly kicked up and he looked at the illuminated medieval buildings trimmed with gleaming gold leaf. A recent survey named the historic *Grand Place* the most beautiful square in Europe.

Donovan agreed, but hoped it didn't become the site of The Most Significant Political Massacre in History.

* * *

A mile west, near the *Gare du Midi* train station, Yusef and his younger brothers, Ahmed and Iram, sat in the kitchen of the small apartment that Valek Stahl rented for them.

They finished eating a meal of lamb and black bean hummus, chicken with eggplant, and rice pudding, then sat back and sipped their cold milk.

Yusef studied his brothers. Their bellies were full, their brains and bodies ready. He was proud of them, even though they'd complained to him about the long hours of practice he'd subjected them to for the last two days. But the practice had paid off. Ahmed had his timing down perfectly, and Iram was only two seconds slower, well within the acceptable range.

"Very soon my brothers," Yusef said, "we will avenge the decades of injustice."

"Allahu Akbar!" said Iram and Ahmed together.

Yusef stood. "Now, it is time to begin."

They picked up three large cases, headed outside, placed the heavy cases in the gray Peugeot panel van and drove off.

Four hours later, they returned to their apartment.

Their cases were empty.

He looked at his brothers. They looked as excited as he felt. And no wonder.

We're prepared and practiced.

History is in our hands.

EIGHTEEN

*T**his is tougher than five star Sudoku,* Maccabee realized as she translated the latest Sumerian message at her hotel room desk.

The new message was longer and complicated, too complicated for her jet-lagged brain. She needed to snap her synapses back to life before she met Donovan and Jean de Waha downstairs in the Amigo Bar in a little while.

Yawning, she stretched her arms and legs, then put on her running shorts, T-shirt and Nikes and began jogging in place. The plush Persian carpet felt good on her feet.

Jogging over to the window, she looked down on the tiny shops below. Tourists window-shopped. Children ate french fries smothered with mayonnaise. People shuffled down narrow cobblestone streets that their ancestors had shuffled down for centuries.

She jogged faster and looked across the street into some business offices where men and women hunched over their desktop computers. Her eyes were drawn to a dimly lit office directly opposite her. A tall man faced her. He held something long and black in his arms. He raised it up to his eye and aimed it directly at her.

A rifle!

She jumped to the side, waiting for the bullet to shatter the glass.

Nothing!

He's waiting for me to appear again...

Her heart pounding, she peeked through the side of the curtain. He was still aiming right at her! But now she noticed the barrel was much thicker than a rifle.

My God – a rocket launcher!

As she turned to run, the man pulled something out of the barrel... and the air rushed from her lungs.

He unraveled a wall poster.

She leaned against the wall, catching her breath. *Death By Mailing Tube!*

She felt foolish. Clearly, her imagination was still hyperventilating thanks to her father's murder and her attacker in the apartment. She told herself to relax! Hotel security was everywhere, she was registered as Antoine Charbonneau, and her guard, Theo, big enough to go bear hunting with a switch, sat right outside in the hall.

She ran hard for another fifteen minutes, then showered, dressed and went downstairs to meet Donovan and Jean de Waha in the Amigo Bar.

* * *

Donovan saw businessmen spin their barstools and look toward the door. Then he saw why: Maccabee. She walked toward their table, her white cotton dress hugging long tan legs worthy of lingerie commercial. Her hair, full and lustrous, gleamed like black silk in the soft overhead lighting.

Donovan was shocked by her transformation. At the funeral home her eyes had been red and puffy from crying, her cheeks pale and drawn. Now, she was composed and well... very attractive.

"Maccabee, meet Jean de Waha," Donovan said, "Jean is Director of Belgium's *Sûreté de l'État,* sort of Belgium's version of the CIA and FBI. He's also my old friend."

"All true," de Waha said, "except for the 'old' and 'friend' parts."

Maccabee smiled and introduced herself. *"Je suis très heureux de faire votre connaissance, Monsieur de Waha."*

"Enchanté, Mademoiselle, and I'm happy to meet you," he said, raising his eyebrows at her excellent French.

The waiter appeared and she ordered a white wine.

"What's that?" she asked pointing to a small square piece of electronic equipment on the table.

"An electronic barrier. Keeps the nasty people from hearing our conversation."

"Those noisy car dealers also help," Donovan said.

"You speak French as though you lived in Paris," de Waha said.

"I did during my father's sabbatical at the Sorbonne. I was twelve. I attended the *Lycee Internationale* in Paris."

"Excellent school system," de Waha said, "despite the fact that my idiot cousin runs it."

Maccabee laughed as the waiter served her wine.

"So how's the new Sumerian message coming along?" Donovan asked, hoping it might reveal vital information on the G8 attack.

"It's long and complicated. Later tonight, I'll receive some pictographs and logograms by e-mail. With them, I hope to have the message translated by early tomorrow morning or maybe sooner."

As she talked, Donovan noticed again how she had matured into a poised and beautiful young woman.

De Waha checked his watch. "Time for dinner. We have reservations at an excellent restaurant near the *Grand Place.*"

"I've always wanted to see the *Grand Place.*"

"You will in sixty seconds."

They walked outside and the crisp night air felt refreshing on Donovan's face. As they strolled down the narrow cobblestone street, he noticed Maccabee checking the five men walking beside the black Suburban following them.

"They're ours," Donovan said.

She looked relieved, but Donovan sensed she was still anxious over the attack in her apartment.

A few feet later, they stepped into the *Grand Place* square. Donovan watched Maccabee stop and stare like a kid at Disneyworld, just as millions of visitors before her had done. Her gaze moved from one ancient, enchanting, illuminated, gold-leaf-trimmed building to another.

"Did I just walk into the Middle Ages?"

"Yep," Donovan said.

"Jean, *c'est magnifique!*"

"*Merci.*"

As they walked across the square's worn cobblestones, Donovan couldn't stop the flood of memories. Sunday strolls with Emma and little Tish on these same cobblestones. Tish bending down to talk to the parrots at the Sunday bird market. Emma buying red tulips on flower day. His stomach ached at the memories.

They stopped in front of the huge *Hôtel de Ville,* the largest building on the square, its illuminated spire rising three hundred feet into the night sky.

"The *Hôtel de Ville* is our Town Hall," de Waha said. "It was here before Columbus discovered America."

"So was Jean!" Donovan said, backing away before de Waha could elbow him.

"See the doors," de Waha said.

"They're enormous," Maccabee said.

"But look – they're off-center to the left. The architect was so angry when he saw how off-center they were, he climbed the tower and leapt to his death right on the stones where you're standing."

Maccabee took a step back. "Didn't anyone try to stop him?"

"Going up, yes. Coming down, no."

Donovan heard hammering. He turned and saw that carpenters were finishing up the G8 grandstand at the far end of the square. The stand was surrounded by guards holding Belgian FAL automatic rifles.

He knew the grandstand would be guarded non-stop until the eight leaders stepped onto it for the ceremony.

But what if Stahl was one of the carpenters? And what if he'd made grandstand boards with explosives? Donovan knew that C4 or PETN explosives could be molded to look like everything from wood planks to toothpaste to Barbie Dolls. He told himself to relax. Guards and Hazmat teams would be scrutinizing and using dogs and sophisticated machines to sniff the grandstand tonight and tomorrow.

They walked over to the restaurant, *Aux Armes de Bruxelles,* and enjoyed a marvelous meal of lobster bisque, roasted lamb and crepes Suzette. As Donovan finished eating, he remembered something he'd almost forgotten: some of the best French cuisine in the world is in Brussels.

Back in the Amigo Hotel, they squeezed through media crews in the lobby and went up to de Waha's suite. There, they picked up folders for their meeting with the G8 national security directors.

Donovan asked Maccabee to come along and show the directors a sample of Sumerian pictograph writing in case they'd seen similar messages.

* * *

Benoit Broutafache, a broad-shouldered, dark-haired man, sat in the Amigo lobby typing on his laptop, posing as a reporter. He watched Maccabee and the two men weave through the crowded lobby and enter an elevator.

Broutafache flipped open his cell phone and dialed.

In Manhattan, Nikko Nikolin picked up.

"She's here!"

"Where?"

"At the Amigo Hotel with Rourke and the Belgian guy."

"Can you get to her?"

"I can get to anybody."

"Our friend will be pleased.

"I'll be pleased with the rest of my fee."

"Half was wired to your Belize account an hour ago."

"I know."

"The rest on completion."

Broutafache hung up, felt the custom-made plastic Glock in his pocket. The hotel's metal detector had failed to detect the weapon because he'd put the gun's only metal part, the small thin firing pin, on his key chain between several similar looking small thin toy golf clubs. The security guard didn't even notice the difference when he passed the key chain through the metal detector.

Broutafache closed his laptop, stood and checked Maccabee's room number again.

Then he walked toward the hotel's back stairwell.

NINETEEN

COLOGNE

Valek Stahl was concerned. Through his BMW windshield, he saw a young cop on the steps of the *Kolner Dom Cathedral* staring at Stahl's parked car. Stahl was parked legally, but the cop seemed anxious, like he might walk over and ask him questions. Stahl wondered if the cops were closing in on Herr Rutten. Maybe they suspected the old man of selling products more dangerous than antiques.

Stahl started to drive away, but stopped when an elderly woman hurried over and embraced the cop. Smiling, the apparent mother and son turned and entered the cathedral. Stahl paused a moment, remembering the last time he embraced his mother like that - the morning the Israelis murdered her.

Stahl got out of his BMW. A bus swept past, engulfing him in smelly diesel fumes. He noticed dark clouds moving overhead as he walked across Komodienstrasse and entered Herr Rutten's small antique shop, jiggling the doorbell.

"Coming… " Rutten shouted from the back.

"It's Stahl."

"Ah, Herr Stahl, good to see you again." Rutten hobbled up to the door, flipped the *Geschlossen/Closed* sign facing the street, then locked the door.

Rutten looked like he'd worked late into the night to finish Stahl's project. His rheumy eyes had tightened into puffy black slits. His face was as parched as a Dead Sea scroll. Flakes of dandruff dotted his black sweater like tiny potato chip crumbs.

"This way, Herr Stahl."

Rutten led Stahl down an aisle with World War II German Army helmets, bayonets and Luger pistols. Stahl found it odd that Rutten placed the war memorabilia next to his prized collection of antique, not-for-sale Beatrix Potter bunnies.

Rutten reached behind the bunnies, revealing a faded swastika on his forearm.

The old Nazi had often bragged about his days as a young Sobibor SS guard. His job was separating children from their mothers as trains unloaded Jewish prisoners at the camp. One day, when a mother refused to give up her young daughter, Rutten pulled out his Luger and shot her and her daughter to death. Then, to teach a lesson, he shot the next two women in line. Rutten was never charged with war crimes since the remaining eyewitnesses were shot or gassed within hours.

Rutten took out a tattered 1937 Berlin phonebook, opened it and pushed a button inside. Suddenly the entire bookcase moved back two feet, exposing a narrow staircase. Stahl remembered the dark, narrow, descending stairs as he followed the old man down to the bottom where Rutten flipped the light switch.

Once again Stahl marveled at what he saw: the exact opposite of the antique shop. He was standing in Herr Rutten's modern factory of death. Sophisticated, electronic tool-making machinery, the newest Baileigh metal lathes, a chrome punch press, and expensive laser-cutting machine. The machine shop and laboratory was sixty-feet-by-sixty-feet of white-tiled floor and walls gleaming under halogen lighting. The soft hum of air conditioners and purifiers filled the room.

So did the tar-like scent of C4 explosives.

In this secret underground factory, Rutten had assembled every weapon imaginable. From sophisticated explosives, to simple, but deadly chemical and biological weapons. He even stored certain components for a suitcase dirty bomb here.

The old man led Stahl over to an open cabinet. Rutten reached in and took out a large brown leather case. His bloodshot eyes brightened as he lifted the top, smiled down at his newest creation for Stahl. He gestured for Stahl to look.

Stahl saw precisely what he'd asked for. Even better than he'd expected. *Incredible!* The man was a master craftsman, an artist.

"Excellent work, Herr Rutten!"

Rutten smiled. "It will perform perfectly."

"Backup systems?"

"Two. If the primary system fails – which is impossible – the first and second system will activate within four seconds."

"Well done."

The old man gazed at his masterpiece. Stahl knew that Rutten only cared about one thing: that his creations worked. Who his weapons killed was irrelevant. *All* killing was irrelevant to him after Sobibor.

"And," Rutten continued, rubbing the case's soft leather, "my unique process makes the weapon undetectable, even by their most sophisticated instruments." His grin revealed bad teeth that looked and smelled like rotten mushrooms.

"Well done, Herr Rutten."

Stahl moved slightly behind the old man as Rutten brushed specks of dust from the case.

From his sleeve, Stahl removed a long syringe and eased it slowly up behind Rutten's neck.

"Tell me more about it," Stahl said.

Staring at his new creation, Rutten babbled on about its unique lethality and how, "The authorities will not anticipate it in a hundred years! And even if they get a hint, they will never be able to detect it!"

"Excellent, Herr Rutten."

Rutten chuckled himself into a coughing fit. "Now, if I could just legally patent my detection-avoidance process, I'd make millions and retire."

"Retiring makes sense. You've earned it." Stahl said, easing the needle up toward Rutten's neck.

Seconds later, Rutten seemed to notice the long, pointed shadow creeping across the leather case. He stopped talking.

As he started to turn, Stahl plunged the syringe into Rutten's neck just above the hairline.

Rutten froze, blinked, then tried to reach up, but Stahl locked his scrawny arms to his sides. The old man's face reddened. His arthritic knuckles bleached white as he gripped Stahl's wrists. He flailed about for a few seconds, then his body went limp.

Stahl pulled the needle from Rutten's neck and let his body drop to the floor. He checked Rutten's pulse. Fast, erratic, weakening. The 300 mgs of potassium cyanide would more than enough to stop his aged heart in minutes. And because of Rutten's advanced age and poor health, the medical examiner would probably see no reason to run toxicology tests.

Stahl watched Rutten's eyes go blank and felt a strange sense of personal loss. Rutten had been his highly skilled resource for sixteen years. His partner in success. But killing the world's eight most powerful leaders would eventually lead the Interpol and the police to Rutten's door. The cops might persuade Rutten give up Stahl. No way that would happen.

Stahl waited until the old Nazi's heart stopped, then carried him upstairs and laid him between the aisles. He wiped a spot of blood from Rutten neck hairline where he'd injected him. He then went back downstairs, wiped his fingerprints off everything he'd touched, grabbed the large leather case and went back upstairs. He shut the secret door to the lab, made sure the sign on the store entrance door read *Geschlossen/Closed* and left.

Outside, the cool fresh air invigorated him.

Across the street, the young cop he'd seen in front of the *Kolner Dom* Cathedral earlier was gone. But he did see the same two old women he'd seen yesterday chatting there.

The tall woman who looked at him yesterday, seemed to pay special attention to him again. She couldn't possibly suspect him. Maybe she was watching Herr Rutten's place. Or she was just a neighborhood busybody. He wasn't worried.

He turned away and walked to his car.

Minutes later, he was driving the Autobahn back to Dusseldorf.

* * *

In his Dusseldorf apartment, Stahl placed Herr Rutten's leather case into a three-by-two-foot pine storage trunk. On top of Rutten's case, he placed a false bottom, then laid several layers of clothing on the false bottom. He carried the pine trunk to the garage. He started to put it in the car's trunk, then realized the trunk was half filled, so he placed the pine trunk in the BMW's back seat.

He drove off toward Brussels.

Fifty minutes later, Stahl approached the Belgian border. He was surprised to see cars backed up, since this was normally a non-stop drive-through border like many European Schengen-crossing countries. Officers were probably checking cars as part of extra security for the G8. Perhaps he should have squeezed the pine case into the trunk. Too late now.

A light rain began to dot the windshield. Thunder rumbled in the distance.

Stahl watched the young male driver ahead hand his passport to the heavyset customs officer. The officer then handed it to an officer in the window of an adjacent building who scanned the passport into a computer that obviously checked his name against terrorist-watch lists.

Stahl wasn't worried. He had a new passport and a set of ID with a name the authorities had never seen before.

Seconds later, the officer signaled the young man to pull his car over to an area where several other cars were being searched.

Stahl grew concerned.

The customs officer waived him forward and Stahl eased the BMW up beside him.

The officer glanced at Stahl's German license plate and said in German, *"Ihren Pass, bitte."*

Stahl handed him a German passport with the name Johannes Steinecker. The officer studied it, flipped through the pages, then flipped back through them again. After a few seconds he asked, "What is your destination, Herr Steinecker?"

"Antwerp."

The officer checked the passport and began walking slowly alongside the car. He looked into the back seat area. The glass was tinted, but he appeared to study the pine trunk at length.

Stahl's muscles tightened. If the officer demanded he unlock the pine trunk, he would. If the man found the false bottom and Rutten's leather case beneath, Stahl would spray the guard's face with Novichok. The deadly mist would incapacitate the officer instantly. Stahl would then shout that the guard was having a heart attack, which would be quite true.

And quite fatal... within seconds.

Stahl remembered how easily he'd purchased a stockpile of the secret Novichok nerve agent from a laid-off worker from Russia's closed Chapayevsk plant.

The officer continued to look at the pine trunk. Finally, he walked back to Stahl.

"There's a problem," the officer said, still staring through the back window.

Stahl gripped the Novichok spray and raised it up close to the windowsill.

"A problem, officer?"

"Your molding. It's loose on this window. Rain could get in."

Stahl relaxed. "Oh, thanks officer."

The border guard nodded and handed Stahl his passport. "You may proceed."

Stahl drove into Belgium.

One hour and twenty minutes later, near the center of Brussels, Stahl turned onto Rue de la Plume. Halfway down the street, he pushed the garage opener and drove inside the garage. He closed the garage door, took the pine trunk out and entered the well-furnished living quarters he rented six months ago.

He opened the windows, turned on a ceiling fan, flipped on the television and began putting away his clothes. The TV screen flickered to life as U.S. President, John Colasanti, shook hands with Leo Van Caweuleart, Prime Minister of Belgium. The camera panned to show British Prime Minister Mary Ryan Kearns and her husband, Thomas, to French President Samuel de Batilly and his beautiful wife, Claude, the Italian President Angelo Miele, and the witty Canadian Prime Minister Marcel Marcotte. They all smiled and waved.

"Soon," he whispered, "I will wipe the arrogance from your faces!"

TWENTY

D onovan smelled wet diapers.

Then he realized it was Gauloises, vile smelling French cigarettes, in the hotel conference room he, de Waha and Maccabee had just entered. Through the hazy smoke he saw his colleagues, the security directors for each G8 leader. This was their final pre-Summit review.

"Donovan, Jean, *mes amis!*" said Philippe Tournier, the slender, dark-haired director of *Commissaire Divisonnaire* of the GSPR, the no-nonsense, ninety-person secret service group protecting the French President, Samuel de Batilly.

"Welcome back, Donovan," Philippe said, shaking hands.

"Thanks, Philippe" Donovan said, happy to see him and the others. Over the years, he'd developed excellent working relationships with most and considered them competent professionals and trusted friends.

"Gentlemen, meet Maccabee Singh. Her father, Professor Sohan Singh, translated the Sumerian message that uncovered this plot. And, as you know, he paid the ultimate price for that.

The group stood and took time to offer their condolences.

"Maccabee is continuing his work. She's translating a recently intercepted Sumerian message that is much longer. So hopefully it will contain information that can help us stop Stahl. One warning though. She speaks most of your languages fluently – so please try to control your usual lewd and lascivious comments."

"I like lewd and lascivious," Maccabee said.

The directors smiled and seemed to relax.

"Let's begin," de Waha said.

Everyone sat around the long, mahogany table. Donovan watched their eyes grow dark as their ominous assignment descended on them like a thick black cloud.

"First of all," de Waha said, "be aware - we face a brilliant, ruthless adversary. His birth name is Valek Stahl, but he's also known as Katill and by several aliases, such as Horst Speerman, Pierre DuMaurier, Ernst Fleisher, Axel Braun and others, as you've read in his Interpol profile. We assume he's already here in Brussels. Our only photo of him was taken seven years ago from a distance of seventy-five meters. That low-res photo is now being digitalized and age-enhanced by computers to give us a higher resolution photograph of him. Even so, chances are he'll be in disguise, something he's very good at. Wigs, collagen implants, plastic noses and so forth."

Philippe Tournier said, "I heard Stahl once posed as an elderly *nun* in a wheelchair and killed two Israelis hiding in the convent."

"True. He also killed the Mother Superior and the priest who hid them."

Werner Vogler, the tall, handsome director of the German Chancellor's security team, raised his hand. "Does the situation with Stahl change any of our security responsibilities?"

"No," de Waha said. "You each have yours, protecting your leader. We have ours. Belgian Security still has overall G8 responsibility. We've brought in 12,000 federal and local uniformed police, plus 1,000 security guards who've set up perimeters around the leaders and their events. In addition, we have several thousand army and national guard troops ready to control any trouble from protest demonstrations."

"Which ones do you expect trouble from?"

"The usual suspects. The anti-capitalists groups, the anarchist groups, the anti-war, anti-world hunger, anti-Wall Street and the anti-everything groups."

"That many groups?" Tournier asked.

"Yes. They've promised to show up."

"How polite of them to warn us."

"Yeah. And of course, Donovan and I will be working in liaison with each of your secret security teams protecting your national leaders."

De Waha turned to Donovan. "Donovan will now fill us in on what we know."

"Which is damn little," Donovan said, leaning on the table.

For the next twenty minutes, he explained everything he knew about the plot. Maccabee showed them a copy of an ancient Sumerian note and asked if they'd seen or heard about similar messages. No one had.

After Donovan finished, the group reviewed the security for each Summit event, identifying potential gaps of security and how those gaps had in theory been closed. When they finished, Donovan sensed they were well prepared for the most likely and predictable attacks: automatic weapons, explosives, biological and chemical weapons.

There was only one problem.

Stahl never did the predictable. His previous attacks were unique. Donovan feared the man had come up with another undetectable, unpredictable weapon delivery system. A one of a kind system so ingenious they might never suspect it.

De Waha stood up. "Breakfast in this room at 6:30 tomorrow morning."

The group nodded and left.

Donovan, Jean and Maccabee walked down to the elevator.

"I'm expecting the pictograms I need from the USA any minute," Maccabee said. "I'll go work on the Sumerian message. If all goes well,

I should have the message translated by morning."

"Terrific."

"What if I translate it sooner?"

"Call my cell immediately. No matter what time."

"I will."

"I'll walk you to your bodyguard."

"Thanks."

Jean de Waha tapped Donovan's shoulder. "When you're done, meet me in the bar. I'm concerned about tomorrow's palace dinner."

"Okay."

The elevator opened. Donovan and Maccabee went up to her floor and got off. Ahead he saw Theo, the muscular guard, a former pro rugby player, seated beside her door.

Theo wore a dark-blue suit stretched tightly over his thick chest and shoulders. His short brown hair and steel gray eyes gave him a no-nonsense military look. In fact, Donovan knew that Theo was Belgian Special Forces member who'd trained with the US Navy SEALs at Virginia Beach. And rumor was, he'd once singlehandedly wiped out four Al Qaeda terrorists planning to blow up a US-built medical center for women near Kabul. Theo confirmed what Caesar once said: 'The Belgians are the bravest of all the Gauls.'

"I'll be right here," Theo said to Maccabee in flawless English. "If you need anything, just let me know." He rubbed an L-shaped white scar on his cheek.

"Thanks, Theo."

Maccabee walked toward her door, Donovan following. She stopped a little too abruptly and he couldn't help but bump into her.

"Whoops!" he said.

"No, my whoops! I just wanted to say thanks again for letting me help."

"We thank you, Maccabee."

They smiled at each other and in that brief moment, Donovan felt something shift in him. A nice shift. He wasn't sure what it was, but something emotional and big, some kind of tectonic plate had shifted in his psyche. He was sure of one thing: he was no longer looking at her as just the daughter of his good friend.

"So, will we see you at our breakfast meeting?"

"You will."

Again, he felt the shift… a shift that he realized she might be reading in his eyes. *What the hell is going on here?*

"See you then," he said, leaving quickly.

* * *

At the other end of the hallway, Benoit Broutifache pretended to search for a room key as Donovan Rourke headed toward the elevator and Maccabee Singh entered her room.

The big guard sat near her door and read his newspaper. Probably some rent-a-cop boozer picking up extra cash.

Broutifache walked the other way, then stepped into a hotel service room. He stepped behind a tall rack of towels and sheets and quickly took his gun's firing pin from his key chain and fitted the pin back into his plastic Glock.

Then he waited.

Several minutes later, a room service waiter pushed a cart with silver covered food trays into the room, took some clean linen napkins from a rack and placed them on the cart. The food smell good.

"What's for dinner?" Broutifache asked.

The startled waiter spun around and stared into the barrel of the Glock.

TWENTY ONE

The Amigo Bar went graveyard quiet.

Donovan turned and saw why. Maccabee. She and Theo were plowing through a group of slightly inebriated car dealers from Norway.

A young blond dealer, name-tagged Bjorn, offered her his whiskey and barstool. She declined both with a smile. Bjorn looked sad, but handled it well.

Theo led her over to the private corner booth where Donovan and de Waha sat. She took a sheet of paper from a folder and placed it on the table. "I just finished this."

Donovan and Jean read her translation silently.

ARRIVED AT NORTH COUNTRY. OUR
TEAM HERE NOW. THE MEDUSA IS
IN PLACE, TESTED, OPERATIONAL,
UNDETECTABLE. MEDUSA WILL

DELIVER ALL EIGHT INFIDEL HEADS.
UPON DELIVERY, BALANCE OF
TWENTY-FIVE MUST ARRIVE AT BANK
WITHIN ONE DAY. NO EXCEPTIONS.
THE MEDUSA MAKER WILL PERISH. NO
FURTHER CONTACT UNTIL SECOND
MOON OF NEXT YEAR.

K

"Team!" Donovan said, concerned.

De Waha nodded. "The K must stand for Katill."

"Yes, but Katill, Valek Stahl, never works with a team! He's a lone wolf!"

They thought about that for a few moments.

"But obviously" Donovan said, "this assignment requires some helpers."

De Waha nodded.

"Where was this sent from?" Donovan asked.

"Dusseldorf."

"To where?"

"Here in Brussels. Also to Manhattan, and to some island in the Caribbean."

"Was it e-mailed, text-messaged?"

"Faxed!"

Donovan was not all that surprised by the fax delivery. More terrorist groups were faxing because the NSA, the FBI's Cyber Division, and other government 'listening' agencies were rumored to be concentrating their resources on the newer tech communications. Cell phones, Internet traffic, and texting, Facebook and Twitter, and e-mail drafts read by two people but never sent, even messages-hidden-in-a-photo steganography. But faxes were also monitored.

"He probably figured faxing would not draw our attention," Donovan said.

De Waha nodded.

Donovan said, "Al Qaeda now combines high tech with high flying tech."

"How?"

"They tape flash-drives to carrier pigeons that fly from cell to cell."

De Waha shook his head.

"Where were Katill's faxes picked up?"

"A library here in Brussels, *Bibliotheque Royale de Belgique,* and the Mid-Manhattan library in New York City. Public access fax machines. Anyone could have picked them up."

Donovan looked up and saw Werner Vogler, Germany's intelligence director for the *Bundesnachrichtendienst,* the BND, hurrying over to their table.

"We've got something," Vogler said, breathing hard. "Last night in Dusseldorf, a former East German *Stasi* policewoman was standing near the *Kolner Dam* Cathedral. She saw a man who looked like Stahl come out of Rutten's Antique Shop. She's been watching Herr Rutten's shop for two years because she and her ex-boss long suspected him of making weapons, probably explosives. She got a tip that Rutten made explosives for a neo-Nazi group, then for Hamas and the PLO, later for Al Qaeda. But no evidence was ever found until last night."

"Did you talk to Rutten?" de Waha said.

"No. He's dead. Died around eleven or so last night."

De Waha shook his head. "Cause of death?"

Vogler shrugged. "No signs of a struggle. He was eighty-seven and in bad health. Maybe heart attack or stroke."

"Maybe Stahl," Donovan said, pointing to Maccabee's translation. *'Medusa maker will perish.'*

Werner Vogler nodded. "We found Rutten's secret underground laboratory. Very sophisticated. He could make anything, explosives, biological and chemical weapons. In one part of the lab we actually got a reading for radioactive material!"

Could this get any worse? Donovan wondered.

"Jesus!" de Waha said, shaking his head.

"Any evidence that links Rutten to Stahl or the G8?" Donovan asked.

"Not yet. But we're still looking. My gut says it's only a matter of time before we find a link."

"Meanwhile," de Waha said, "we're distributing a computer-aged photo of Stahl to all police throughout Belgium."

"And all hotels, restaurants, and bars," Donovan added.

"We're also trying to put his photo in our national papers, and on television."

"Trying... ?" Donovan said, surprised it wasn't already in the works. "What's the hold up?"

De Waha's face reddened and Donovan could see that his friend was frustrated.

"Certain government officials are terrified a full-blown media and television blitz will unleash a twitter blitz or go viral in a way that will ruin the G8's image, throw a blanket of panic over the entire Summit."

"Would they rather throw blankets over eight dead world leaders?"

De Waha shrugged with obvious frustration.

Everyone racked their brains for ways to alert the public about Stahl.

Donovan noticed a band-aid on Vogler's finger and had a thought. "Medical emergency."

Everyone turned toward him.

"What emergency?" de Waha said.

"We say Valek Stahl has been exposed to something highly serious and contagious... maybe Ebola or meningococcal meningitis. We say he needs urgent medical care."

"Ebola would cause total panic," de Waha said. "But meningococcal meningitis will frighten people enough and keep them on the lookout for him. Let's try it."

Donovan nodded. "We tell people, 'if you see him, don't get near him, but phone the police immediately.'"

"I can sell that."

"If not, let's call our friend."

"Our friend?"

"The King."

"Good idea." De Waha glanced at his watch and stood. "Okay everyone, let's reconvene at breakfast."

They walked out of the bar and boarded the elevator. De Waha got off at his floor and the elevator headed on up.

Donovan turned toward Maccabee. "Yet again I'll deliver you to your trusty guard."

"Yet again I thank you."

The doors opened, and they walked slowly down the hall toward her room. He saw Theo, who looked up from his newspaper.

"Any trouble?" Donovan asked.

"Just a couple of axe-wielding ninjas."

Donovan and Maccabee smiled.

He turned to her. "Thanks to your translation, we now know Stahl has a *team* here. And we may know his weapon maker. Knowing this helps a lot, Maccabee. And we're reviewing videos of people picking up faxes at *Bibliotheque Royale de Belgique* and the Mid Manhattan Library. The fax time-stamps may help us identify who picked it up and then the sender in Dusseldorf."

"I'll sleep better if it does."

"You've gotta be jet-lagged."

"I am."

"Sleep well. We've got a long day tomorrow."

When she nodded, he noticed her eyes, like liquid jade in the chandelier lights.

"Maccabee, I must confess."

"Please do... ."

"You're the only woman I've said goodnight to outside her hotel room twice on the same night."

She smiled. "How many *inside* their hotel rooms?"

"Sixty-seven."

She laughed.

"Good night, Ms. Singh." He leaned forward and kissed her cheek.

"I feel deprived."

"Did I hear depraved?"

"Deprived!"

"But why?"

"We're in Belgium."

He wasn't sure what she meant.

"One kisses the cheeks three times."

"Ahhh… how culturally insensitive, especially of an urbane so-phisticate like me." He leaned forward and kissed her left cheek, then her right, then her left.

"Well done. And Donovan, one more thing."

"Yeah?"

"Letting me help means more to me than you realize."

He nodded. *And you mean more to me than I realized.* "You're wel-come, Maccabee. See you at breakfast."

Donovan walked down the hallway concerned about what the hell was going on in his head, or was it his heart… which seemed to have a mind of its own.

What am I getting myself into – and why now of all times – when I should be focused on stopping an assassin!

Not starting a relationship.

TWENTY TWO

In the housekeeping room down the hall from Maccabee Singh's hotel room, Benoit Broutafache sucked in his beer belly so he could button the room service jacket… a jacket he'd borrowed from a waiter now lying unconscious, gagged and tied up in a nearby closet. The waiter would wake up in about three hours.

Earlier, Benoit had watched Singh walk through the lobby with Rourke and de Waha, then go up to a hotel conference room. Later, she returned to her room, but a short time after that, she came out again and the big guard escorted her downstairs to the Amigo Bar.

Now, finally, she was back in her room.

Just in time for room service.

He grabbed the passkey he'd taken from the waiter, then straightened the silverware and food trays on the service trolley. He slid his suppressed Glock beneath the big linen napkins near the silver dome food cover. Beneath the cover was the cheeseburger and french fries the waiter had been delivering to another room.

Benoit rolled the service trolley out into the hallway, turned the corner and saw her guard still reading a newspaper. If the guard gave him any trouble, he'd pump a quiet slug into the guy's skull and drag him into her room.

Benoit pushed the trolley down to her door and put on his happy face.

"Some people sure eat late," Benoit said, smiling at the guard.

"This room ordered food?"

"Yeah. Miss Singh ordered about fifteen minutes ago. Cheeseburger and french fries. Probably American. Here's the order."

He showed the guard the waiter's order sheet he'd written up for Singh's room number, then lifted the chrome lid and showed him the cheeseburger and fries.

The guard studied the order and food, still looking puzzled.

"Okay," the guard said, "But I have to frisk you first."

"No problem."

The guard frisked him, found nothing, then paused as though still concerned about something. Then he nodded for him to go ahead.

Benoit rolled the trolley toward the door.

"Oh... just one question," the guard said.

"Yeah?"

"How'd you know the person in there was Ms. Singh?"

Benoit scrambled for an answer. "Oh, the cook told me."

"But this room is booked to a Mr. Antoine Charbonneau."

"Who... ?"

Benoit inched toward his Glock. "All I know is what the cook told me. Ms. Singh musta mentioned her name when she ordered."

The guard stared hard at him for a moment, then nodded.

Benoit rolled the trolley to the door, picked up the passkey.

"Wait... ."

"What's wrong?"

"I need a closer look at your service cart."

"No problem."

Actually, it's a big ass problem.

———

121

Benoit turned and lifted the serving cover to show the cheeseburger again. His right hand eased beneath the napkins and gripped his Glock. Time to wax the Rent-A-Cop!

Benoit spun around to shoot him - and felt cold steel jammed into his own cheek – *the steel of a fucking Beretta!* Benoit felt his cheek quiver.

"Hand me your gun," the guard said.

Benoit paused.

"The gun, *asshole!*"

"Yeah, yeah, okay, man." Benoit nodded, sweat beading on his forehead. "You win! You win!"

Acting defeated, Benoit let his body go limp and started to hand over his gun, handle first.

As the guard reached for it, Benoit spun the barrel toward the guard's face and squeezed the trigger. But the guard had nudged the barrel upward, sending the silenced bullet into the ceiling.

As they wrestled for control of Glock, the guard's Beretta fell on the carpet.

Got your ass now! Benoit thought.

But when he tried to push him back, the big guard slammed him back against the wall.

The guard was no rent-a-cop! He was scary strong. *Who is this guy?*

Then somehow the guard managed to slide his finger *behind* Benoit's trigger so he couldn't even squeeze it.

The powerful guard began to twist the barrel back toward Benoit.

Benoit tried to turn the barrel back, but couldn't. The guy was too strong.

He tried to turn the barrel up, but only got as far as his own ear.

He tried again... squeezing hard.

Nothing.

Then he squeezed with everything he had.

A big fucking mistake!

Because the guard had jerked his finger out from behind the trigger... and Benoit couldn't stop himself from squeezing it!

As his head snapped back, Benoit realized he'd just shot himself in the temple! He slumped to the floor and looked up at the large chandelier. It was very bright.

And then, everything faded away.

* * *

Donovan and de Waha looked down at the corpse of Benoit Broutafache as Theo explained what happened.

Donovan's fears about Maccabee's safety raced through him again. Whoever was behind the assassination plot would do anything to keep her from translating other Sumerian messages. And they knew she was in Brussels.

And knew she was in this hotel.

And they wanted her dead.

Which meant there were other coded messages out there. Messages that might reveal how, when and where the assassination attempt would take place, and maybe who was bankrolling Katill and his team.

"Did Maccabee come out into the hall?" Donovan asked.

"No. She apparently slept through everything."

"You're sure she's okay?"

Theo nodded. "This guy's Beretta had a silencer. It happened very quickly and quietly. She also told me she was turning on her white-noise machine to drown out hallway and street sounds. Help her sleep."

Donovan nodded. "Let's post additional guards on this floor."

"Done!" de Waha said, pointing to four guards he'd just ordered to both ends of the hall.

De Waha and Donovan walked back to the elevators.

"Go sleep," de Waha said.

Donovan nodded, but knew he'd sleep little. He'd promised Maccabee greater safety in Brussels, and all he'd done was nearly get her killed.

They'd missed her this time.

But they would come at her again.

TWENTY THREE

Stahl drove his Renault rental van to meet his team, Yusef and his brothers, near the *Gare du Midi* train station.

It warmed his heart to see *Allah's chosen people* walking the city streets. Muslim men, women and children, many dressed in traditional Middle-Eastern clothing. He saw two women wearing gossamer thin face veils, defying Belgium's non-burka, no-face-veil law. Brave women. He was proud of them.

The city's Muslim population had grown to seventeen percent and was growing just as fast in most European cities. A fact that delighted Stahl… and, of course, terrified the historically indigenous Europeans.

Stahl loved numbers. And numbers didn't lie.

For every non-Muslim baby born in Europe, there were eight Muslim babies born in Europe. And because of the eight-to-one birth rate advantage, estimates were that nearly half the boys born in certain European cities were named Mohammad.

Muslims make lots of babies. Like Catholics in the old days.

Stahl smiled at the thought. *By 2030, we will control Europe...*

And, then, it's only a matter of time. First Western Europe, then Eastern Europe and Russia.

And finally we will conquer The Great Satan – America! In the USA, the Muslim birth rate is six percent versus the anemic two percent for all other Americans.

"Wake up, America!" he whispered. "You've got a big Trojan Horse in your midst! Muslims! And we're growing bigger every day."

Stahl parked in front of a gray brick apartment building and checked to see if anyone had followed him. No one had. He grabbed a large travel bag, got out and entered the building. He walked down a dark hallway that smelled like cat urine and beer and stuck to the soles of his shoes.

Perhaps he should have rented a nicer apartment for the brothers, but he wanted them hidden in a low rent flat where they fit in and would not draw attention to themselves.

He knocked on door A 2. The peephole slid open and a dark luminous eye peered out at him. The door clicked open and Yusef, smiling, ushered him inside.

"Welcome, Valek."

Stahl nodded and unzipped the hanger travel bag. "These are your Brussels Police uniforms. The large one, the one with the shoulder bars is yours Yusef. The two shorter uniforms are for your brothers. My uniform is at my apartment."

"Excellent," Yusef said, as he hung the navy blue uniforms in a hall closet. "Come, take coffee with us and we'll update you."

Stahl followed Yusef into the living room. Ahmed and Iram hurried over and everyone sat around a small Formica table. Yusef poured cups of Arab coffee, its fragrant scent of cardamom reminding Stahl of the last morning his mother brewed her rich, delicious coffee... the morning the Israeli rockets killed her.

Stahl sipped coffee and it tasted delicious. He nodded for Yusef to begin his report.

"Everything is in place and ready."

Stahl nodded. "Problems?"

"None."

For the next twenty minutes Yusef explained how they'd followed Stahl's instructions to the letter. They'd taken their large cases to the Arab food shop two blocks from the *Grand Place*. The shop owner led them down to his basement crawl space that opened into the ancient walled-up sewer that hadn't been used in decades. The shop owner removed a few loose concrete blocks from the sewer wall. The brothers stepped through the sewer wall opening and carried their cases down the bone dry sewer one hundred yards to a small door that opened onto a cellar of an ancient four-story building on the *Grand Place*.

In the *Grand Place* building, they'd climbed up to the third floor and entered room 3C, where they moved a massive armoire aside. Behind the armoire was a door. They opened it and carried their cases inside the hidden alcove room. Then they'd walked to the alcove window and looked down at the *Grand Place* below. Specifically, they'd looked at the wooden grandstand directly beneath them.

The grandstand where the leaders would soon sit.

Yusef also explained how they'd rehearsed the attack until their movements were fluid.

Exactly as I directed, Stahl thought, pleased with their work.

"Excellent, Yusef. I will meet you in the room just before the *Grand Place* ceremony begins."

"*Insha'Allah,* we will change the world!" Yusef said.

"Allah wills it!" Stahl said.

The group all clasped hands.

Stahl pointed to a spot on the map. "Afterward, wearing our police uniforms, we'll walk to a dark blue Mercedes van at this location." He pointed to a spot a few blocks north of the *Grand Place*. "The van will have three Daffy Duck decals on the corner of driver's side windshield. We will be driven to Montpellier in southern France. There, a man will fly us to Teheran. Questions?"

There were none.

"Let's synchronize," Stahl said. On his signal, the brothers set the

U.S. Special Ops titanium wristwatches he'd given them.

Stahl finished his coffee, stood and they walked to the door.

Again, he praised them for their work, left and drove back to his apartment.

Fifteen minutes later, he emerged from the apartment carrying the pine case containing the late Herr Rutten's final masterpiece. Stahl was wearing a uniform he'd taken from the home of a local man eight months ago. The man's body and suicide note were found a few days later when he washed up on the shore of the Scheldt River.

Stahl placed the pine case in a rental van and drove off.

* * *

Two hours later, Stahl returned with the pine case empty. He took off the uniform, dressed in his regular clothes and flipped on the television. CNN International showed the G8 leaders at the Royal Palace, chatting as they walked through the gardens, smelling the red, yellow and blue flowers.

Smell the flowers why you can...

He walked to the bay window and looked outside. Thick gray rain clouds had pushed in. Gusty winds swayed the Dutch elms. He breathed in deep and let it out. The most important assignment of his life was at hand and everything was ready. Yet he felt oddly restless. Perhaps it was the magnitude of his task, or the excitement of his imminent revenge.

Whatever it was, he needed to ease the tension creeping into his muscles. Perhaps a long walk would help. He put on his windbreaker and sunglasses, left the apartment and headed toward nearby Boulevard du Midi. Fat drops of rain began to splash onto the grey sidewalk, turning it into black slate.

Just ahead, he saw a neon sign for *Albert & Lucienne's,* a small bar. He entered the busy tavern and smelled fried food and cigars. At the long mahogany bar, several men watched a soccer game on a large television. In the corner, young men threw darts. Stahl sat on a barstool.

The redheaded, mustached bartender walked up and Stahl ordered a beer and a *croque monsieur*: melted cheese with chicken instead of ham. Not eating swine was one of the few Muslim restrictions he still followed. He wasn't sure why. Perhaps his mother's mandate that he never eat pork.

Three stools down, a skinny guy attacked a huge pile of *boeuf americain,* raw ground beef with onions. Oddly, he'd never seen an American eat *boeuf americain,* probably because Americans were afraid to try things they didn't understand... which, of course, was most things in life.

The bartender served his beer, a De Koninck amber. Stahl sipped some and realized how much he liked Belgian beer. He also liked the country. Of course, the G8 assassinations would damage its image forever. Damage well deserved, he felt, since Belgium had sided with America and its puppet democracies too many times over the decades.

Perfume suddenly filled his nostrils. In the mirror, he watched a young woman walk behind him, then sit on the stool beside him. She smiled and leaned close.

"You are a visitor here, no?" she asked in good English, somehow guessing, probably by his clothes, that he wasn't Belgian.

"Yes."

She brushed her fingers along his bicep as he sipped his beer. "Your muscle is huge," she said, rubbing her arm against his. She fingered some foam from his beer and licked it off.

He gestured for her to take the beer. She did and thanked him. He ordered another De Koninck and she scooted her stool closer, resting her thigh against his.

"So where are you from?" she asked.

Her hand brushed his knee.

"Denmark."

"You have business in Brussels?"

He nodded.

"What kind of business?"

He paused. "People business."

"You mean like… personnel work?"

Stahl liked the analogy. "Yeah. You could say we're making some personnel changes."

He studied her. Very attractive face and figure. Alluring blue eyes, nicely applied makeup that didn't quite hide the two-inch scar on her chin. Plump, red lips. Big gold banana earrings that drew attention away from her natural beauty.

"I'm kinda in the personnel business, too." She pressed her breast against his arm.

Stahl noticed her glass was nearly empty. "Another beer?"

"I'd like that. And anything else you might suggest." Another naughty girl smile.

Stahl ordered two more beers, and the bartender served them. She drank some, brushed his thigh again and left her hand there.

"So, are you staying near here?" she asked.

"Around the corner."

He looked at her for a few moments. Why not have a little fun, relieve his tension? Everything was set. All he had to do was lie low until it was time. Why not lie low with her? She might even provide him with an alibi should he need one.

They drank beer for a while.

"Maybe we could go there now," she said, "Your body is so, ah… masculine! But you seem a little tense Perhaps you need a little comfort?"

Perhaps you're right.

Her hand brushed against his crotch

"What's your name?"

"Camille. What's yours?"

"Thomas."

Stahl paid and they left.

Outside, they stepped into a heavy mist. The wet sidewalk glistened now and looked as slick as polished black marble. Raindrops had pooled in the sunken stones.

* * *

As Camille and the stranger left *Albert & Lucienne's Bar,* the bartender, Albert Hellings, walked down the bar to pour another Glenfiddich for old Henri.

As Hellings reached for the bottle, the TV sportscaster said they were interrupting the soccer game for a news bulletin.

Hellings poured the whiskey, but missed seeing something one foot above his head, a news bulletin that showed the face of the man… a man he'd served beer to minutes ago.

TWENTY FOUR

One block over from *Albert & Lucienne's Bar*, Stahl led Camille through his apartment door, making sure no one saw them enter. He shut the door and locked it.

He walked to the kitchen and came back with a bottle of Jack Daniels and two tumblers. He filled them and handed her one. They sipped a healthy sip and relaxed on the sofa. The overhead lights accented her natural blonde hair and innate beauty.

"Your French is *Parisian*," he said.

"Pigalliane."

Stahl knew the Pigalle, a touristy section of Paris known for its trendy cafes, restaurants, Moulin Rouge type nightclubs, sex clubs and prostitutes who catered to every conceivable sexual orientation and perversion.

"I left two years ago."

"Why?"

She pointed to the scar on her chin.

"Boyfriend?"

"Pimp. He enjoys hitting girls."

Stahl did not like men who beat women. More than once, he'd beaten men unconscious when he saw them hitting women. On one occasion, he'd beaten the man to death.

"Where'd you work?"

"Around the *Palais des Congrès.*"

"The hotels?"

"Yeah. Businessmen. Mostly nice guys. But sometimes, you know, I was sick, or didn't *feel* like working. So he beats me! My nose, see – it bends left! The bastard hit it with a wine bottle. The beatings got worse, so I left. Came to Brussels. Work independent now. It's much better."

"What's his name?"

She frowned. "Why?"

"Just curious."

"Remy DeRachet."

Stahl committed the name to memory. "Maybe I'll chat with Remy next time I'm in Paris."

"Be very careful. He's crazy. Dangerous."

"I'll be careful."

"Promise?"

"Yes."

"Don't tell Remy I'm here. I'm afraid he might come up for me."

Stahl turned and looked into her eyes. "Remy will never bother you again."

She stared back surprised, apparently wondering how he could make such a promise. Then she shrugged.

"Your parents still in France?"

Camille looked down a moment, seemed hesitant to answer. "Most guys just want to know what's between my legs."

Stahl shrugged.

"Never knew my birth father. Mother died when I was nine. Lived with my aunt and uncle. When she died, he took me to his bed. I was eleven. *Sale con!* I ran away at thirteen. I'm nineteen now. Never been back."

Stahl realized that she, like him, had been robbed of a normal childhood.

He felt a rare emotion, something like sympathy for her, maybe even something more, because the longer he looked at her, the more she reminded him of Zafina, the only woman in his life that he'd felt close to besides his mother. Zafina had natural beauty too, and like Camille had lost both parents early. Growing up in a Palestinian camp taught Zafina to hate the West, but failed to teach her to stay off streets when Israeli rockets were expected, like the one that killed her.

He looked at Camille. Perhaps after this assignment, he should take her away from all this, maybe to his Caribbean villa. Or maybe give her enough money to get off the streets, live a more normal life.

She sipped more whiskey. "How long will you stay in Brussels?"

"Couple days," he said.

"Stay longer." She put her drink down, leaned over and kissed his lips.

"Can't."

They moved toward the bed, peeling off their clothes. She quickly excited him and he enjoyed exploring her voluptuous young body, even though he saw scars on her back and arms presumably caused by her soon-to-be-dead former pimp, Remy DeRachet.

Camille and Stahl made love and her responses were strong and seemed genuine. But then, he reminded himself, prostitutes could win Oscars. Still, she seemed genuinely pleased by the intensity of their lovemaking. And he seemed genuinely relaxed.

After, they lay in silence, listening to the wind and rain rattle the windows.

"You're different," she said.

"How?

"I don't know. But with you, I *feel* something."

He said nothing.

"Can I see you again soon? No money please."

"I'll be traveling."

"Take my phone number for when you're here again"

He took her card.

"Please call me," she said seriously. "We can be friends, yes?"

He realized she meant it and nodded, thinking perhaps he'd call her in the future. Perhaps take her to the Caribbean, or set her up with enough money.

She bounced up from the bed, smiling. He marveled at her exquisite body as she walked over and lit a cigarette. Fate blessed her with beauty – then cursed her with environment.

Stahl took a thousand Euros from his wallet, placed the money beside her purse, then went into the bathroom.

* * *

Camille turned on the television. The screen flickered to a Paris fashion show. She watched the beautiful, long-legged models strut down the runway. Friends often told her she had a model's body. Do a photo book, they said, show it around, you'll get hired, make big money. She'd been thinking about doing that. Last week, a photographer had asked her to stop by for a photo session. Maybe she would. She was still young. Many of Europe's hottest new fashion designers were in Brussels. If it didn't work out, she could always fall back on her present line of work.

A news flash interrupted the fashion show. Seconds later, her eyes fixed on the screen.

On a man's face.

Her eyes widened as the announcer said, "Anyone knowing the whereabouts of this man should contact the police immediately. He needs urgent medical attention... ."

The face seemed familiar, she thought, but the eyes, well yes, very familiar, definitely the same eyes. Eyes like no one else.

I know where the man is!

She continued staring at the man's face.

* * *

And the man was staring at her.

From the bathroom, Stahl saw his computer-aged face, but still *his* face on the television screen.

He looked at Camille as she looked at the screen. He could tell by her stiff-back posture that she recognized him. But even if she didn't, she soon would. A most unfortunate turn of events for him.

And for her... .

He inched silently toward her back, staring at her thin neck... so beautiful.

I'm very sorry, Camille.

TWENTY FIVE

Hans Hellings blinked his eyes again and again. No question about it – the face on television was the same face he looked at across the bar thirty minutes ago. Same black olive pit eyes that burned right through him. Eyes that hurt to look at.

The announcer said the man was suffering from very serious meningococcal meningitis – the deadly, contagious kind – and needed immediate treatment.

Did I touch the guy? Do I need immediate treatment?

No. I didn't touch him.

But I touched his money. And his empty beer glass!

Sweet Jesus - his disease mighta rubbed off on me!

Hellings rushed to the sink, sprinkled Borax soap powder on his hands, arms and face, scrubbed them pink and rinsed them off. Then, he dumped on more Borax and scrubbed his arms and hands and face again, even harder.

Nearby, Lucienne, his wife, stared at him like he'd crawled from a latrine.

"I'll explain later," Hellings said as he dialed 911.

* * *

Donovan watched the cars ahead pull over, as he, de Waha and Maccabee raced past them in the Mercedes police car. Red lights flashing, the big car bounced over tram tracks and careened around a tight corner, tilting Maccabee into Donovan.

A most pleasing tilt, he noted.

Minutes later, the driver stopped in front of *Albert & Lucienne's* bar.

Donovan hoped the bartender had some idea where Stahl went, or maybe saw the car he got into.

They stepped inside the busy bistro, and Donovan smelled fried food and cigars. Posters of Eddie Merckx, Belgium's five-time *Tour de France* winner, Edith Piaf and Humphrey Bogart crammed the walls. The Wurlitzer thumped out Johnny Cash's *Folsom Prison Blues*.

"Monsieur Hellings?" de Waha said to the bartender, a large, beer-bellied man with red cheeks and thick auburn-red eyebrows that looked like they were reaching for each other. He seemed nervous.

"Oui, c'est moi," Hellings said.

"Je vous present Mademoiselle Maccabee Singh, et Monsieur Donovan Rourke, mes amis Americains... ."

"Ah, Americans. Let's speak English," said Hellings, a Flemish-speaking Belgian, clearly comfortable with English.

Donovan handed Hellings the age-enhanced photo of Stahl.

"Is this the man you saw?"

The bartender's brow narrowed as he studied the face for several seconds, then pointed to the stool beside Maccabee.

"On that stool he sits!"

"You're certain?" de Waha asked.

"Yes! Did I catch his meninga... kaka?"

"No. You're safe."

"But I touched his beer glass and money."

"It's okay. Don't worry."

"Did he talk to anyone else here?" Donovan asked.

"Just me... and Camille."

"Who's Camille?"

He paused. "She comes in sometimes, you know to give conversation and perhaps... ah... companionship to the men. Nice girl. They leave together." Hellings whispered, "Perhaps they have, you know... a rendezvous. Will Camille catch his meningaka - ?"

"No, she's okay. Does Camille live near here?" de Waha asked.

"Yes."

"What was he wearing?" Donovan asked.

Hellings closed his eyes. "Dark blue shirt, grey pants, and a black jacket that, how you say in English... breaks wind."

Maccabee smiled. "A windbreaker."

"Yes."

"What about his hair?" de Waha asked.

"Blond-brown. Pushed straight back like this." Hellings ran his hand back through his springy red hair.

"Anything about him that stands out?" Donovan asked.

"Huge arms and shoulders. Big! Big!" The bartender held his hand three inches above his bicep. "Weightlifter muscles. But it's the *eyes* – the eyes of *de haai - a requin!* How you say *requin* in English?"

"Shark!" Maccabee said.

"Yes, yes, shark eyes!"

"Did you see him get into a car?" Donovan asked.

"No, but maybe Gio did." He pointed to a tall handsome man with jet-black hair seated at a window table.

They walked over and Hellings introduced him as Gio Tartini. A thick cloud of smoke wafted up from the Gauloise drooping from Tartini's lower lip. He put down the *Le Soir* sports page.

"Gio, that man who left with Camille... "

"The big guy with a black jacket?"

"Yes."

"Did you see them get into a car?" de Waha asked.

"They walked."

"Which way?"

"That way."

"Past all those empty parking spots?" Donovan asked.

"Yes."

"Does Camille live in that direction?"

"No."

"I just remembered something," Hellings said. "I heard the man tell Camille he lives nearby."

"So Stahl probably walked to the bar," Donovan said. "Remember anything else?"

Tartini shook his head.

De Waha phoned his Deputy Director, Maurice Sendrowicz, and gave him orders to start dragneting the surrounding area. Then he hung up and faced Donovan.

"Police will search from rue de Fleuristes down to rue Haute, and over to Boulevard du Midi. House to house. Hotel to hotel. Fast and quiet. No sirens!"

Three minutes later two police vans stopped silently in front of the bar. Anti-terrorist teams exited the vans and formed into two groups: Alpha Team and Bravo Team.

Their quiet arrival was destroyed by two ambulances roaring past the bar, sirens blaring.

Donovan cursed the sirens, fearing Stahl might mistake them for police sirens.

* * *

In his apartment, Stahl was thinking about the large-screen television in the bar. It was on when he and Camille walked toward the door to leave. He remembered the announcer interrupting the soccer match for an important news bulletin. Obviously the bulletin was about him. Many customers were watching the game. One of them or the bartender would have likely seen his picture, possibly recognized him, maybe remembered he'd left with Camille and phoned the police.

Time to leave. He packed a small bag, then walked over to the large bay window.

He pulled back the lace curtain an inch and looked out.

Cops!

Both sides of the street. Knocking on doors. Working their way toward him. Two minutes from his door.

* * *

This is it! Officer Willi De Rycke thought. *My big chance!*

He would help collar Valek Stahl and in doing so would earn the promotion that Inspector Mertens planned to give to Alphonse, his thumb-sucking idiot nephew.

Grabbing Stahl might even earn him a date with Delphine, the cute new red haired dispatcher.

But Stahl, De Rycke knew, had undoubtedly left the area by now.

Still, I'll do my job, check every damn house on this side of the street.

He walked up to #962 and pounded on the door. Seconds later, an elderly, very heavy-set woman with scraggly gray hair hanging over bloodshot eyes, opened the door. She wore a purple bow in her hair, purple housedress the size of a pup tent. On her feet were purple bunny slippers.

"I ain't deaf!" she announced, not the least intimidated by his police uniform.

"Sorry, ma'am."

"Whaddaya want?"

"Did you see this man in the last few hours?" He handed her Stahl's photo.

She handed it right back.

"Ma'am, please just look at – "

"Him and the slut from *Albert & Lucienne's* went in 965!" She pointed across the street. Then she turned, went back inside and slammed her door.

De Rycke's heart pounded. He yanked out his cell phone and called de Waha.

Then he took out his Glock and tried to act cool.

* * *

Donovan's pulse quickened as the Alpha Team, an elite Brussels ESI anti-terrorist teams carrying HK MP-5 submachine guns, took their positions on Rue de la Plume. They stood one hundred feet from Stahl's apartment.

The Bravo Team had positioned themselves in the alley behind the apartment, closing Stahl off.

Donovan and de Waha stayed with the Alpha Team and put on Kevlar-vests and checked their Berettas.

As Donovan started to follow the team, Maccabee touched his arm.

He turned and faced her.

"Be careful."

"I will." He remembered that the last person who said that to him was Emma.

On a three-count signal, Alpha team burst through the door. Seconds later, Donovan and de Waha entered. Donovan saw no hint of Stahl, but sensed someone had just been in the apartment. He hurried to the bedroom, saw the rumpled bedcovers and a black windbreaker on a chair. He caught the hint of a woman's perfume.

Gun drawn, Donovan opened an enormous oak armoire. Empty. On the table near the television, he saw two glasses with traces of whiskey and a lipstick-smudged cigarette still smoldering in the ashtray. The television felt warm.

"BMW in the garage," someone shouted. "German plates. Dusseldorf."

Donovan hurried to the kitchen and pointed to an open back door and an alley beyond. "Looks like he left back here."

"Merde!" de Waha shouted. "Set up road blocks within a five mile

area and on all major roads leading from Brussels."

Donovan's gut told him they'd be too late. Stahl had probably seen the TV bulletin and escaped in a backup vehicle or a stolen one.

"Monsieur de Waha!" someone shouted from the basement.

The group hurried down the narrow wooden stairs. Halfway down, Donovan saw some men standing beside an open vegetable bin. Their heads were bowed, their eyes riveted at something on the cement floor. They were not speaking.

Donovan moved closer and saw a woman's legs. He hurried over, bent down and felt her neck. Her skin was warm, but he could detect no pulse. Her eyes were fixed, unresponsive and red. He saw red welts on her neck.

Stahl had strangled her.

"Camille... ." Jean whispered.

Donovan nodded and touched her cheek softly. He closed his eyes and felt fresh hot rage burn through him.

We'll get the bastard, Camille!

TWENTY SIX

Who betrayed me? Yusef or his brothers? Impossible. Stahl knew they were fanatically committed to the cause. Nor was it Wassif, his insider with G8 Security. Wassif had a three-decade hatred of the G8 countries.

Which left Herr Rutten. The doddering old Nazi, now lying stone cold in a Dusseldorf morgue, had probably left some clue referring to Stahl's visit.

Or maybe he was smart enough to leave a pre-written note suggesting that I might murder him.

Stahl drove the Renault van along the E40, heading west, away from Brussels. Traffic was light and the driving relaxed him. He cracked the window and let the cool country air wash over him.

Forty minutes later, he drove into the town of Knokke, an Atlantic seaside town he visited years ago. Knokke was a vacation site, crammed with tourists, families, kids. What he liked best about Knokke was that there were more tourists than locals this time of year. Perfect to hide out in.

He drove by a police car with two officers who paid no attention to him. Soon, he came upon a row of small hotels and pulled in at a charming, red-bricked bed-and-breakfast: *Christine's,* a 1900s Victorian with white rocking chairs on the porches, lace curtains and red tulip gardens hugging the house.

He reached into his large backpack, slid back a zipper and checked his four passports with matching sets of IDs and credit cards. He selected the burgundy-colored *Den Europaeiske Danmark,* a Danish-Euro passport, in the name of Thom Larsen. He adjusted his beard, put on his sunglasses and cap, grabbed his suitcase, got out and walked toward the door.

Inside, he stepped up to the reception desk where an elderly woman in a yellow-flower smock smiled and addressed him in Flemish. *"Goie middag, Mijnheer."* Her desk card name read *Christine de Witte.*

"Good day, madam. Do you have a room for tonight?" He spoke English.

"Yes, we do," she answered in English. "Nice ocean view. Sixty euros a night. Includes breakfast and dinner."

"That's fine." He filled in a guest card using the Danish passport.

"Just follow me, Mr. Larsen," she said as she led him through a small sitting room with a faded green sofa, lounge chairs and a purple Persian carpet. A large television was turned off. He would incapacitate it later. Across from the television sat a man in his mid-sixties with thick gray hair. He was reading a book and sipping what looked like whisky.

"Edwin, this is Mr. Larsen from Denmark," she said. "Edwin D'Hondt is a permanent resident."

D'Hondt looked up with intelligent grey eyes. "Pleased to meet you. Staying long, Mr. Larsen?"

"Just tonight."

D'Hondt smiled, looked Stahl over a moment, then went back to reading. The woman led Stahl upstairs to a spotless, comfortable-looking room at the back corner of the house.

"Perfect," he said, handing her a hundred euros. "Keep the change."

Her eyes widened at the amount of the tip. She thanked him and scurried from the room.

Stahl stretched his arms and realized he needed exercise. He stripped off his shirt and began doing pushups. As he completed his ninety-fifth, a single dot of perspiration appeared on his upper lip. He paused in mid-air, placed his right arm behind him and did five more one-arm pushups. His shoulders were on fire. He loved the pain.

After showering, he toweled off, walked back to the window and opened it. A gust of sea air fluffed the lace curtains and rewarded him with the sweet aroma of roasting hops from a nearby brewery. He looked at the Atlantic where a flock of gulls screamed past.

Soon, eight world leaders will scream...

He looked at the street behind the boarding house and saw a row of shops. A *Stella Artois* sign glowed red above a bar. Next to the bar was the store he would visit.

Stahl dressed, put on his sunglasses, adjusted his beard and locked his room. Downstairs, he walked into the small sitting room where Christine and the old man were reading. The television was still off. The old man looked up, nodded, then seemed to study him closely. Maybe a little too closely, maybe just nosy, or maybe an ex-cop.

"Oh, Mr. Larsen," the woman said, "will you join us for dinner? Dover sole with lemon and Parmesan crust. It's my specialty." She smiled.

"Sorry, ma'am, but I've eaten, and I'm afraid I have some important business later."

"I understand."

"What part of Denmark are you from, Mr. Larsen?" Edwin Dhond't asked, sipping his whisky.

"Copenhagen."

"Nice city. Which area?"

"The Latin Quarter."

"Smuk område," Edwin Dhond't said in Danish.

"You're quire right, sir. It is a beautiful area," Stahl said in English as he left.

* * *

As the tall guest walked outside, Edwin D'Hondt's phony detector started beeping. He could spot a phony in seconds, thanks to decades as a customs officer at Brussels International Airport.

Something about the new guest didn't feel right. D'Hondt put down his riveting new novel, *The Confessions of Al Capone,* by Loren Estleman. The new guest gave off strange vibes like one of Capone's hitmen.

D'Hondt turned to Christine De Witte. "Something funny about the new guest."

"He's perfectly normal."

"Then why does he wear sunglasses inside? And even when it's cloudy outside?"

"Probably has sensitive eyes like Burt."

"Maybe, maybe not. And I'll tell you something else. He's not Danish. Not enough singsong in his voice. Chops his words off like a damned Kraut."

"Maybe he moved to Germany."

D'Hondt shook his head. "Forty years as a customs inspector taught me accents. That man's mother-tongue is not Danish."

"I saw his Danish passport."

"Could be fake. And I'll tell you another thing."

"What?"

"His beard moved an inch!"

"Oh, Edwin, for God's sake! Get your eyes checked."

"My eyes are fine!" He sipped his whiskey. "That man doesn't want to be recognized."

"You suspect everyone."

"Do not."

"Do so."

"And another thing!"

"What?"

"Why is his hat pulled down so far over his forehead and eyes?"

She didn't answer.

"And why is his collar turned way up?"

"Tell me."

"Because he doesn't want his face seen."

"By whom?"

Edwin Dhond't shrugged. "Police, or maybe some mafia guys. Who knows?"

Christine De Witte rolled her eyes and flipped through the TV guide. "You read too many mysteries, Edwin."

"And that's why I know that man's hiding."

* * *

Stahl walked along the narrow street behind the boarding house. He passed an ice cream store, then the noisy bar with customers cheering a soccer game.

He entered the next store, the *Battens Apotheek-Pharmacy.* The store lights were bright, so he pulled his cap down further.

He walked down an aisle to the hair dyes and selected *Garnier Nutrisse Noir,* an ink-black shade, and paid the clerk.

Outside, Stahl strolled back toward Christine's.

Halfway up the street he saw something that stopped him in his tracks. A television retail outlet with at least twenty large screen televisions all on - all facing the street - all showing *his face!*

Quickly, he checked to see if anyone was looking at him. No one was. Why should they? He bore little resemblance to the face on television.

The announcer said, "This man, Mr. Valek Stahl, has contracted *meningococcal meningitis,* a highly contagious disease which, if untreated, can be fatal. If you see him, do not approach him, or come in contact with him. Call 911 or your local police... "

Stahl found it interesting that they hadn't mentioned the real reason they wanted to capture him. They probably didn't want to throw the city into a terror-stricken state of panic or ruin the dream of their safe and secure G8 Summit.

Too late for that dream. *My weapon will soon destroy any hope for a successful Summit.*

He returned to Christine's B & B. As he walked through the sitting room, Christine looked up from her magazine and smiled. The television was still off.

Heading up toward his room, Stahl removed his sunglasses to see the stairs better, and again noticed the old man paying close attention to him. Too much attention. Stahl pretended to walk to his room, then decided to come back to the top of the stairs and listen.

"Strange man, you ask me," Edwin said to Christine.

"No one did."

"He wears very expensive clothes, shoes, and a gold Rolex. And he gave you one hundred Euros for the night. Why didn't he stay in a fancier hotel? Why here?"

Christine looked offended. "Maybe he prefers my cozy atmosphere!"

"Rubbish!

"What? It's not cozy?"

"Yes, yes! It's very cozy!" Dhond't said, clearly not wanting to anger Mevrow de Witte. "But that man's *hiding!*"

Stahl was mildly concerned. He grew even more concerned when he heard the old man click on the television. He didn't think they'd recognize him from his photo on television. But the old man seemed particularly perceptive.

If he did recognize him, Stahl would have no choice but to eliminate them both.

Besides they were old. They'd lived long enough.

Stahl walked to his room and locked the door. At the bathroom sink he began applying the dye to his hair. He blow-dried it, then applied a second treatment. He dyed his eyebrows and eyelashes and again dried them. He combed his new jet-black hair straight back. It looked good.

On the sink, a large fly landed on some gooey hair dye and got stuck. Stahl had hated flies ever since they crawled from his dead mother's mouth. He took a safety pin and jabbed the sharp point into the fly's back and watched it thrash its wings. He lit a match and let the flames lick the fly's wings. The flame vaporized the wings and shot a vile odor into his nose. Quickly, he flushed the charred remains down the sink.

He placed the used hair-dye materials in a baggie and put it in his large Lowepro backpack. He then took out his theatrical case and looked in at the rows of contact lenses, fake ears, chin extensions, wigs, toupees, beards, moustaches, and syringes of collagen to puff out his lips and cheeks. He put on a pair of dark-blue contact lenses.

He then took off his fake beard and applied a black bushy moustache to his upper lip.

He walked over to the wall mirror and checked himself. The man in the mirror bore no resemblance to the man on television or the man who walked upstairs twenty minutes ago.

The fading sunlight bounced off the mirror into his eyes – the same sunlight that long ago bounced off the blank eyes of his dead father.

"Soon, papa, I will repay them! *Ich verspreche, Vater!*

Brussels was just minutes away. It was time.

But first he had to see what nosey Mr. D'Hondt and sweet Christine de Witte were up to downstairs.

TWENTY SEVEN

The palace dinner begins in just two hours, Donovan realized as he, de Waha and Maccabee reviewed the dinner's VIP list for the third time in de Waha's office.

Donovan was still worried about dinner security. Despite knowing that all guests, attendees, chefs, waiters, service personnel and musicians had been thoroughly vetted, and would be subjected to X-ray body scans, and admitted only with hologram ID cards, he feared that Stahl might be among them.

The office door opened and de Waha's attractive assistant, Eliane, rushed into the office, her face flushed with excitement.

"A man just called who knows how the leaders will be attacked."

De Waha shrugged. "Add him to the other seven who know."

"This one's different."

"Why?"

"He called the assassination plot – The *Medusa!*"

Donovan and de Waha bolted forward in their chairs. *Medusa* had not been released to the media.

"He'll call later to tell us how and where the assassination will take place."

"When later?"

"He didn't say."

"Did we get his Caller ID name?"

"No. Untraceable phone."

"His language?"

"French with a slight Arab accent."

"Someone's turning on Stahl," de Waha said.

Donovan nodded, but wondered why Stahl, on his most important assignment, would suddenly reveal the specifics of his attack plan to another person? Stahl worked alone. Always. On the other hand, Maccabee's translated Sumerian note said he was working with a team. Maybe someone wasn't a team player. Maybe he had a traitor in his midst. And maybe we had a mole in his camp.

"Call me the minute he calls back, wherever I am."

Eliane nodded.

De Waha looked at his watch. *"Mon dieu!"*

"What's wrong?" Donovan asked.

"The Palace Dinner! We have to get ready now!"

Maccabee stood up. "I'll be working at the hotel."

"What?" De Waha looked shocked. "But you must come!"

"Jean, I didn't bring a formal dress – "

"I need a dress!" de Waha shouted.

"Pardon?" Eliane said from her office.

"For *Maccabee!*"

Maccabee shook her head. "Jean, it's not necessa – "

"It is *nessa* – "

"But, Jean - "

"You are a highly esteemed member of our highly esteemed security team. This dinner is an official function. We're obligated and delighted to provide you with the requisite attire as we can continue our discussions on G8 security this evening."

"But - "

"Carina Van Haver's Shoppe is perfect for you," Eliane said, smiling. You'll love Carina and her dresses!"

Maccabee finally shrugged an okay and smiled.

Donovan watched Maccabee walk out the door with Eliane.

He decided he liked watching Maccabee walk out the door. He also liked watching her walk in the door. Or around the desk, or down the street. He liked everything else about her, too. Her smile, courage, intelligence, linguistic skill, sense of humor, and of course, her beauty.

But he didn't like that he was being drawn to her now. This was not the time. He should be focused on Stahl. And protecting the lives of the eight most powerful leaders in the world. Nothing else should matter now.

Besides, his infatuation with her was absurd. It would lead to nothing. Maccabee obviously saw him as just an old friend of her father.

* * *

After seeing the nosy Mr. D'Hondt at Christine's B&B engrossed in a soccer game on television, Stahl had crawled through his room's window and dropped onto the soft dirt of the tulip bed. Then he drove off in the van.

Now, as he drove toward Brussels, he realized the soccer game would have been interrupted with a news flash about him. Nosy Mr. D'Hondt would have seen the bulletin and his face on television, maybe identified him, then discovered his Renault van missing and phoned the police.

Time to change vehicles.

Ahead, he saw a forested rest area. He pulled in, looked around and saw the restroom light reflecting onto the fender of the only other vehicle in the area, a silver Opel Insignia. Its windows were steamed up. Someone inside.

Stahl spun the suppressor onto his Glock. Slowly, he approached the Opel and peered into the back seat. A man was sleeping.

Stahl knocked on the window and smiled. The man woke up, yawned, rolled down the window a few inches. "Yes… ?"

Stahl raised his Glock. "Get out of the car!"

The man, dressed like a middle-aged businessman, paused, then slowly crawled out.

As Stahl glanced back at the highway, the man suddenly came at him with a switchblade. Stahl side-stepped him and pumped two silenced shots into the idiot's forehead.

The man slumped to the ground.

Stahl removed his wallet and ID, dragged the body into the van and drove it deep in the forest and left it there.

He walked back, took the big Opel and drove toward Brussels.

* * *

In her Amigo Hotel room, Maccabee checked her new dress in the mirror. She thought the crimson dress looked good, maybe a bit naughty. Maybe very naughty. It was low-cut and strapless with bare shoulders and back, but hopefully not too risqué for the royal dinner at the palace.

Eliane and Carina Van Haver had both assured her it was palace-appropriate and looked fabulous on her.

Will Donovan like it? she wondered.

Will he finally look at me as a woman… not just as my dad's daughter?

She smiled as she remembered her high-school crush on Donovan. He'd never realized it, thank God. She also remembered the sensitive way he'd talked with her after her mother's death a few years ago, and again after her father's death. His eyes, always warm and caring, seemed to listen *and* speak to her at the same time. Those same eyes, she'd noticed a couple of times today, had dimmed with sadness, as he obviously recalled memories of his wife and her horrific murder here.

Would he ever get over that loss? Could he? Did anyone ever get over the savage murder or unexpected death of a loved one? She doubted it. They probably just learned to live with it better. She wasn't sure she'd ever get over the sudden death of her fiancé, David.

Glancing at her watch, she realized it was time to leave. She grabbed the matching red-lacquered purse, checked herself in the mirror and whispered, "Let's go boogie with world leaders and important potentates!"

She stepped into the hall.

Theo smiled at her. "Ooooh la la... Monsieur Charbonneau! You look very *feminine,* Monsieur!"

Maccabee laughed. "*Merci,* Theo."

He escorted her down to the Amigo Hotel lobby.

Minutes later, she and Donovan, De Waha and his wife, Florian, strolled through the ornate and elegant entrance of the Royal Palace.

Maccabee was overwhelmed. The Grand Staircase, a majestic ascent of polished white marble steps, was lined with ten tall Palace Guards in white trousers, black coats and tall fur hats. They held long gleaming swords, unsheathed, and looked ready to skewer anyone trying to crash the event.

"No White House party crashers here," Maccabee whispered to Donovan.

"They wouldn't make it into the parking lot."

She looked around at the gilded décor. "Jean, the palace is... spectacular!"

"Thank you. But the truth is part of it was built by those heathens to the north."

"The Dutch?"

"Yes. But we kicked their butts out in 1830 when we won our independence. Today northern Belgium speaks *Dutch* or *Flemish* while the south, the Walloon area, speaks French. And we love to fight each other. But when we're invaded by Germany, which happens now and then, we unite. When the Krauts get kicked out, we go back to normal."

"What's normal?"

"Fighting each other like bloody hell."

They stopped at a pair of enormous doors. Two guards opened the door and led them inside.

"*Voila!* The Throne Room," de Waha said.

Maccabee caught her breath. The décor and grandeur were like nothing she'd ever seen. The room was larger than a professional basketball court. She saw mirrors everywhere and made the room seem even larger. The room reminded her of the Palace of Versailles. A small orchestra in the balcony played something by Beethoven.

Dignitaries and guests stood on a floor made of several shades of gleaming woods. From the ceiling, hung the largest crystal chandeliers she'd ever seen.

I just stepped into a Merchant Ivory film!

A waiter offered them flutes of champagne. They each took one.

Donovan lifted his glass. "May we have even more reason to celebrate tomorrow evening when the leaders, God willing, are flying home!"

"I'll drink to that!" de Waha said.

"You'll drink to a toilet cleaner sale!" his wife said.

Everyone laughed, except Donovan, who Maccabee noticed was hurrying over toward a man who was placing a large potted plant next to the leaders' table.

Donovan started examining the potted plant closely.

Maccabee recalled him telling her that a potted plant *bomb* was disarmed in the lobby of a Jerusalem hotel minutes before it was set to explode.

TWENTY EIGHT

The potted plant was only a potted plant. Maccabee was relieved by how thoroughly Donovan and the security officers had checked it and other décor items out.

Security had also checked out each dinner guest's hologram-ID card three separate times as they were admitted through increasingly tighter rings of security.

If Valek Stahl was here, he had inside help from the innermost circle of Summit security.

Suddenly a trumpet blared, and she, Donovan and over two hundred fifty dinner guests snapped to attention.

The massive doors of the Throne Room opened and the G8 leaders and their spouses, followed by the King and Queen, looking very elegant, strolled in and walked toward their regal head table. Guests applauded as cameras panned every inch of the gilded grandeur.

The orchestra eased into Debussy's cheerful *L'Apres-midi d'un faune* as white-coated waiters swept into the room with trays of hors d'oeuvres.

Maccabee hoped Donovan could relax enough to enjoy all the beauty and splendor around him. But he seemed to scrutinize every waiter and guest who approached within ten feet of the head table.

She looked down at the food on their table: escargots in garlic butter, and petite slices of *Ballotine de Faisan*. She tried the pheasant and it dissolved in her mouth like cotton candy. She felt like purring.

"Many say the best French food is in Brussels," Donovan said to her.

"They're wrong."

"Where is it?"

"In my mouth."

Donovan smiled as de Waha tapped him on the shoulder and stared at him. Something was up.

"My secretary just called. The informant who said he'd tell us where Stahl will attack just called back."

"And?"

"Before he could tell her *where*, the line went dead."

Maccabee wondered if the line went dead because the informant did.

"Did she call him back?" Donovan asked.

"Yes, but no one answered."

"So, Stahl could strike here tonight."

De Waha nodded.

Maccabee saw tension grip Donovan's face once again as he scanned the two hundred fifty guests. Then he looked at the musicians in the small balcony loft, which she realized was a perfect perch for a sniper.

Everyone seemed like they belonged.

A waiter placed the main course in front of Maccabee. *Saumon a la Genevoise* cooked in Madeira wine and butter, and *asperges flammandes* drenched in more butter and sprinkled with egg, pepper and bacon. The food smelled wonderful.

So did Donovan's sandalwood cologne.

* * *

In the Knokke board house, Edwin D'Hondt shouted "Bastards!" at the television announcer who said, "Today's G8 Summit meetings have been frank and - "

"I'll be *frank!*" D'Hondt shouted. "You're interrupting my soccer game with only two minutes to go!" He had ten euros riding on Ostende who were tied with Anderlecht.

"Assholes! Can't you wait two minutes? "

"Edwin, your language!" Christine said

D'Hondt gulped down the rest of his scotch. The television screen faded to a photo of a man.

> *"And now this: Police are urgently looking*
> *for this man, Valek Stahl. He has contracted*
> *meningococcal meningitis. The deadly infection is*
> *contagious. He needs urgent medical attention…*
> *if you see him, do not approach him, and please*
> *call 911 or the police… "*

Edwin D'Hondt studied the man's face and eyes for a few seconds. His heart start pounding. He'd seen those eyes.

Then he grabbed the phone.

* * *

Donovan heard the orchestra segue into Glenn Miller's version of *Tuxedo Junction*. De Waha and his wife and several other couples got up and began dancing.

"Maccabee, would you consider dancing with a federal government employee?"

"No. Sorry."

"Why not?"

"I only dance with Cabinet level or above!"

Laughing, they wove their way through tables and began dancing to the up-tempo music. Donovan enjoyed the dancing and when she smiled up at him, something seemed to melt inside. He knew he'd been growing closer to her each day... make that each hour, feeling the warm shift in their relationship, from the daughter of a friend – to *my friend,* my very good friend.

But was he ready for this? Would he ever get over the loss of Emma? And what about Maccabee? Would she ever get over the loss of her fiancé? And how does she feel about me?

Where would it all end? And why was he feeling all this now, when he should be focused on the most important job in his life - protecting the G8 leaders from the world's most terrifying assassin...

Three very pleasant dances later, he watched the leaders stand and leave. He felt enormous relief, as though he'd just tucked a bunch of senior citizens in bed for the night.

De Waha stood, "*Mes amis,* we have a very busy day tomorrow. We should retire to our bedchambers."

What about Maccabee's bedchamber? Donovan wondered. How safe was it? How well screened were the hotel housekeepers and room service waiters and maintenance personnel? Had one called in sick and been replaced by a hitman? Had a maid placed something lethal in Maccabee's room?

No matter how much security was in place, there was always a chance someone could get through.

They'd already tried to kill her twice!

TWENTY NINE

Jean de Waha walked into his Amigo Hotel room, collapsed in a big chair and let the tension drain from his body.

He was feeling every minute of his sixty-four years, thanks to the eighteen-hour workdays he'd been chalking up for months preparing for the Summit. And thanks to the lousy four hours sleep per night for the last week.

This morning, he woke up feeling like he'd run a marathon.

After tomorrow, he'd relax, take time off, maybe just vegetate and watch old movies, or maybe take his wife Florian for a week in the Seychelles, or maybe ask his anesthesiologist cousin to put him in a restful coma.

Beside him, his phone vibrated. *So who's about to ruin my night's sleep?*

"De Waha."

"Wim Jacobs."

"What's up, Wim?"

"Valek Stahl."

"Where?"

"At Christine's Bed & Breakfast in Knokke. A resident, Mr. Edwin Dhond't, a retired customs director, saw his picture on television. He's positive it's Stahl."

"Why?"

"The eyes."

"And... ?"

"And the man had a Danish passport, but a German accent. Plus, his beard was fake. He also wore sunglasses inside the house at night!"

"And... ?"

"Dhond't found traces of black hair dye on the sink in the man's room."

De Waha sat up, more interested. "And... ?"

"And even though the guy paid in advance, he jumped from the window of his room and drove away without checking out. Dhond't is positive it's Stahl."

"Drove away in what?"

"A gray Renault van."

"Bingo!"

"What?"

"That matches the gray Renault van that a man fitting Stahl's description rented from a Eurocar agency here in Brussels."

"Gotta be him, Director."

"Good chance. How long ago did he disappear?"

"Sometime in the last three hours. I just put out a bulletin for the van. We're setting up roadblocks leading back to Brussels."

"Good. But he's probably switched vehicles by now. Check all vehicles stolen within fifty kilometers of Knokke in the last three hours."

"Roger that. My gut says he's heading back to Brussels."

"My gut says he's here."

After hanging up, de Waha phoned Donovan who was escorting Maccabee to her room. No answer. De Waha tried his room. No answer. He'd call him later.

De Waha leaned back in the chair, lit a Cuban Montecristo and exhaled a thick rope of smoke toward the ceiling. Just a week ago, everything was proceeding well. Security was rock solid for all G8 events. They'd reviewed all possible scenarios several times.

Then everything changed.

Donovan learned of a very serious, well-financed G8 plot by a man that many experts consider the world's most lethal assassin. A man who'd killed hundreds of innocent people and avoided global police authorities for fifteen years, a man who left no trace. A man who did not fail.

And now the bastard plans to destroy my country's first, and maybe only, G8 Summit. If he succeeds, heads will roll. And mine will roll first. Not exactly how I planned to ride off into my sunset retirement.

But if you succeed Stahl, I will find you, even in my retirement. I have contacts in your slimy underworld. They owe me favors and will help me find you. And I will bring you to justice, dead or alive.

Although, I prefer dead.

De Waha stared out the window. All he wanted was a safe and successful G8 Summit... and that people in other countries realized that Belgium and Brussels were terrific places to visit and vacation.

He looked up and noticed the yellow halo of light hovering above the *Grand Place* square. The more he thought about it, the more he agreed with Donovan – the *Grand Place* was where Stahl would strike. The G8 leaders would soon be sitting on the grandstand. They would be out in the open for thirty minutes. They would be surrounded by thousands of people.

And they would be surrounded by hundreds of windows.

An assassin's dream.

THIRTY

Donovan escorted Maccabee down the long carpeted hall toward her hotel room. After checking with Security, he learned a Hazmat team had inspected every inch of her room and found no hint of explosives, biological and chemical toxins and nothing suspicious in the air vents.

He was even more relieved to see Theo, her guard, on duty.

"Any evildoers, Theo?"

"Bad ones."

"Who?"

"Drunk Norwegian car dealers."

"That's terrifying!"

"Yeah… "

Maccabee and Donovan laughed as they walked on down to her door.

She turned, looked at him and said, "I feel like Cinderella!"

"Me too," he said.

She laughed. "All that palace pomp... "

"Don't forget the circumstance... ."

"Like the circumstance last night?"

"What circumstance last night?" he said, wondering.

"Saying goodnight the Belgian way."

"Oh... "

"Tonight, let's try the American way!" She leaned forward and kissed his lips softly.

Her kiss surprised him, but not as much as it pleased him. Things quickly became more impassioned. He knew he should back away now, but he couldn't. His lips seemed to have a mind of their own. And, so did the rest of him now that he noticed.

"Maccabee, maybe we should ah... "

"Check my room for drunk Norwegian car dealers?"

"Yep. They're scary."

THIRTY ONE

The soft rays of the sun warmed his face. Slowly, he opened his eyes and stared out through the dew-covered windshield at the pink slice of dawn seeping through the pine trees. Last night he'd found the narrow forest road and driven in about a mile and hidden the Opel.

Yawning, Stahl stepped outside, breathed in the cool, fresh air, then walked into the woods and relieved himself.

He got back in the car, found some new *Handi Wipes* in the glove compartment and cleaned his face and hands. He felt refreshed, completely awake and excited. His big day had finally arrived.

He opened his theatrical case, took out a cotton swab, dipped it in rubbing alcohol and swabbed his upper lip and cheekbones. He took two syringes of collagen and injected the clear substance into his upper lip and beneath each cheekbone. His skin puffed up noticeably. Next, he put on a black Van Dyke beard, wraparound sunglasses and a baseball cap.

In the mirror, his new face bore no resemblance to his face on television.

Satisfied, he drove off toward Brussels, taking back roads to avoid police checkpoints.

Twenty minutes later, near the small town of Wolvertem, he pulled into a service plaza where several vans, trucks, cars and motorhomes were parked. Inside, he smelled bacon and strong coffee as he passed truckers and businessmen eating at small wooden tables. Two small boys played a game on an iPad.

He was hungry and stacked his tray with scrambled eggs, sausages, fried potatoes, two chocolate-filled croissants and a large coffee. He paid an obese cashier with red beehive hair, and sat at a corner table.

He ate quickly, checking from time to time whether anyone was paying particular attention to him. No one was. And why should they?

When he finished, he stood and walked toward the door.

Then he stopped.

Walking toward him were two Belgian federal cops.

Stahl eased behind a tall magazine rack as they passed by. The tall cop showed the cashier a photograph and appeared to ask if she'd seen the person. She stared at the photo, then shook her head. The other cop, short and muscular, strolled through the tables, checking the men.

Stahl squatted down to the lowest magazine rung and started paging through *Auto Magazine.* The tall cop walked over to the other side of the magazine rack.

Head down, Stahl continued flipping through the pages.

The tall cop stepped closer, so close Stahl could see his own face in the cop's shiny boots.

The short cop started to walk over.

"You see Stahl?"

"Yeah!"

"Where?"

"He's behind this magazine rack!"

Stahl couldn't believe his ears. He gripped the Glock hidden in his coat and prepared to pump bullets into their heads.

The short cop hurried over. "Where?"

"*Here!* Behind the magazine rack. See - his poster on the wall!" The tall cop laughed.

"Smart ass!" the short cop said.

Stahl relaxed his trigger finger.

Moments later, the cops walked out.

He waited until he saw their car drive off. Then he stood and looked at the wall poster that contained two photos of him. He saw the same two photos on the front page in *De Standaard* newspaper on the news rack. One with a full beard, one beardless. Both with light brown hair. He resembled neither photo.

He left and drove off toward the *Grand Place*.

Thirty minutes later, he sat in the crowded smoking section of a noisy bar just three blocks from the *Grand Place*. His face stung a bit from the collagen injections, but his facial makeover and the bar's thick smoke made him completely unrecognizable.

He sipped his beer and dabbed foam from his tender lips. He was pumped up, excited, actually felt blood coursing through his veins. He was about to change the course of human history. Never before had the eight most powerful leaders in the world been assassinated *en masse*. Never again would the eight most powerful nations forget their heinous crimes against Islam. Never again would Muslims live with the shame of being occupied by non-believers.

Never again would people forget his name.

Even the people sitting around him now. Most were glued to the big screen television covering the imminent *Grand Place* ceremony. Their country's big moment in the sun. Soon to be shattered. On the television a brunette reporter jabbered on about how the *Grand Place* security was impenetrable.

Stahl had to force the smile from his lips.

Watching the screen, he easily located the hundreds of white-helmeted security police on the square. They were positioned strategically at the corners and throughout the large square. Even the undercover agents in the crowd were pathetically obvious. They were *looking* for someone, looking only at tall men, looking up at the windows, looking up at the ancient rooftops. Subtle as neon lights.

He watched the television, enjoying its irony. By giving him live instant visuals and updates on the leaders – television was his partner in jihad today.

The *Grand Place* was filling up with thousands of people. He checked his watch and smiled. Time to go to work. He placed money on his bill and stood.

As he walked out, the TV announcer said, "In just minutes, the big event begins."

You have no idea how big!

THIRTY TWO

Will these ancient cobblestones soon be drenched with blood? Donovan wondered, as he, de Waha and Maccabee walked across the *Grand Place.*

He looked up at the hundreds of gilded windows gleaming in the late morning sun and felt his muscles tense. Despite the massive security, despite the guards at each building, despite the numerous room searches, he feared Stahl might be behind a window, looking down on the G8 leaders' grandstand, mocking their efforts to stop him, counting the seconds until he unleashed his weapon.

Donovan scanned the windows for any hint of a face. He watched for a curtain shifting, a shadow moving. He saw nothing, mostly due to the sun's reflections.

He looked up at the *Hôtel de Ville's* 310-foot spire. On its top, stood the statue of Michael the Archangel, his foot crushing the head of a demon.

There's a new demon in town, Michael! And if you're not busy, we could use your help…

They walked inside the 14th century *Maison du Boulanger* building and entered the G8 command center. It reminded Donovan of a NASA control room. More than twenty specialists sat at keyboards linked to flat-screen monitors scanning every foot of the *Grand Place.*

Their leader, Pierre Dumon, worked the main control console. Donovan knew Dumon, an information-technology wizard. He'd worked with the thin, forty-year-old man with intense blue eyes and red hair tied in a ponytail. He waved Donovan and the others over.

"Check this out!" Dumon said, pointing to a 103-inch, high- definition monitor. The screen replayed Maccabee, de Waha and Donovan walking across the *Grand Place.* The picture was so sharp, Donovan saw a razor nick on his chin and the detail of Maccabee's silver brace-lets and tear-drop earrings.

Donovan placed his hand on hers and nodded toward the screen, "You look like an innocent tourist."

"*Moi?* Innocent? After last night?"

Donovan smiled and flashed back to last night's passionate love-making. Miraculously, it had ignited something in him that he feared he'd lost and would never again regain. The courage to love a woman again… and the magic of two people becoming one. He was amazed at how quickly the feelings and emotions had re-emerged in him. He'd thought they might be extinguished forever. But they weren't. And he was blissfully happy that they had rekindled.

"Each screen," Pierre Dumon said, "can zoom in on a suspect. We then compare his frontal and profile facial composition to Stahl's. If our facial recognition software scores high enough comparing eye-width, ear, nose and mouth to Stahl, we move in on the guy. They eyes are the big thing. Their dimensions don't change."

"How long for the comparison?" Donovan asked.

"Our new units give us a preliminary comparison in about thirty seconds."

"You're covering the entire *Grand Place,* right?"

Dumon nodded. "We've divided it into thirty-three sections. If we see Stahl in section B-6, officers surround him and close in fast!"

Donovan nodded. "What about all the windows?"

"Each window is scanned every thirty seconds. As you know, no one has been allowed inside the *Grand Place* buildings since last night at six p.m. Since then, over two-hundred armed guards have blocked all building entrances, front and back."

"But what if you see someone in a window?" Donovan asked.

"We identify the person fast. If we can't, and he's holding a weapon or something that looks like a weapon, we take him out."

"How?"

"Anti-terrorist teams are just outside all buildings. They'll enter and break into the room."

Donovan nodded. "But what if the team can't reach him in time?"

Dumon pointed at the roofs.

Donovan saw a row of snipers and remembered they were Belgian's best special ops snipers and among the world's best.

"Were all rooms searched this morning?"

"An hour ago," Dumon said. "And we're checking them again now."

Donovan nodded. "Who's checking the checkers?"

"We are. All checkers must report for roll call outside on the *Grand Place,* and all their weapons must be accounted for, five minutes before the ceremony begins."

Down on the square, Donovan watched people move through metal detector arches at the six street entrances to the *Grand Place.* Once they passed through the metal detectors, they stepped into full body scanners. Next, they were sniffed for biological and chemical toxins. Overhead, Geiger counters sifted the air for the radioactive isotopes of a dirty bomb.

People seemed in a festive mood and not too bothered by the extensive security measures.

The security measures reassured Donovan, but he knew Stahl had anticipated them and planned for them.

Donovan walked over in front of the team. "Last night," Donovan said, holding up Stahl's photo in front of them, "we learned Stahl dyed his hair black. By now it may be blond or red or gray or he may be bald. Or he may wear a beard. Go by height. He's one-point-nine meters tall, six-three, he weighs one hundred kilos, two hundred twenty pounds. He has powerful arms and shoulders. But he's a genius at disguise. So check everyone that height, anyone older, fatter, a policeman, a doctor, a man in a wheelchair, a tall nun, a Hasidic Jew, a monk, a one-legged man on crutches. Look for anyone paying special attention to our security."

The group nodded.

"And above all look for these eyes," Donovan said, pointing to the black eye sockets on Stahl's face. "Lenses can change their color – but not their intensity - or how deep-set they are. He knows that, so he's probably wearing sunglasses."

* * *

Directly below him on the *Grand Place,* he listened to the crowd noise grow louder. He peeked out the ancient window of the secret storage room and was pleased to see people filling the square and crowding close to the grandstand. The more the better.

Just minutes now, he realized.

He took off his sunglasses and saw sunlight pouring into the small room. He followed the rays of the sun back to the middle of the room where they bathed his beautiful rocket launchers in gold. The launchers were armed and ready. So were the brothers operating them.

He looked down at where the leaders would soon sit – the large grandstand.

On that grandstand, I will avenge the loss of my family and the slaughter of my Muslim brothers and sisters… On that grandstand we will repay Israel and the infidel nations for their occupation and desecration of our sacred lands.

Earlier, wearing their police uniforms, they'd entered an Arab food shop two blocks from the *Grand Place.* In its sub-basement, they removed the loosened concrete blocks, crawled into the ancient, abandoned sewer and walked through it to the cellar of the *Grand Place* building. There, they then climbed to the third floor and stepped into room 3C where they moved the large armoire aside and entered the secret storage alcove. They inched the armoire back in front of the door, sealing themselves inside the alcove. Everything had gone smoothly.

And still was.

One second later, it wasn't.

He heard floorboards creak in the hallway. The kind of creak caused by human weight. Someone was walking this way.

Finger to his lips, he alerted the brothers.

In the hallway, he heard men checking rooms, shouting commands. Moments later, they stepped into room 3C with the large armoire beside him. He heard a dog sniffing around the armoire.

"The dog's acting strange," a man said.

"Where?"

"Over near this armoire."

"Probably some food in there."

"I don't think so."

"Come on, let's keep moving. We got more rooms to check. And we gotta get down to the *Grand Place*."

"No – something's in this armoire."

The dog scratched at the armoire, then began to growl.

"Open it for chrissakes."

He heard the armoire's door squeak open.

The dog scratched harder.

"It's filled with huge stacks of magazines and papers and shit like that. Probably food or a dead mouse underneath."

"No. This dog is trained for explosives."

"So wave the explosives sniffer around in there."

"Dogs are better. They can sniff what sniffers can't."

"Wave the damn sniffer anyway. Hurry!"

Seconds later. "Negative readings. Absolutely nothing."

"Okay. Check behind the armoire!"

"What? This thing's flush against the wall! And heavier than Napoleon's tomb!"

A phone rang and a man said, "Yeah, okay, we are hurrying!" He hung up. "We got our arms-check roll call outside in two minutes! Let's go!"

The men hurried out of the room and hustled down the hall.

When he no longer heard the men, he inched up to the window, lifted his sunglasses and peeked outside. He saw the sun-drenched grandstand below where the G8 leaders would sit in just minutes. A nine-foot-high bulletproof Plexiglas wall surrounded the grandstand.

An excellent wall, except for one thing. No roof. His rocket grenades, four powerful thermobaric fuel-air explosive warheads, the most powerful and deadly in the world, would easily sail over the wall and explode.

And obliterate everyone on the grandstand and beyond.

The leaders would be identified by their teeth.

If teeth could be found.

THIRTY THREE

Donovan saw a big problem. Big Belgian men. Too many of them. He watched them entering the *Grand Place* through the metal detectors, and realized many were Stahl's height, size and age. And many had the same brown-blond hair as Stahl.

De Waha's phone rang. He answered, listened, hung up and spun around toward Donovan.

"That was *him!*" de Waha said, excited, his eyes wide.

"Who?"

"The informant who called last night."

De Waha hurried Donovan over to a window and pointed. "He says Valek Stahl and his team are in that building with the gold trim over the window."

"*Where* in the building?"

"A secret storage room on the third floor."

Donovan looked at the third floor windows and saw no hint of a person, no shadows behind the lace curtains.

"When do the leaders arrive?"

"Six minutes," de Waha said. "Let's go!"

Donovan started to leave and felt Maccabee touch his arm. He saw her concern.

"Don't worry. The anti-terrorist team will handle things."

Donovan and de Waha hurried outside and met up with a Belgian ESI anti-terrorism team behind the building. The team wore black FN P-200 bulletproof body suits and riot helmets. Each man carried an HK MP-5, two gas grenades, flash-bangs, and a handgun. One man held a Steyr semi-automatic rifle that Donovan knew could fire six hundred rounds per minute.

The team leader, Willi Ridder, a muscular thirty-year old, unfolded a sketch of the building's third floor.

"Here's the room! The building manager says it's an unused storage alcove that connects to room C3. The door to the alcove is hidden behind a large armoire."

"You're positive someone's in the room?" Donovan asked.

"Yes."

"How many?"

"Not sure."

"Jean, can we use thermal imagers to detect the number of body heat profiles?"

"The thermals are twenty minutes away at the Congo Museum."

"Our listening devices have picked up men whispering," Ridder said.

"Language?"

"Arabic."

"What's your plan?" Donovan asked Ridder.

"We'll move into the room next to them and attach special location-listening monitors to the wall. Try to determine how many men and *where* they're located. Toss in a flash-bang grenade and go in fast."

Donovan nodded agreement, then pointed up at the tower of the *Hôtel de Ville*. "Jean, can your people in the tower see down into the alcove window? Maybe see how many men are in the room?"

De Waha phoned to find out.

Donovan turned to Ridder. "What's your back-up plan?"

"Philippe's team."

"Where are they?"

"Climbing up to the roof above room C3 now. If for some reason we can't break inside, Philippe's team will drop down and enter through the windows."

De Waha waved his hand for attention. "Our guy in the tower sees a tall man wearing sunglasses near the window and some other men in back."

"How many men all together?" Ridder asked.

Pause. "He's not sure, but he thinks maybe… four."

"What weapons do they have?"

De Waha asked, then lowered his head. "Awww shit!"

"What?"

"Rocket launchers, maybe surface-to-air missiles!"

Donovan cringed at the potential devastation. "We might have another problem."

"What?" Ridder asked.

"When you break in – they might fire the rockets and kill hundreds, maybe thousands of people near the grandstand. Claim a partial victory."

"But if we flash-bang them fast," Ridder said, "they shouldn't have enough time to recover, then move the launchers up to the window, turn the safeties off, grab the pull tabs, aim and fire."

"True," Donovan said, "but just to be safe, let's start moving people away from the grandstand. Tell them we need more room for the limousines."

"Agreed."

De Waha took his phone from his ear. "The men in the room are wearing Brussels police uniforms."

"Any chance they are police?" Ridder asked.

"Absolutely not!" de Waha said, obviously angry the terrorists were defiling police uniforms. "No one should be in that building now!"

"Where's the motorcade?" Donovan asked.

"Four minutes away."

"Slow them down," Ridder said.

"But not so slow," Donovan said, "that they become easy targets for other assassins who might be out there."

De Waha gave the order and handed his headset to Ridder. "Our guy in the *Hôtel de Ville* tower will tell you if they're getting ready to fire the launchers."

Ridder nodded, put on the headset, then he and his team disappeared into the ancient building.

Donovan saw the fire in their eyes, like all Special Ops men he'd known. They trained and lived for these moments. To charge into the face of danger despite the personal risk to themselves.

He felt an overwhelming urge to go with them, a long-held, burning desire to look Valek Stahl in the eyes… and repay him for killing Emma.

But Ridder's team was a precision unit, trained like Navy SEALs to perform in concert, to act and react as one… and to cover for each other with practiced, precise, team movements. A non-team member like him could risk their lives. And he'd probably risk his own life, since he hadn't been on any "hot ops" actions in two years.

Still, Donovan would be a nanosecond behind Ridder's team, and with a little luck, he might get a chance to whisper *Emma Rourke* in Stahl's ear as the bastard died and went off to try and justify his crimes to Allah.

THIRTY FOUR

Willi Ridder's plan was simple: shock and awe Stahl and the others into a clear choice: surrender or die.

He assumed they were wearing bulletproof vests – but maybe they weren't. Maybe they were wearing suicide vests. If a bullet hit the explosives, *everybody* in the room, including his ESI team, would be identified by DNA.

He and his team would have to try for headshots. Almost impossible when all hell broke loose, and Ridder anticipated all hell breaking loose.

They climbed to the third floor, moved soundlessly down the hall and entered C3. Then, using the coordinated helicopter flyover noise and the roar of the crowd as cover, they inched the large armoire silently to the side.

Ridder and the team saw the door to the secret alcove. They placed location-listening devices on the wall to determine where the terrorists were positioned.

Suddenly Ridder's earphone clicked on. The man in the *Hôtel de Ville* tower said, "The tall man is looking out the window. He seems puzzled about why the police are backing the crowds away from the grandstand."

"Are the other men still behind the rocket launchers?"

"Yes, but… "

"But what?"

"Oh shit… ."

"What's wrong?"

"People in the crowd are pointing up at Philippe's team on the roof right above 3C window. The tall guy at the window realizes someone's right above him. He's very excited. Now he's saying something to the men behind the rocket launchers. It looks like he wants them to fire the rockets now!"

Ridder feared they would fire any second and kill thousands - because they feared a roof assault through their window.

Ridder faced his team and mouthed, *"One… two… three… GO!"*

Instantly, they yanked open the secret door, tossed in the flash-bang grenade, covered their ears and eyes for the blinding flash, then rushed into the room.

The terrorists, disoriented, were ducking for cover.

"Hands up!" Ridder shouted.

At the window, the tall man wearing wraparound sunglasses started to put his hands up, then leaped for cover behind some wooden crates and fired off two rounds, missing Ridder's head by inches.

The other terrorists shot their handguns as they lunged behind the rocket launchers and prepared to fire them.

But Ridder's team unleashed a barrage of bullets that drilled them against the back wall. They slumped to the floor, firing wildly into the room.

The tall man behind the wooden crates sprang from behind the crates and reached for the rocket launcher's pull-tab, just inches away.

His fingers grabbed the pull-tab.

Ridder and a team member fired and bullets ripped into the man's fingers, then up through his shoulder, neck, face.

The tall man froze, then slumped beside the launcher, his mangled fingers still twitching on the pull-tab.

Ridder kicked his hand away.

* * *

Running into the room, Donovan slipped on the wall-to-wall blood and had to steady himself on a large wood crate. He smelled gunpowder and sweat.

De Waha rushed in. "Status?"

"Bad guys dead or dying!" Ridder said. "Good guys, one grazed shoulder, couple of slugs in our vests."

The ESI team hunched over the bodies, checking for pulses, any sign of life, finding none.

Donovan walked over and checked the crumpled, bloody bodies behind the rocket launchers. They seemed too short to be Stahl. He walked over to the tall man beside the launcher. Stahl's height and weight, and his hair was black, the color Stahl had died it last night.

Donovan looked at the man's bloody, bullet-ravaged face. The man looked like Stahl, even though the bullets had ripped open his cheeks, mouth and forehead. Donovan studied the man's bloodied eyes. Dead, dark, deep-set, stone-cold eyes. But too damaged to compare to the eyes in Stahl's photo. He searched the pockets of the man's police jacket for some ID. Nothing. As he pulled his hand out, his knuckles brushed against something stiff in the lining. He reached through a slit in the lining and pulled out a frayed Euro passport.

His heart pounding, he opened the passport – *Axel Braun. Stahl's alias!*

Donovan looked at the passport picture, then at the bloody face on the floor. They matched, except where bullets had sliced and diced his face and eyebrows.

De Waha walked up to Donovan, looked at the passport and breathed out.

"Axel Braun," de Waha said, "a.k.a. Valek Stahl!"

"a.k.a. *dead!*"

"Yeah… bastard got off easy!"

Donovan agreed, feeling oddly cheated. He'd wanted to look at Stahl, remind him of his cowardly slaughter of Emma, see the recognition in his eyes. But that was not to be.

At least Stahl was dead.

Donovan walked over to the rocket launchers and looked out the window at the grandstand less than one hundred feet below.

He saw the empty chairs where, in just three minutes, the eight most powerful leaders in the world were scheduled to sit.

And die.

Then Donovan felt himself tense up. He remembered something from the Mossad profile on Stahl.

Stahl always had a backup plan.

THIRTY FIVE

"You got Stahl?" Maccabee said as Donovan and de Waha entered the control room to warm applause.

"Willi Ridder's team got Stahl," Donovan said.

"Were you hurt?"

"Nope! Jean and I hid from the scary stuff."

"Scary stuff like that?" She pointed to blood on his shirt.

"Valek Stahl's blood."

Maccabee nodded, but seemed to check his body for any wounds or leakage.

"Attention, people!" de Waha shouted. "The leaders are arriving. Let's assume other assassins are out there. Find them and stop them! Everybody back to work!"

Donovan studied the main screen. The caravan of limousines crawled into the *Grand Place* from a narrow side street. The secret service teams honed in on their big black cars like heat-seeking missiles. Limo doors opened. Distinguished leaders emerged. The huge crowd applauded. Everything appeared to be going well.

But Mossad's warning that Stahl always had a backup plan was digging away at Donovan.

First out of his limousine was French President, Samuel de Batilly, who smiled at the loud applause. Next was the German Chancellor, Heinz Schuster, giving the crowd his best *Bundesrepublik* grin. The applause was subdued, since Belgians still detested the German occupation of their country in both World Wars. Next came American President John Colasanti and England's Prime Minister, Mary Ryan Kearns, and the other leaders who were enthusiastically applauded.

The crowds surged closer to the leaders, but the police forced them back behind a nine-foot transparent Plexiglas wall.

Donovan's gaze again moved up to the hundreds of *Grand Place* windows. Stahl's main attack had been behind one and it almost worked. Was his backup plan behind another window? Would the man who'd warned them about Stahl and his assassins in the secret room, call again with another warning about which window? *Or are we on our own?*

Donovan's gut was churning.

The leaders took their seats on the grandstand and began chatting with each other. The grandstand, he knew, had been guarded 24-7 from start to completion. It had also been swept hourly for explosives. Nothing was found.

The grandstand was safe.

Unless Herr Rutten's explosive or weapon was somehow undetectable… maybe built into the construction materials and embedded with an ozone-masking coating. Experts said their new sniffers were effective even with ozone masking devices. Other experts weren't so sure.

Donovan wiped perspiration from his lip.

As the President of the European Union, Luc DeVries, began speaking, the leaders seemed to relax. And why not? Their work was done. They'd adopted plans to fight famine and genocide. They'd also agreed to fight both political and corporate terrorism. There would be less dumping of low-wage-country products in high-wage countries. A corporation had to create jobs or revenue in a country commensurate in value with the revenue the corporation took out of the country. If not, there would be penalties.

Donovan noticed that DeVries leaned on the podium as he spoke. Was the podium checked? He ran his finger down a grandstand checklist. No mention of the podium.

"Jean, the podium?"

De Waha pulled out another list and pointed at an item. "The podium's been triple checked."

Donovan nodded, but something else began to gnaw at his memory. Something specific a Mossad agent had said about Stahl. A minor personal detail. But for some reason, the detail eluded him and now it felt very important. *What the hell is it?*

Luc DeVries finished to enormous applause.

Minutes later, the *Grand Place* ceremony ended. The leaders, flanked by their secret security personnel, left the grandstand, smiling and unscathed.

Donovan's lungs deflated like a balloon. He couldn't believe it. Jean and he had survived their greatest fear: the vulnerability of the leaders sitting exposed on the grandstand on the *Grand Place.* Nothing had happened. They'd stopped Stahl. Killed him. And, they'd avoided any quick backup attack he might have planned outside on the *Grand Place.*

Still, Donovan knew, his backup attack could take place *inside a Grand Place* building. Like the *Hôtel de Ville,* the seven hundred year old superstructure the leaders were walking into.

THIRTY SIX

D onovan watched the G8 leaders stroll through the dark, narrow hallways of the *Hôtel de Ville.* Armed guards stood in position. Security procedures were being followed. Privileged attendees smiling behind velvet ropes. Everything was working well.

Except Donovan's memory.

He still couldn't remember the one detail about Valek Stahl that he'd read in the Mossad briefing reports, a detail that his gut told him was crucial. It must be crucial, or it wouldn't be gnawing at him now?

What the hell was it?

He watched the leaders stroll through high-ceiling rooms lined with magnificent paintings and sprawling tapestries from the middle ages. In each room, stern-faced guards scrutinized anyone who even glanced at the leaders.

The leaders wandered over and clustered around an enormous ancient tapestry.

Donovan didn't want them clustering. He wanted them spread out and them hurrying along. Instead, they stared at a famous tapestry depicting the Duke of Alba, a ruthless Spanish Duke who ruled the country in the 1560s and just to make sure citizens knew he ruled, slaughtered eighteen thousand of them.

"Jean, have all tapestries and artwork been checked for explosives?"

"Sniffed every hour, and fifteen minutes before the leaders walk by them."

"Still, I - "

"Still what... ?" de Waha said.

"Stahl knew the leaders would be led right up to the tapestries and artwork."

"Right. You think Stahl's backup attack is an explosive behind one?"

"An *undetectable* explosive, maybe."

"Experts say no way," de Waha said, but concern lingered in his eyes.

Donovan watched the leaders move into the spectacular Hall of the City Council.

For seven hundred years, local officials met in this same room and governed the country, surrounded by rich, exotic woods and paintings depicting the land's rich history.

Suddenly, a tall, broad-shouldered guard Donovan hadn't seen before hurried in and stood behind the leaders. The guard scanned the room as though checking whether anyone was watching him. He seemed very anxious, nervous even, and his skin glowed with perspiration.

He reached into his pocket.

"Jean, who's the guard with - ?"

Jean was gone.

Donovan looked back at the guard. For some reason, the guard reminded him of Stahl. Same height and build, same big physique, same jet black hair.

Forget it — Stahl's dead.

The guard inched closer to the leaders, scanned the room again, then yanked a black device from his pocket. A detonator?

Donovan started running down toward the room and bumped into de Waha.

"What's wrong?" de Waha said.

Donovan pointed. "That guard holding that black – "

" - two-way radio! That's Henri. Calls ahead, tells the next chamber the leaders are on their way."

Donovan felt the air drain from his lungs.

"A little mistaken identity, Donovan?"

"Yeah."

Mistaken identity!

The phrase started bouncing around his head. Is it possible they'd mistakenly identified the dead man in 3C as Valek Stahl? Donovan turned and stared outside at the building where Stahl had been shot and killed.

De Waha was looking at him. "You're acting kinda weird. What's bugging you?"

"I'm not sure… " Donovan said, shaking his head.

"About what?"

"Stahl."

"Stahl's dead!"

"Yeah, but – "

"But what?"

"Hear me out."

"I'm all ears."

"Stahl has never used rocket and grenade launchers before."

"Right."

"Stahl did not visit Herr Rutten to exchange fondue recipes."

"Right again."

"Herr Rutten's expertise is explosives and custom made weapons."

"Right."

"Stahl has nearly always used explosives."

"So what - Stahl's dead."

"Is he?"

De Waha stared at Donovan like he was losing it. "His passport says Axel Braun, Stahl's alias."

"Yes, but - "

"How much proof do you want? We get a phone call saying Valek Stahl is in that room and bingo – Valek Stahl was in the room! He's the right height and weight. His hair was black, the color he dyed it. His face, even though it was partly destroyed by bullets, matches his passport picture, a passport using Stahl's alias, Axel Braun. What do you want, 'Stahl' tattooed on his damn forehead?"

Donovan spun around and looked at de Waha. "That's it!"

"What's it?"

"What I couldn't remember – a tattoo!"

De Waha frowned.

"Didn't a Mossad agent report say Stahl had a small tattoo?"

De Waha closed his eyes, then slowly turned back and stared at Donovan. "I think so."

"A word tattoo."

"Yeah."

"Which I dismissed," Donovan said, "because Islam forbids tattoos."

"True, but Stahl is not your most observant disciple of Islam."

"He drinks alcohol, too."

"But you're right, the report said he had one. A name tattoo, I think."

"On his shoulder! And now that I remember, I read somewhere that he has a small L-shape scar on his nose."

De Waha punched a number on his phone, waited, spoke briefly, got excited, then hung up.

"Let's hurry - they're carrying the bodies out now!"

Donovan and de Waha hurried through the thousands of people still leaving the *Grand Place* to the building where Stahl died. They caught up to the ambulance crews carrying the body bags down the back stairs.

Donovan unzipped the first bag. A short man. He unzipped the next bag - the tall man with Stahl's Axel Braun passport. He ripped open the dead man's shirt and pulled it down over his shoulders and arms, blanketed with blood.

Donovan realized there was too much blood to see skin well. Using the man's shirt, he wiped the blood off his left shoulder and arm. No tattoo. No hint one had been removed.

He wiped off the right shoulder, arm and bullet-riddled chest. Nothing.

Then they checked his back. Again nothing.

"No tattoos!" Donovan said.

"Let's check for the nose scar."

Donovan saw that a bullet had ripped into the lower part of his nose and left it hanging down on his upper lip. Donovan wiped blood off the nose, repositioned it and looked for a scar. He saw none.

"No scar!" de Waha confirmed. *This is not Stahl!*

They stared at each other.

"Stahl set us up," Donovan said, "wanted us to think this man was Stahl. Probably gave him the Axel Braun passport to carry for him."

"He set them up too!" De Waha pointed to the body bags.

"So we'd think we had stopped *him!* And relax security!"

"So he can strike at the *Hôtel de -* "

"Forget the *Hôtel de Ville,*" de Waha said, looking at his hand-held television. "The leaders are ready to leave it."

"Which means he's going to strike at the Congo Museum."

"Why?"

"It's the last time they're together."

THIRTY SEVEN

Valek Stahl turned off Avenue de Tervuren, drove a few blocks and parked next to a small, neighborhood restaurant, the St. Bernard, where he'd eaten several months ago. He parked and went inside.

The Daily Special, *Boeuf aux Champignons,* steak and mushrooms, smelled delicious. And it was delicious. He'd eaten it last time he was here.

But not today. He never ate before an assignment. Food sedated the brain, and he wanted to be razor sharp in the next few hours. He ordered black coffee.

The restaurant looked the same. Regular customers sat at tables with red checkerboard tablecloths. The walls held pictures of St. Bernard rescue dogs. A juke box played Elvis singing *Love Me Tender.* In the corner, two older couples speaking Flemish, played cards, including a gray-haired woman who seemed to glance at him from time to time. Did she maybe recognize him from the last time he was here. He didn't remember seeing her then.

A wall-mounted television showed the G8 leaders preparing to leave the *Hôtel de Ville*. The announcer said:

> "This just in… three armed terrorists,
> members of Al Qaeda, were killed by an ESI
> SWAT team in the small alcove of a Grand
> Place building minutes before the G8 leaders
> arrived."

Exactly as planned, Stahl thought.

He thought back to when he'd phoned de Waha last night and given him a heads up on the attack. Then today, he called him again and told him *"Stahl and the brothers are in the secret room."*

Then, as he expected, the SWAT team broke in, massacred the brothers and found Axel Braun's passport in Yusef's police jacket. They looked at the passport photo, a photo that Stahl had computer-altered to merge his face with Yusef's, and then concluded they'd killed Valek Stahl.

Finally, they congratulated themselves, let their guard down.

Idiots!

Perhaps, he should feel some remorse for sacrificing Yusef and his brothers, but he didn't. They were merely bullets in Jihad's gun. A means to a much more important goal. His! And they had long voiced their willingness to die for the jihad.

Of course, they died martyrs. Maybe not willing, but still, martyrs who died believing they were furthering the Al Qaeda cause and that paradise and seventy-two virgins awaited them. They died achieving their goal. They died happy. And he was happy to accommodate them.

Stahl removed his sunglasses and noticed the gray-haired woman paying extra attention to him. Perhaps because he was a stranger. To be safe, Stahl lifted a newspaper in front of his face.

And saw his own face.

His *old* face actually. Nothing like his new look.

Which made him wonder again, why the old woman was so interested in him?

He drank more coffee and read about the one-on-one meetings between the President of the United States and the President of Russia. Their last, of course.

A minute later, as Stahl lowered the paper, he caught the woman staring at him again.

What's with her? She can't possibly recognize me. My hair, beard and collagen injections have transformed my face.

But he decided not to take any chances. He'd read about studies that prove some people have a rare genetic gift, a unique and uncanny ability to identify faces, even identify an aged adult from their baby picture. She could be one.

He put his sunglasses on, finished his coffee, placed money on the table and walked out. The nosy woman watched him leave. Let her watch. It would all be over very soon.

Stahl drove out onto the Avenue Tervuren where crowds were already forming to watch the leaders drive by.

He drove through the large forest, the *Forêt de Soignes*. He'd knew this forest well. He liked how the tall thick trees bent over the road, blocking out the sun, creating darkness.

He was about to cast the world into darkness.

Minutes later, he saw the sprawling Royal Museum of Central Africa. Locals called it the Congo Museum. He drove through the iron gates at the side of the Congo Museum. The leaders would soon enter through the same gates.

And soon after, they would enter the gates of hell.

Stahl pulled into the side lot. He drove behind rows of parked cars and vans to his pre-determined spot next to the wide stairs that descended into the massive gardens.

He was precisely eighty-six-yards from what American television announcers would soon call Europe's 'ground zero.'

A yellow mini-bus with elementary school children parked beside him. He smiled at them and they smiled back. He wondered if later they'd tell their parents they parked next to the man who assassinated the eight most powerful leaders in the world. They probably would. After all, he'd be part of history. Like Lee Harvey Oswald, Kennedy's assassin.

Only I'm killing eight world leaders.

He felt good about that.

A Peugeot with a family parked in front of him. He reached over, picked up his hand-sized television he'd bought at the nearby INNO store and turned it on. The picture flickered to life and he watched the smiling G8 leaders waving at people in the crowds from the limousines crawling out of the *Grand Place.*

He turned his special cell phone on, and the little red light glowed. The battery icon indicated full power. The system was set.

He leaned back and smiled at the television, his partner in the righteous jihad today. He would watch the leaders walk into the museum and gather around the fascinating display.

He would speed-dial G 8.

He would watch them die.

And… he would vanish in the panic and chaos.

Soon, Papa… soon I will repay them for you…

Stahl watched more police and anti-terrorist teams arrive and take up positions. On the roof, snipers perched like hawks. They held what looked like Belgian A3G sniper rifles, or the Carabine Automatique Leger, a scaled-down weapon Stahl liked. Excellent weapons.

Just one problem. By the time the police realized what happened, they wouldn't know who to aim the guns at… and he'd be long gone.

Stahl glanced at his television. The leaders were driving toward the Congo Museum in their shiny limousines.

They would leave the Congo Museum in hearses.

THIRTY EIGHT

In the St. Bernard Restaurant, Camille Segers shuffled the cards, trying to remember where she'd seen the stranger who'd just left. She had an excellent memory for faces, thanks to retouching them for thirty-four years at Chaffee's Portraits. She'd made wrinkles and warts vanish, eyes change colors, hair thicken, frowns smile, and years disappear.

And she was positive she'd seen the stranger's face somewhere recently. But where?

She sipped more wine as a Stella Artois commercial blasted onto the television. Suddenly her memory clicked in.

"Got it!"

"Got what?" her husband, Pierre, asked.

"TV!"

Her fellow card players stared at her.

"That's where I saw him!"

"Who in hell are you talking about?"

"That tall stranger who just left."

"Who cares!"

"The police care! They put his picture on television. The poor man has a real bad disease. Some kind of meningitis. He needs medical attention real fast for chrissakes!"

Pierre stared at her. "You're losing it, Camille! The man in here had black hair and a beard. The man on TV had brown-blond hair and no beard."

"Old photo maybe. When he removed his glasses, I saw his eyes, deep close-set eyes, slight slant. Strange eyes. Hell, you can't change that. And when he walked past, I saw his nose. Little white, L-shaped scar on the bridge. Same as on the TV picture. It's him alright!"

"Rubbish!"

"Same word you used in grade school when I told you the Germans were invading in '40."

Pierre clammed up.

Camille fished out her cell phone and dialed the number on the television. A male officer answered.

"Hello, I'm Camille Segers at the St. Bernard Restaurant in Sint-Pieters-Woluwe."

"Yes… "

"And I just saw the man you're looking for."

"Which man?" The officer yawned.

"The man on TV with the real bad meningitis."

Another yawn. "You're certain ma'am?"

"Of course. You think I call the police every day?"

"Some people do."

"I'm not some people. And I also saw him drive away."

"In what?"

"A silver Opel Insignia."

The cop sputtered. "Did you say a silver Opel Insignia?"

"Sure did."

"My God, we just learned about the Opel a minute ago."

"You want the license plate number?"

"What? Yes!"

"BBL-738."

"You're *right!* You really did see him!"

"How many times I gotta tell you?"

"When did - ?"

"Ten minutes ago."

"Did he drive toward the Congo Museum?"

"He turned in that direction."

"Thank you, ma'am. Please wait there for an officer to come talk to you."

"Make it fast! I'm playing canasta at Yolanda's in thirty minutes. She gets real snippy if I'm late."

THIRTY NINE

*M*y *enemies arrive…* Stahl realized as the Belgian police helicopter descended like a bird of prey over the sprawling Congo Museum grounds.

The downwash from the rotors flattened the red and white flowers in the gardens and pushed tiny ripples across the massive reflecting pool.

The chopper touched down, sending dust devils swirling into the air. Moments later, two men and a tall woman stepped out.

Stahl recognized the first man: Jean de Waha, Belgian's Director General of G8 Summit security. Stahl had studied the man's impressive bio and work habits for months.

The second man, tall, powerfully-built and wearing an American-cut suit, had his back to Stahl. As the man turned, Stahl blinked a few times, then squinted to be sure. No question about it. He was looking at a CIA operative he'd been hired to terminate two years ago, a man named Donovan Rourke. A man lucky to be alive.

Stahl remembered breaking into Rourke's apartment not far from here. When Rourke wasn't home, he'd carried out plan B – terminated Rourke's wife. Her death achieved the client objective: rendered Rourke ineffective. In fact, the man became such a basket case, the CIA transferred him back to Langley headquarters. Once there, he ceased to be a problem for Stahl's employer.

But now, Stahl realized with no small pleasure, *I may have a chance to finish the job, get some 'closure' as the Americans say. And repay him for the difficulty he's caused me in the last few days.*

Stahl looked at the attractive woman. Tall and thin with smooth, honey-hued skin and dark, silky hair. She wore a stylish royal blue suit and the way she and Rourke glanced at each other suggested something personal between them, maybe romantic.

A chubby, bald museum official hurried outside and ushered them in through the museum's side door.

* * *

Inside the museum, Donovan, de Waha and Maccabee stared at a wall of television monitors revealing the galleries the leaders would soon walk through. Donovan saw armed guards in each gallery.

He turned and looked outside at the anti-terrorist teams patrolling the perimeter. Plainclothes officers walked through the crowds looking for Stahl. Blue vans jammed with paramilitary squads were parked in strategic locations around the museum. Security looked tight. Everything looked safe.

An illusion, Donovan knew.

Because Stahl was here. He *had* to be. This was the last time the leaders were *together.* From here, they would depart separately for their flights back home.

It would happen here.

The Congo Museum.

Stahl's plan all along.

Which meant he was either near the museum, or in the museum.

Or, he'd planted Herr Rutten's weapon, an explosive probably, inside the museum.

So why hadn't a gallery-by-gallery sweep minutes ago detected some hint of an explosive? And why hadn't a similar sweep detected an airborne chemical or biological weapon?

The answer was simple. Stahl's weapon was undetectable.

Herr Rutten must have used a sophisticated ozone or microscopic nanobot-masking device. Some experts said ozone and nanobots might mask the scent of an explosive so well even dogs and electronic sniffers could not detect it.

Whatever the case, the weapon had to be here.

So was Stahl. His ego required that he see his end game, see his creation's devastation, see his history-changing catastrophe take place, see the bleeding corpses.

See it all in person.

Donovan dabbed perspiration from his brow, walked out into the hallway and ran his fingers along the cool marble wall. He remembered when little Tish ran her toy train along this same wall. She made such a racket, Emma and he took her outside to play in the gardens.

Two weeks later Emma was dead. Murdered by the same man now planning eight more murders here in this museum in a matter of minutes.

Maccabee walked up beside him. "Hey there, Mister"

He turned and smiled.

"You look kinda lost."

"Lost and found… last night," he said, suddenly flooded with love for her.

She smiled back as de Waha rushed over with the head of museum security, a man named Frans Kramers.

"We just completed the final check of the museum," Kramers said. "The museum is cleared. No explosives, no bio or chemical weapons found."

"Basement?" Donovan asked.

"Clean."

"Ventilation systems??"

"Nothing."

"The dogs?"

"Nothing."

"How much time before the limos arrive?"

De Waha checked his watch. "Six minutes."

Despite the excellent security, despite Kramer's assurances, despite the weapons sweeps, Donovan couldn't relax. Stahl's weapon was here!

"Jean... ?"

"Yeah?"

"Stahl *has* to hit here!"

De Waha nodded.

"Let's try again to cancel this tour."

"I tried five minutes ago."

"And?"

"The authorities turned me down again. Unanimous decision by the leaders."

"Why?"

"Their image," De Waha said.

"For chrissakes, they've already got *thousands* of image photos and video!"

"No, their image toward Africa. They've been criticized for neglecting Africa's problems: genocide, famine, AIDS, disease. They want the leaders seen in this *African* museum, showing they care. If they cancel this museum tour, the world will see it as further proof that the world leaders don't care about Africa. As they tour, TV announcers and commercials will talk about G8's bold new plans to help solve Africa's problems. So that's a good thing."

"But not if the leaders die here!"

De Waha nodded. "I tried... "

Donovan knew he had. "I wouldn't be surprised that Stahl chose this African museum tour because he knew the leaders could not afford the bad PR from canceling the tour."

De Waha nodded. "Probably. But the leaders also insisted on something else."

"What?"

"They insisted that Stahl not be allowed to determine their agenda."

"Understandable, but then their agenda may include their own funerals."

De Waha shrugged.

Donovan felt frustrated, like someone was holding a blowtorch to his skin. He had to move, walk, do something. "Frans, could you hurry us through the galleries for one last look. Maybe we'll get lucky, see something."

Kramers glanced at his watch. "We'll have to rush!"

He led them quickly into the first gallery, which displayed mining products from the Congo. Donovan scanned the display cases filled with big chunks of copper, uranium and cobalt. *Are these big chunks really what they appear to be? Could they be C4 or PETN explosives?*

"How many items in the museum?" Donovan asked.

"You won't believe it."

"Try me."

"250,000 rock samples, 56,000 wood samples, and somewhere around 10 million animals and life forms."

Jesus! Impossible to screen them all.

Still, he wondered if Stahl might have replicated a larger object, like a statue or animal, using an explosive and then somehow made it undetectable. But experts said no way.

Experts also said the Titanic could not sink.

They walked quickly into the second gallery, a display of beautiful African woodcarvings. Everything seemed normal, safe. The next gallery was filled with a large collection of objects from several Congo villages and the Matadi-Leopoldville railway.

The adjoining room displayed native spears and weapons from the tribes of southern central Africa. Again, nothing looked threatening except the spears and knives, but they were locked up in cases.

"How much time?" Donovan asked.

"*Three* minutes," Kramers said.

"Let's hurry through the remaining galleries," de Waha said. They rushed into a gallery containing rare metals and minerals. Donovan saw rows of brilliant diamonds sparkling at him from a display case.

Outside, a car alarm started beeping. Donovan looked out a side window and saw the parking area jammed with cars.

"Jean, those cars in the lot... "

"Yeah?"

"Were they swept for explosives?"

"Yes. Officers with hand-held sniffers and dogs have been checking them for the last fifteen minutes."

"Is security checking the drivers and passengers?"

"Yes. Both ground security and roof snipers."

Donovan was anxious about the proximity of the cars to the museum, especially those within one hundred feet. Cars could hide hundreds of pounds of explosives. On the other hand, the cars seemed too far away, and the museum walls far too thick for a car explosion to injure the leaders. The blast would only kill people in the immediate blast area.

Stahl's explosive was *inside* the museum where the blast would kill the eight leaders.

Donovan heard the motorcade sirens drawing near.

Kramers hurried them into a large room, The Elephant Gallery, where several large African animals looked like they'd just crept out of the jungle. In the middle stood the enormous elephant that little Tish had been afraid of.

He looked at the majestic beast with its long trunk and ivory tusks flaring out. The twelve thousand pound elephant stood on its natural African terrain of tall grass and rocks in sandy soil. As Donovan walked past the elephant, its dark eyes seemed to follow him, as though trying to communicate, maybe warn him. A cold draft swept across Donovan's face.

Something in this gallery made him uneasy. *Very* uneasy.

He turned and looked back into the elephant's eyes. Were they warning him? Or was he hallucinating?

Outside, the motorcade sirens whined down to a stop.

"The leaders are here," de Waha said.

They hurried back to the control room and Donovan watched the television screens fill up with leaders entering the museum. His pulse pounded against his temple. His throat and eyes were bone dry. He stared at the screen, afraid to blink and miss something.

The moment of truth was at hand.

Stahl and his weapon were here.

And Donovan had no idea how to stop him!

FORTY

Donovan hated what he saw. The leaders *clustering* close together again... this time around a mahogany carving of an African woman's face.

He didn't want them clustering. He wanted them hustling their distinguished VIP butts out of the Congo museum and racing to the airport to fly home.

He was still frustrated and angry that he and Jean couldn't persuade officials to cancel the Congo museum tour.

A minute ago, he'd tried again. He'd phoned President Colasanti's Chief of Staff, Nester Smale, and explained his concern. Smale argued that the Congo Museum tour was absolutely necessary to demonstrate the President's concern for African famine and genocide, as well as people of color worldwide. Smale neglected to admit that the tour would also help win African American votes back home.

Donovan looked over at the fire alarm. He was tempted to run over and pull the damn thing and get everyone outside, then claim an electrical malfunction triggered the alarm.

Because Stahl was *here,* in control, ready to unleash his weapon any moment.

But how did Stahl know *which moment?* And how did he know which galleries would be toured? And how could he know the sequence? The museum director had only decided on the gallery tour sequence thirty minutes ago.

The answer was clear. Stahl knew because he was with or *near* the leaders!

Or someone with or near the leaders was telling Stahl where they were.

Or… Stahl *saw* the leaders!

"Jean – is this tour being televised?"

Jean checked his clipboard. "Yes. Only the *Grand Place* ceremony and this Congo Museum tour are televised."

"Stahl's watching this on television."

"So?"

"So he's within a few hundred feet of this building. I don't know how, but somehow he's masked Rutten's explosive. He has a detonator and when the leaders walk into the gallery with the explosive, he'll – "

"But we've swept every gallery five times!"

"Yeah, but - "

De Waha's phone suddenly rang. He answered, listened and hung up.

"A woman in a nearby restaurant saw Stahl drive in this direction."

"What was he driving?"

"The stolen Opel Insignia we just learned about! The one stolen out near Knokke."

Donovan and de Waha ran to the window and looked out at the parked vehicles. No silver Opel Insignias. They ran to the next window facing the side lot. A blue Opel Senator. An old Opel Vectra. No Insignias.

De Waha grabbed the security phone. "Search every silver Opel within five-hundred meters of the museum now!"

* * *

Stahl watched the leaders gather around a display of a large African yellow-billed stork. Such a beautiful bird. Even more beautiful was how the leaders clustered tightly together around the bird. The fools were contributing to their own imminent deaths.

What more can I ask for?

Only one more gallery...

He visualized his glorious, triumphant moment. They walk into the Elephant Gallery...

They're drawn to the massive elephant - my beautiful five-ton avenging angel. They walk up to it. They marvel at its size, its long trunk and massive ivory tusks. They notice the sandy soil the elephant stands in, they see the large dark rocks in the soil. Maybe they notice Herr Rutten's identical large dark rocks peeking up through the sandy soil.

And even if they do, it will be too late.

Because at that precise moment, I will push G 8 on the detonator phone – and those beautiful dark rocks of PETN will explode at 26,400 feet per second – shredding the infidels to confetti.

He visualized the magnificent carnage... the American's leg here... the German's foot there... the English woman's fingers landing on the Italian's crotch as his head rolls down the hall like a bowling ball.

'Nothing rolls like a head,' Stahl's father had often told him. Actually, Stahl recalled, heads wobbled more than they rolled straight.

The leaders approached the door of the Elephant Gallery. The Canadian and German leaders smiled and walked toward the enormous beast... like rats drawn to poison.

Out of the corner of his eye, Stahl noticed policemen running toward a silver Opel Insignia near the entrance gate. Weapons drawn, they ordered the young male driver to get out.

They know...

Stahl's pulse kicked up a bit. Checking the television, he saw more leaders enter the Elephant Gallery. By the time the cops spotted his car, all leaders would stand beside the elephant – he'd push *G 8* and escape in the chaos.

His righteous moment… the most glorious in his life… was at hand.

Just seconds now…

* * *

Donovan turned to de Waha. "Jean, *back* the leaders out of the Elephant Gallery – back them through the rooms they just visited! Those rooms are safe! Phone your coordinator in the Elephant Room and tell him!"

De Waha grabbed the phone, hit speed dial.

"MERDE!"

"What?"

"Busy!"

De Waha turned to Frans Kramers. "Frans, run up there. *Back* the leaders out of the room. *Hurry!*"

Kramers sprinted off toward the Elephant Gallery at the opposite end of the massive building, several hundred feet away.

Donovan focused his binoculars on the vehicles in the side lot. Vans and mini-buses blocked his view of many cars. He saw SUVs with families, busses with children, vans with seniors. He scanned the last row beside the wide steps leading down to the huge garden and froze. He blinked to be sure.

"Got him!" Donovan said.

"Where?"

"Silver Opel Insignia, seven rows back. Next to the garden steps. He's wearing sunglasses. Black hair. Beard. It's *him!* Keeps checking something on the seat – gotta be a TV!"

Donovan and de Waha raced down to the door that opened onto the side parking lot and stepped outside. Donovan felt Maccabee grab his arm from behind.

"Be safe," she said.

He nodded, then realized the building could explode and collapse any second. "It might be safer to wait outside this door away from the concrete and glass."

"Okay."

Weapons drawn, Donovan and Jean ran toward Stahl's car, less than two hundred feet away.

Donovan saw Stahl's eyes lock on him.

FORTY ONE

S tahl watched Rourke and de Waha run toward him, weaving between cars, their guns raised and zeroing in on him. He started the car and grabbed his Glock.

Glancing at the mini-TV, he saw the rest of the leaders walking into the Elephant Gallery... just fifty feet from his avenging beast.

Move closer!

Rourke and de Waha raised their guns, but held fire when a group of grade school girls walked in front.

Just a few more seconds... a few more feet... when all leaders are beside the elephant!

He spun the big Opel out of his parking spot and drove down the wide steps into the massive gardens. He sped alongside the long reflecting pool, forcing people to jump out of the way and some to jump in. He looked back and saw Rourke and de Waha commandeer a small police Renault and race after him.

Stahl checked his mini TV. The leaders, just thirty feet from the elephant, strolled toward it.

"Closer! Faster!"

From the right, Stahl saw a large police van race toward him. He turned and headed straight toward the main entrance gates to the street.

The leaders stepped closer to the elephant

Twenty feet... fifteen... ten...

Then the American president stopped at an antelope.

Stahl wanted to kill him most.

"Closer, you bastard!"

A bullet ripped through Stahl's roof. He swerved around a minibus, then, dodging spectators, sped on toward the gates and road in front of the museum.

Two more bullets pierced his rear window.

The American President walked toward the elephant... ten feet... five... he reached it!

All leaders stood beside the elephant!

"Allahu Akbar!" Stahl shouted.

He punched in *G 8!*

The explosion shook the ground so much it rocked the big Opel. He saw smoke, fire and glass, blast out of the Elephant Gallery windows.

Then he saw chunks of elephant... and a bloody human leg with its foot blown off... then another leg... and a mangled arm.

Magnificent! Stahl thought, racing ahead.

People screamed and ran away from the fiery smoke and slabs of concrete blasting out of the Elephant Room windows. Long tongues of fire licked up the side of the museum.

All police vehicles stopped, their drivers gawking at the fiery devastation. Stahl looked at his TV screen: Nothing but snow. He checked the rearview mirror. Rourke and de Waha still chased him in the small Renault, two hundred yards back.

Then, Stahl had some luck.

A long *BBC WORLD NEWS* truck backed away from the explosion and blocked Rourke's car. Rourke pounded on the horn, but the truck didn't budge.

Stahl sped ahead.

Then he couldn't believe his eyes! More good luck!

Rourke's friend, the tall attractive woman, stood fifty feet ahead beside the museum door.

Stahl stopped beside her, pushed open the passenger door, stuck his gun inches from her face. "Get in or die here!"

She looked back toward Donovan. Stahl leaned over, yanked her into the car and sped off. He raced through the gates onto the main street.

Stahl checked the mirror. Donovan's car was still blocked behind the *BBC WORLD NEWS* truck.

* * *

"Jesus! He took Maccabee!" Donovan shouted, as he found some room to squeeze around the BBC truck and race ahead.

De Waha seemed to be in shock. His eyes locked open and stared at the snowy screen of his small television.

"What... ?"

"Stahl pulled Maccabee into his car!"

De Waha snapped out of it. "She's his insurance. He knows we won't shoot."

Donovan's heart was pounding so hard he couldn't speak.

Enraged and nauseated by his pathetic failure to protect the lives of the G8 leaders, and now Maccabee, Donovan sped toward the open gate, barely missing two teenagers.

His siren blaring, he careened wildly onto the street, weaving between cars, and raced after Stahl. De Waha was on the phone, directing all police cars to pursue the silver Opel.

But the big Opel had pulled away, accelerating to at least one hundred forty kilometers per hour.

Donovan's small Renault lost ground fast.

* * *

Stahl turned onto the long forest straightaway and raced ahead.

In the mirror, he no longer saw Rourke's police car. But he had to ditch the Opel fast. Fortunately, he knew this forest well and remembered a forest clearing a mile ahead where hikers parked their vehicles and bikes.

He turned in at the clearing and hid the Opel behind some bushes. He looked back toward the road and thirty seconds later saw Rourke's police car race past.

Stahl scanned the area. Through the branches of some evergreens, he saw the trunk of what looked like a red BMW parked ahead. There were no other cars in the area.

"Get out!" he said to Maccabee.

She turned to open the door. As she did, he karate-chopped the back of her neck. She slumped unconscious. He bound her wrists with flex-cuffs and left her on the car seat.

Soundlessly, he walked toward the rear of the red BMW. He saw a young couple in the front seat.

Stahl spun the silencer on his Glock.

FORTY TWO

G ripping his suppressed Glock, Stahl stepped soundlessly on the spongy pine needles toward the red BMW. He paused near its trunk and saw a young man and woman embracing in the front seat.

He stepped up to the open driver's window. The surprised couple looked out at him.

"Out of the car! Now!"

They stared back.

"Now!" He placed the silencer near the man's head.

They stepped from the car.

"Turn around and walk down that path."

They turned and walked.

Stahl raised the silenced gun and shot them both in the back of the head.

He dragged their bodies behind some bushes, removed their IDs and destroyed their cell phones. He walked back to the Opel and lifted the American woman out and placed her on the ground. Her driver's license read: Maccabee Singh.

She was not moving. Perhaps he'd hit her too hard. He'd done that a few times. In Caracas, he barely hit a guy who died within minutes. He looked down at the woman. Should he keep her as a hostage? Or would she slow him down?

He should probably just finish her off here.

* * *

"We've lost him!" Donovan said, slamming his fist on the dashboard as he drove through the forest.

"We're blocking off Avenue de Tervuren!" de Waha said. "He's trapped!"

"Not if he turned into the forest."

Donovan knew the *Forêt de Soignes* sprawled over sixteen thousand acres of thick woods and numerous pathways. Perfect for hiding the Opel.

And Maccabee's body.

As they drove out of the forest, Donovan raced past Avenue Isidor Gerard, then the small lakes in Auderghem. He skidded to a stop at the roadblock where an ESI anti-terrorist team stood armed and ready.

De Waha asked the team if they'd seen the Opel. They shook their heads.

Donovan squeezed the steering wheel. "Stahl turned into a side street or the forest. She's dead weight to him now."

"No. She's protection against our assault! He needs her as a hostage!"

"He needs to dump her body and get out of the country!"

De Waha shook his head. "The only way that bastard'll get out of my country is in a *coffin!*"

"Like the G8 leaders... " Donovan whispered, swallowing bile in his throat.

He felt nauseated by *his* horrific failure to stop the assassinations of the world leaders. He saw the explosion, saw bloody human legs and an arm, saw the elephant tusks, all blasting out of the gallery windows.

His life was over. He'd live forever as the agent who'd failed to protect the president of the United States... and the seven other most powerful leaders in the world. Forget that he and de Waha had tried repeatedly to cancel the tour. Forget that the authorities had insisted on touring the Congo Museum for political reasons. Scapegoats were needed. Heads would roll. And his head and de Waha's were first in line for the chopping block.

Donovan was angry with himself for not following his instincts. He should have pulled the damn fire alarm and hustled the leaders out of the museum.

And because he didn't, their lives ended.

So had his career, not that it mattered now.

De Waha grabbed the police car phone and dialed the Congo Museum.

Donovan felt the blood drain from his face.

"Nothing but *static...* " de Waha said.

"They're dead... " Donovan whispered.

De Waha adjusted the channel frequency several times and still got static, then the line went dead. "The explosion wiped out our phones."

"Try the museum phone."

He punched in the number and waited. "Dead!"

Dead... Donovan felt nauseated, tried to swallow, couldn't.

"I'll call Frans Kramer's cell," De Waha dialed and pushed the speaker button. A loud buzz filled the car, then the phone rang once and started hissing.

"Kramers here."

More hissing...

"Frans... how many?"

Again the phone crackled and hissed.

"Frans?

The line beeped.

"Frans, how many?"

More hissing... "All of them... "

Donovan's heart stopped.

More hissing… buzzing… beeping.

"*All* G8 leaders?"

"Yes. All of them!"

More buzzing.

Donovan started to pull off the road to vomit.

"Jesus," de Waha said, "all eight world leaders dead."

More hissing and buzzing.

"I said… *alive!* All leaders are *alive!*"

"What - ?"

"Not a scratch!"

"But I saw them on my small TV," de Waha said. "They were standing at the elephant. I saw the Elephant Gallery explode. I saw a human leg fly out the damn window!"

"A guard's leg!"

"But the leaders… ?"

"They're okay, Jean! They're all fine!"

Stunned, Donovan looked at de Waha who crossed himself, shot his fist in the air and shouted, *"Thank God!"*

"Thank commercial television, too," Kramers said.

"What?"

"Commercial television. Stahl was watching the leaders on TV. He watched them walk up to the elephant, right?"

"Right," de Waha said.

"Then he detonated, right?"

"Yeah."

"One small problem."

"What?"

"The leaders were not at the elephant."

Donovan got it. "Time-delay TV!"

"Exactly."

"But I saw the word *LIVE* on my TV screen!" de Waha said.

"*LIVE* ain't what it use to be. The networks use that word loosely these days."

———

"So what happened?"

"The leaders weren't in the elephant gallery. They were in another room several hundred feet away, separated by six walls of very thick concrete went the bomb went off. What Stahl saw on television happened three minutes earlier. The network tape-delayed so they could fit in commercials for people to donate to African charities."

Donovan thought back to when the leaders entered the building. He remembered seeing commercials for African charities that ran for about three minutes. During that time, obviously, the leaders were *already* touring the galleries. When the commercials ended, the coverage began with the leaders in the first gallery.

The G8 leaders were alive.

Stahl had failed.

And when he finds out he'll be enraged. What will he do to Maccabee?

FORTY THREE

D onovan smelled thick, suffocating smoke as he parked beside the Congo Museum. Fire trucks, policemen and counter-terrorism squads swarmed around the massive building. Yellow crime scene tape blocked all doors. Police had corralled the media in the parking lot. Television reporters spoke into cameras and pointed at the smoke and destruction behind them.

He and de Waha stepped over fire hoses as firemen pumped stiff streams of water through the windows of the Elephant Gallery. Around the scorched window frames, large chunks of concrete had been blown out. Despite the enormous blast, the magnificent 114-year-old building stood rock solid.

They walked into the control room.

Donovan saw Frans Kramers. "Where are the leaders now, Frans?"

"Just arriving at the airport."

"But I just saw their limos right outside."

"Yeah. We feared Stahl might have a backup plan to hit the limos.

And, we didn't want television showing the eight most powerful leaders in the world sprinting for their limos. So we snuck them out of here."

"How?"

"In two armored police vans."

Donovan nodded. "Good move."

"They'll be airborne in about fifteen minutes."

"What's the media know?" de Waha asked.

"Only that there was an explosion. They don't know what caused it. But they're demanding a press conference *now!*"

"Off the record, tell them that one guard was killed by the blast, another guard is critical, another is injured, but those two are expected to recover. Tell them all leaders are fine. But ask them not to announce that fact for ten minutes. I want Stahl thinking he's succeeded. If he hears they're alive, the bastard may unleash an airport attack scenario."

"Okay."

"What'd you tell the media so far?"

"That we weren't sure what caused the explosion, but we suspected that the large number of media cables somehow overloaded their power transformers and caused a spark to ignite some nearby propane gas tanks."

"Did they buy that?"

Kramers shrugged. "Probably not."

"Doesn't matter," Donovan said. "The media will learn the truth at the airport if they haven't already."

"Go tell them I'll brief them in two minutes," de Waha said.

Kramers nodded and left.

Donovan walked over to the window and stared over toward the *Forêt de Soignes*. Stahl had probably pulled in there and switched his Opel with one of the cars parked along the many walking paths, then escaped in the stolen car. But did he take Maccabee with him, or leave her body behind?

"Jean, how many people do you have checking the forest?"

"Six search teams. Plus military units. They're combing every inch."

Donovan spun around and faced de Waha. *"Damn! I forgot!"*

"What?"

"Maccabee's cell phone. Let's ping it."

He handed the number to de Waha's assistant who sprinted from the room. Donovan knew Maccabee carried her cell phone in her pocket and prayed she'd been able to hide it from Stahl.

For the next fifteen minutes de Waha focused on setting up a European-wide police dragnet and finding the silver Opel and Stahl.

Donovan focused on finding Maccabee.

* * *

Stahl kept the BMW at the speed limit as he drove onto the E19, heading north. Soon he'd abandon the BMW and leave the country in a way the police and G8 authorities would never suspect.

Time to hear the good news, he thought. He reached over to turn on the radio and celebrate his glorious triumph. But instead of a radio knob, his fingers found air. The car's portable radio unit had been removed.

He shrugged. No big deal. He'd soon have a radio and television to hear the good news.

And a lifetime to celebrate it.

FORTY FOUR

Donovan and de Waha stared out the Congo Museum window. Still, no word of Maccabee and Stahl. No sighting, no scrap of information, no wisp of hope. Each time the phone rang, Donovan stopped breathing and expected the worst.

For good reason. Stahl knew that Maccabee's description was now in the media and with every police officer in Europe. She was a neon albatross around his neck. He had to ditch her. The question was alive or dead.

And dead was way smarter.

The phone rang. De Waha answered.

When Donovan saw de Waha's face relax, Donovan relaxed.

De Waha hung up.

"Seven leaders are airborne. The eighth is taking off now."

Donovan nodded. The leaders were safe and no longer his responsibility. "Any news on Stahl's Opel?"

"Still searching."

"I think he switched to another car in the forest."

"Makes sense."

Donovan stared out the window and saw the wind pushing small whitecaps across the museum's reflecting pool. Fat black clouds looking like slabs of lead had muscled in from the west. Rain was coming. So was night. Two big advantages for Stahl.

The speakerphone crackled. "Sir, we've triangulated Maccabee's cell phone to a vehicle that just turned off the E19 heading toward Nivelles. We're minutes away from stopping he vehicle."

Donovan's hope rebounded. Stahl had *not* found the phone or removed its battery. Somehow, she'd hidden the phone from Stahl.

De Waha hung up and turned to Donovan. "You think Stahl will stick to his original escape plan?"

"Probably."

"Let him try! Every border guard has his photo."

"Which he doesn't resemble now."

"We also gave guards his latest description."

"Which changes by the hour. The man's a chameleon."

De Waha nodded.

"Your airports are ready?"

"Yes. All airport personnel are checking passengers very closely. So are security officers in train and bus stations, the ferries, Hovercrafts and the Chunnel to England. We've tripled the officers in each departure lounge. Everyone has a description of Maccabee's clothing. And her Palace Dinner ID photo is being e-mailed to everyone."

"Good."

"We've also started stopping vehicles and checking the passengers at our borders crossings to Holland, France and Germany."

"But Stahl will have a new fake passport, probably one we've never seen before. And a disguise that matches the new passport photo."

De Waha nodded. "At least Maccabee will have her passport."

"No, she won't... "

"What?"

"She told me she locked hers in the hotel room safe."

223

De Waha frowned. "Stahl may not be worried about a border crossing, since the borders are non-stop Schengen Border crossings. He assumes he will just drive through.

"But if he sees a backup at the crossing, and sees customs officers demanding to see passports, he may decide to not risk crossing, especially if Maccabee doesn't have her passport."

De Waha nodded.

"I think they'll walk into Germany... or France or Holland."

"But our military personnel and choppers will soon be patrolling the borders."

De Waha's phone rang and he hit the speaker button.

"Sir, we've just found Maccabee's phone."

"Is she - ?" Donovan shouted.

"She's not here, sir. Stahl tossed her phone in the bed of a trash hauler."

Donovan slumped back down. Back to nothing.

De Waha looked equally frustrated. His brow lines seemed deeper, his eyes tighter, and a small tic fluttered his cheek. If Stahl escaped, Jean would be criticized heavily for the escape and the explosion, and probably forced into early retirement.

Me too, Donovan thought, *since the explosion happened on our watch. The fact that we tried to cancel the Congo Museum tour several times would be conveniently forgotten.* Scapegoats were needed.

"Think he's heading to Germany?" de Waha said.

"Yeah."

"Why?"

"He seems to be based there. His car is registered there. The Sumerian messages came from Dusseldorf. And Herr Rutten lived in nearby Cologne."

De Waha nodded.

"What about private aircraft?" Donovan asked.

"Grounded until we check crew and passengers."

"Commercial trucks?"

"Being checked at the border crossings."

"Trains?"

"Being inspected, car-by-car, at the stations."

"Baggage cars, too?"

"Yes."

"Post office trains?"

"Yes."

"Canal barges?"

De Waha froze, turned and stared at Donovan. *"Merde!* I forgot! Our canals take you everywhere."

"To Germany?"

"Yes. Or the Atlantic, or France or even down to the Mediterranean."

"But canal barges are slow... "

"Speed limit is only about four knots-per-hour. All the more reason he may think we would not check them."

"Can pleasure craft travel faster?"

"Only in unrestricted areas."

"Stahl might have assumed we'd never consider a canal escape."

"And he'd be right!" De Waha grabbed his phone and ordered all canal boats checked.

As soon as he hung up, the phone rang. He hit the speaker button.

"Sir, we've found the Opel Insignia."

"Where?"

"In the *Forêt de Soignes* off Avenue de Tervuren. On its front seat we found a hand-sized TV and a cell phone, the probable detonator."

"Anything else?"

Pause. "Yes sir. Bodies."

Donovan's heart stopped.

"Woman and man shot in the head."

"Does the woman have dark hair?" Donovan asked.

"Dark with blood. But she's a blonde. Blue eyes. The man, about thirty-five, had a diabetic tag around his neck. His name is Phillipe Van Halle. Vehicle Records says Van Halle drives a new red BMW Series Berline. We just put out a BOLO for the car."

"Find that damn car fast!" De Waha said.

Donovan's hope grew. They had a car to search for, a car that Stahl didn't know they knew about. Still, Stahl had gained valuable time, and Donovan knew there were a slew of BMWs in the country.

"Sir... "

"Yes... ?"

"Hang on a second... "

They waited.

"We just found something else in the forest."

"What is it?"

"I don't know. Just a moment, sir."

They waited some more.

"Sir, it's a woman's scarf."

Donovan's heart started pounding. "What color?"

"Purple and red with white flowers."

"It's Maccabee's!"

Long pause. "Sir...

"Yes... ?"

"There's a lot of blood on it."

FORTY FIVE

D riving north on the A1, Stahl smiled when he saw two cops spread-eagle a man over the hood of a silver Opel Insignia.

By the time they finally connect me to this BMW, I'll be out of the car... and out of the country.

Minutes later, Stahl drove through the ancient city of Antwerp. From an overpass, he saw the port's towering dock cranes poking into the gunmetal-gray sky. The cranes were unloading long shipping containers from vessels that had sailed sixty miles from the Atlantic Ocean down the natural waterway inlet to Antwerp. Also poking into the sky were the city's historic church spires that had escaped Hitler's V2 rockets. Unfortunately. Stahl hated churches.

Fortunately though, the V2 rockets had killed thousands of citizens, and Hitler's SS had rounded up thousands of Jews in Antwerp's diamond district and shipped them to their deaths in the Holocaust, an event that Stahl considered *der Fuehrer's* greatest success.

He turned onto the E 313 that ran parallel with the Albert Canal, a ribbon of water that stretched one hundred thirty kilometers east to the Dutch and German borders, and served as a major and efficient means of transporting goods deeper to Europe.

Forty minutes later, he drove past houseboats, yachts and sailboats and soon saw his destination: a vacation barge with a red albatross painted on the hull. He confirmed the barge number, then parked the BMW behind some nearby evergreens.

The barge was a long, black-hulled vessel similar to hundreds of European canal barges. On the rear deck, a red-yellow-black Belgian flag snapped in the wind behind the pilothouse where an elderly captain sat hunched over the wheel, reading something.

Stahl turned and checked the woman in the back seat. Still not moving. Perhaps she was dead. No big deal. Sooner or later, he'd have to dispose of her. He reached back and shook her shoulder. No response.

Her driver's license said her name was Maccabee Singh, probably the daughter of Professor Singh who translated the Sumerian message. Earlier, when Stahl searched her purse, he found a small book of Sumerian pictographs, which suggested she could also translate Sumerian. A serious problem, since there were other Sumerian messages out there... messages that could incriminate some very important people. Bottom line, she would have to die. But right now, she could serve as his insurance.

But only if they believed she was alive.

Stahl turned and looked back at her.

She was staring at him.

"I'm going to uncuff you. We're going on a barge. You will say nothing, understand?"

She nodded.

Stahl walked around and opened the rear door, then cut off her flex-cuffs. She rubbed her wrists a moment.

He grabbed his large Lowepro backpack and escorted her up to the dock. As they stepped aboard the barge, the old captain shuffled out to greet them. He was a short, wiry man in his mid-seventies, sporting a Belgian Navy jacket. White tufts of hair stuck out beneath his black beret. Coffee had stained his pale turtleneck and his smile had more folds than an accordion. But his cobalt blue eyes were bright and clear.

"Welcome aboard, folks. Name's Marcel. I was told there'd be just *one* passenger, a man."

"Change of plans. Need more money?"

"Nope. Your people paid enough for a family of four. You folks ready to go?"

"Yes."

"Where's your luggage?"

"Just my backpack.""

The captain nodded and led them toward the door to the living quarters below.

Stahl glanced back to see if anyone was watching.

He saw no one.

* * *

A few minutes later, as the barge chugged east toward Germany, Stahl felt the diesel engines rumbling beneath him. He liked the rumble. The vibrations were gentle, like the fingers of a masseuse. Everything felt good. As well it should.

He'd just achieved the most profound political act in history. And despite last second challenges by the police and anti-terrorist teams, and their billion-dollar wall of security, and their thousands of soldiers and security personnel searching for him, he'd assassinated the world's eight most powerful leaders.

Once again, he'd achieved his goal. The most important goal of his life. He'd changed the course of history.

Of course, every cop in the world would have a photo of his face. A good thing actually, since his face would not exist in three days. Dr. Joao Machado, the renowned Portuguese plastic surgeon, would give him a new face *and* new ethnicity.

While the police of the world searched for a Caucasian, I'll look part

Asian.

After the surgery, he'd fly to his sprawling villa on Martinique. There, he'd enjoy its breezy rooms and spectacular views of his private lagoon, a cove of clear blue-green water, pure sand and palm trees. And as always, he'd enjoy the black-skinned girls on the white silk sheets of his bed.

But first, why not enjoy a tawny-skinned girl? he thought, looking at Maccabee.

She sat on a nearby chair. He liked how her exotic tan face worked with her trim, shapely body, her nice long legs... and nice everything else.

But first it was time to celebrate his historic achievement. To savor the great news... word by word... from the world's media. He couldn't wait to see how the Al Qaeda blogs and Internet sites celebrated the news.

Smiling, he walked over to a galley table set up with a small radio, a Keurig coffee maker, a wide array of liquors and wines. He poured himself a celebration drink, a tall tumbler of Jameson, his favorite whiskey, and took a healthy sip. It felt wonderful. *He* felt wonderful.

"And now let's hear some good news!" he said to her in Arabic.

He saw that she understood Arabic. "Don't you agree?"

She said nothing.

"DO YOU?"

She nodded.

He turned on the radio and solemn classical music flowed around the barge's iron hull, which made the acoustics perfect.

"My... what a sad, gloomy melody. Wonder why they're playing it?"

She said nothing.

"Do you recognize it?"

She shook her head.

"Brahm's Symphony #3. Guess where it's often played?"

She remained silent.

"Funerals," Stahl said, unable to keep the grin from his face. "Wonder who died?"

Maccabee closed her eyes and lowered her head. Clearly, she knew for whom the dirge played.

He dialed to an English-speaking station so she could also hear the good news.

> "… with fog increasing throughout the
> night and tomorrow morning. And now for
> an update from Brussels. Today at the G8
> Economic Summit, a major explosion ripped
> through the world famous Congo Museum
> as the Summit leaders were touring the
> galleries… "

"And… ?" Stahl said.

> "… Two guards have died, and another
> is injured, but is expected to fully recover
> according to doctors… "

Stahl wondered why the announcer even mentioned the lowly guards…

> "… and fortunately, all eight world leaders
> escaped without injury. They are now flying
> home… "

Stahl stopped breathing.

His heart pounded into his throat.

He finally managed to draw air into his lungs.

"*You are lying!* I saw the leaders standing at the elephant! I saw eighty pounds of PETN explode! I saw bloody human body parts blast out of the museum windows!"

He paced back and forth, breathing deeply, the hairs on his neck stiff as bristles.

Then he understood. "The cowards are lying! They're afraid to tell the world the leaders are dead! They're afraid of global panic! I know what they're doing. They're using lookalikes, *doppelgängers.* All governments have them. They're lying!"

He walked to the rear porthole and looked out. His vision was blurry, his mind spinning out of control, his skin blanketed with cold sweat.

Then, slowly, logic began to take hold and he realized that authorities could not hide the death of eight world leaders. The media jackals see the leaders every day. Reporters would spot the lookalikes. Up-close television pictures would reveal facial differences.

He took several deep breaths.

So… the eight Satans ARE fucking alive! But how?"

Stahl threw his tumbler against the cast iron wall of the barge, splintering glass throughout the galley.

> "… according to a reliable source, police first
> thought a spark from media transformers
> had ignited propane tanks, but now they
> have evidence a bomb was detonated by an
> assassin watching the leaders on television.
> What the assassin didn't realize was that he
> was watching time-delay TV. What he saw
> had actually taken place minutes earlier. The
> leaders were at the other end of the museum
> having refreshments when the explosion
> destroyed the Elephant Gallery several
> hundred feet away. Al Qaeda and six other
> terrorist groups have claimed responsibility.
> Authorities are investigating… ."

Stahl slammed his fist down on the small radio, smashing it to pieces.

"But the television screen said *LIVE!* I saw it. The said it would be a *LIVE* broadcast!"

He paced back and forth his rage erupting beyond anything he'd ever felt before.

"I'll kill all eight!" He turned to Maccabee. "And the two men who got off the helicopter with you! You'll all die!"

He stood over her, shouting, spittle spraying her face. He hated the G8 leaders, hated Rourke, hated de Waha, hated her! Crazed with anger, he backhanded her across the mouth, splitting her lip, and sending blood down her chin.

Stahl knew his emotions were running wild, something he rarely experienced, but when he did, he always felt rage. The kind of rage that often resulted in serious injury or death to anyone around him!

He forced himself to walk back and forth, and regain some control of his emotions. He was adjusting to something he'd never faced before – failure.

And he refused to accept it.

I have not failed.

I merely postponed my ultimate victory.

And I will deliver the heads of these eight infidels.

FORTY SIX

Officer Jos Dyckmans couldn't believe his eyes. He and his partner, Officer Wim Smit, were staring at the ugliest house-barge Dyckmans had ever seen.

Long strips of green paint had peeled off the hull and drooped down into the canal water. On the deck, trash bags spewed slimy brown lettuce, soppy slices of pizza and empty wine bottles. A large rat gnawed on some green moldy stuff. Nearby, sat a hideous pink sofa with nasty exposed springs and even nastier black and red stains.

"Le Barge… de Garbage!" Dyckmans said, chuckling at his own wit.

"Yeah!"

Dyckmans and Smit were searching for Valek Stahl, checking all vessels along the south bank of the Albert Canal. This was the thirty-second boat they'd checked with no luck.

"This search is a waste of time! Nobody escapes by barge for chrissakes!" Officer Dyckmans said.

"Yeah, nobody!"

They stepped onto the foul smelling barge and Dyckmans knocked on the door. No response. He knocked harder. Thirty seconds later a skinny young man with long, straggly brown hair and drug-glazed eyes opened it. Beside him appeared a young woman with the same twilight-zone gaze. Her enormous breasts filled a white T-shirt with a picture of an AC Delco oil filter above the words, "Screw Me In Your Car." She looked like the Belgian army just did.

Dyckmans handed Stahl's photo to the man. "Have you seen this man with a woman in a blue suit in the last few hours?"

They stared at the photo, moving it close to their pinpoint-pupils, then back, then close again.

"Ain't seen him. You, Stella?"

"Seen who... ?"

Dyckmans realized they wouldn't recognize the Pope saying Mass.

"If you do see them, please call this number immediately." He handed them a card.

"Sure thing, officer."

As they headed toward the next barge, Dyckmans noticed a cottage perched on a small hill. Someone inside would have an excellent view of the Albert Canal. Lace curtains hung over the windows that were shaped like a ship's portholes. In the front yard, red tulips surrounded a large ship's wheel overgrown with ivy. A roof weathervane shaped like a ship's sail twirled in the wind. Leaning against the side of the cottage was a cast iron anchor.

"Maybe someone up there saw something!" Dyckmans said.

"Yeah, maybe."

They climbed the brick steps to the cottage and Dyckmans knocked on the door.

An old raspy voice croaked from within. The door squeaked open and a leather-cheeked old man in a wheelchair grinned up at them with bright gray eyes surrounded by at least eighty years of wrinkles. He wore a black wool sweater and baggy corduroy trousers. His hands looked like they'd been microwaved.

"Step aboard, lads," he said, smiling. "Captain Dirk Van Ackere, retired, at your service."

They followed him inside where he rolled his chair behind an oak desk with a photo album opened to a faded picture of a Texaco supertanker. A small television in the corner was playing *Moby Dick*. Ahab was shouting at a sailor.

"Sit, lads."

They sat in chairs made of grey driftwood.

"Sittin's all I do since that shit-faced trucker put me in this damn wheelchair. His third DUI!"

"I'm very sorry for you, sir," Dyckmans said, meaning it.

"Police locked his ass up! Damn well deserved it."

Dyckmans nodded and handed Stahl's photo to him. "We wonder if you've seen anyone who resembles this man in the last few hours."

The old man scrunched up his brow as he studied the photo, then handed it back.

"Yep. I seen him."

Dyckmans wasn't sure he heard correctly. "Are you *positive?*"

"Yep. All I do is watch the canal boats. Usta captain supertankers. Saudi crude. Rammed a bunch of Somali pirates once. Tossed them skinny bastards in my brig. Now *I'm* in the brig!" He thumped his wheelchair.

"Was there a tall woman with him?"

"Yep. Damn pretty woman, you ask me." Van Ackere winked.

Dyckmans' heart started pounding. "What was the man wearing?"

"Let's see, that fella wore a dark shirt and ah… dark-brown trousers!"

"That's correct! And the woman?"

"She wore a blue suit. Cut a nice figure, she did."

"Damn - you DID see them!"

"I just told you I did."

"Did you see his car?"

"Still do."

"Where?"

"Behind them evergreens yonder." He pointed out a side window. "That red BMW, German car."

Dyckmans stood and saw a red fender.

"I don't buy no Kraut shit," Van Ackere said. "Bastards hurt my family bad. Both wars!"

"Where'd they go?"

"Krauts went back to Germany. Where they belong!"

"No, no, the man and woman."

"Oh, they boarded a barge right down there." He pointed at the empty canal dock just below the cabin.

Dyckmans was excited. "What kind of barge?"

"Vacation barge. Belgian flag. Moored here a few times over the years, then again yesterday."

"You remember anything else about the barge?"

"Registration number."

Dyckmans didn't believe him. "But barge numbers are *long!* How could – ?"

"I remember 'em. Keeps my noodle sharp. Hey - use it or lose it, right? Run ten barges past me right now. I'll give you all the numbers in sequence."

"But that's imposs - "

"Wanna bet a hundred euros?"

Dyckmans, who couldn't remember his own license plate number, doubted the old man could do it. But something told Dyckmans not to bet. "Nope. What's the barge number?"

The old man closed his eyes. "Let's see, that barge number was... *six... five... zero... three... four... seven... one... BL.*"

Amazed, Dyckmans wrote down the number.

"Got a red albatross on the bow, too."

"How long ago did the barge leave?"

He glanced at the ship's clock on the wall. "Reckon she pulled anchor at least three hours ago. Maybe more."

Dyckmans had to get the news to headquarters. He reached for his cell phone and speed-dialed. Nothing. He checked his battery icon.

No power lines. *Shit!* And Wim's phone was charging in the police car half-mile away. "Could we use your phone?"

"Ain't got one!"

"What?"

"Don't need one."

"You don't need a phone?"

"Nope! My friends are all dead or nuts."

"Where's the nearest phone?"

"Them assholes on that smelly barge." He pointed toward the Barge de Garbage. "I'd like to drop a bunker buster bomb on it!"

Dyckmans and Smit thanked the old man, ran down the hill, and banged on the barge door again. Half minute later, the stoned couple stared out as though they'd never seen them before.

"Police emergency! I need to use your phone."

The young man pointed inside. "Galley wall."

Dyckmans rushed into the barge, ducking to avoid the low ceiling. The sweet scent of marijuana filled his lungs.

He hurried past a snoring four-hundred-pound bearded man wearing red leotards and a tutu. Looking around, Dyckmans realized he could be in a sex shop in Amsterdam's Red Light District. Long plastic devices of terrifying anatomical purpose stood like candlesticks along a mantle. Below the mantle, was a fake fireplace with a turning spit. Skewered on the spit was a plastic nude female who squealed each time the flames licked her butt.

And on the ceiling, glowing pink... and smiling forgivingly on the entire sinful panorama, was Richard Nixon, grinning and flashing his V sign.

Dyckmans phoned the news to his superior and hung up. They thanked the stoned couple and left the barge, knowing they'd just completed the most important police work of their careers.

"Let's celebrate at Froukje's Bar," Smit said.

"Can't."

"Why not? We're off duty in three minutes."

"Boss says we gotta guard the BMW."

"Why?"

"Stahl may come back for it!"

* * *

"Canal barge!" de Waha said, hanging up his phone in the Congo Museum room.

"Both *Maccabee* and Stahl?"

"Yes!"

Donovan melted with relief. "How was she?"

"Apparently fine."

Stahl is keeping her as a hostage. Maybe he would bargain. Maybe he would release her.

Or maybe he'd finally decide she was slowing him down and that the canal was the perfect place to make a body disappear. Sooner or later, Donovan knew, Stahl would decide he didn't need her any longer.

De Waha pointed to the large map. "They boarded the barge here and headed east."

"So where could they be now?" Donovan asked.

"At the speed limit, with no stops, it should be about here. The towns of Eigenbilzen and Gellik."

They jogged outside the Congo Museum to the waiting police helicopter, its rotors turning slowly. In twenty minutes they would be just a kilometer or so from the barge. As the chopper floated up over the Congo Museum gardens, Donovan saw smoke still wafting from some Elephant Gallery windows. He looked at the huge gardens and saw where Stahl's tires had left long black slash marks on the grass.

He prayed that was the only thing Stahl slashed today.

FORTY SEVEN

Officer Pieter Kass sat on a tree stump and shoveled the rest of the Cote D'Or chocolate bar into his mouth. He loved how the chocolate melted and slid down his gullet like an oyster. And the good news, he reminded himself, is that chocolate is so healthy, chocked full of those wonderful riboflavins.

Kaas dropped the Cote D'Or wrapper on the ground. It landed on seven other wrappers.

He shifted his two hundred ninety-seven pounds on the stump, giving his hemorrhoids a breather, then focused his binoculars on the next barge inching past on the Albert Canal. He checked the barge number against the number he got from the precinct.

"Wrong, wrong, wrong!" he shouted like a television talent judge.

He loved assignments like this, where he could channel his keen powers of observation and 20-20 vision.

Another long black barge crawled past.

"Sorry, wrong number!"

Going to be a long night, he thought, as he stuffed a new Cote D'or halfway into his mouth and licked his fingers.

Another barge crept into view. Growing more bored with each barge, he read the numbers aloud... "6... 5... 0... 3... 4... 7... 1... BL."

Something rattled in his brain. He stopped chewing.

"Jezus Christus! That's it! That's Stahl's barge!"

Heart pounding, Kass yanked out his cell phone. As he started to dial, he dropped his chocolate bar. Grabbing for it, the phone slipped between his fingers and splashed into the canal along with the chocolate bar.

"SHITSHITSHIT!" he hissed.

Kass scooched off the tree stump, bent down and grabbed around in the squishy canal muck for the phone. He pulled out the heel of a shoe, a muddy Heineken bottle, and then froze. Something slimy began to *curl around his fingers.*

An eel!

He jerked his hand away from the slimy creature too fast - lost his balance, fell backward into the canal and found himself sitting in water up to his waist.

"FUCK!"

Kaas crawled back on shore, shook off the mud and water and squished over to his bicycle. He hoisted his massive buttocks onto the bike, swallowing its skinny seat, and pumped off toward his police station two miles away.

Minutes later, his heart pounding harder than his hemorrhoids, Kaas collapsed in a chair opposite Inspector De Groot.

The Inspector looked incensed that Kass had just made his only guest chair sopping wet.

"Kass? You're dripping all - "

"Stahl's... barge! I saw it!"

* * *

As the police chopper droned through the black night, Donovan wondered if Stahl and Maccabee were still on the barge. Donovan knew there was a good possibility that it had docked earlier and someone picked Stahl up.

Next to Donovan, Jean de Waha hung up his phone.

"We've got eyes on the barge now. It's near where the Albert Canal feeds into the Juliana Canal. Near the Dutch and German borders."

"Are border officials stopping barges?"

"Yes. And barges are already backing up."

"And Stahl's is under surveillance?"

"Yes."

Donovan nodded.

"We're touching down where Kanne Road Bridge crosses the canal. A police team will be ready for us to board."

Minutes later, at a height of two thousand feet, Donovan looked down at the long line of barges lit up like Christmas lights along the Albert Canal. He hoped Maccabee was on the one with the red albatross on the bow.

The chopper banked right and soon touched down. Donovan saw a waiting police car, lights off. Barges were backed up from the Dutch border. Jean and he deplaned and introduced themselves to three police officers.

"Where's Stahl's barge?" de Waha asked.

"Thirteenth back. Got a red Albatross painted on the bow."

"How long's it been stopped?" Donovan asked.

"Minute or two."

"Did you see Stahl or Maccabee?"

"No."

"Who's the captain?"

"Old guy named Marcel Spaanbroek. We checked him out. His company rents barges for family vacations. He's been piloting barges over forty years. My sense is he has no idea who his passenger is."

"It's better if he doesn't," Donovan said.

FORTY EIGHT

Valek Stahl had felt the engine shift into idle as the barge crept to a stop. Perhaps they'd backed up at the Dutch border. Time to find out. He climbed up to the deck cabin and saw the old captain hunched over the pages of *De Standaard* newspaper. Beyond the captain, Stahl saw barges backed up ahead for at least a quarter-mile.

"Border slowdown?"

The captain turned around and faced him. "Yep."

"This normal?"

"Way worse."

"What's going on?"

"Inspectors lookin' for something."

"What?"

"Hard to say. Drugs maybe. Big money in drugs."

"True."

"Maybe terrorists. Bastards is everywheres! Like down in Brussels today."

"Also true."

Stahl checked the barges ahead. "How long before we reach the border customs inspectors?"

"At this pace, I reckon thirty minutes. Sorry about the delay."

"Not a problem."

But it was a problem. The backup was for him. By now the police would have found the Opel and the two bodies in the Brussels forest, and maybe even found something that linked the bodies to the red BMW. Later, the cops would find the BMW along the canal bank and assume he'd escaped on a boat. Perhaps they already had.

There was even a slight chance someone saw him board the barge.

It was time to leave the barge.

* * *

Donovan kept his eyes riveted ahead, as he, de Waha and three police officers drove slowly along the canal in an unmarked lights-off police vehicle, heading toward Stahl's barge.

They parked a hundred yards in back of Stahl's barge, got out and eased the doors shut. Foghorns groaned up and down the canal.

The mist was so thick, Donovan realized Stahl and Maccabee could have left the barge without being seen.

An officer opened the car trunk and lifted out a Zodiac Minuteman raft, military version. The raft hissed to full inflation within sixty seconds. They slid it into the water, boarded and paddled off toward the *Albatross*.

Donovan shoved a full magazine into his 9mm Smith & Wesson. As the raft moved closer, a chilly gust of wind hit him. Visibility was down to fifty feet. Breathing was down to diesel fumes. He knew the chances of finding Maccabee aboard were maybe fifty-fifty. Like the chances of finding her alive.

De Waha pointed to the screen of his cell phone.

Donovan looked and saw the *Albatross Vacation* Website. The barge's floor plan revealed a living room, master bedroom, two smaller bedrooms, baths, galley and storage room.

Where would Stahl keep Maccabee?

Was she still on the barge?

Ahead, Donovan saw the elderly captain jackknifed over the wheel in the cabin. The yellow overhead light made him look jaundiced. The fact he wasn't moving a muscle made him look dead.

De Waha pointed to a rope ladder hung over the barge's side. "We climb the ladder silently."

Everyone nodded.

"I'll show my badge to the captain, then we'll enter the cabin below."

"What if Stahl holds a gun on her?" an officer asked.

"Do nothing," Donovan said. "If we surprise him, he may not have time to threaten her."

They paddled the raft closer to the long black barge. Behind it, seven more barges had backed up.

Donovan was thankful the thick fog made their approach invisible.

* * *

But not to Valek Stahl.

After hearing the unmistakable sound of a raft hissing to life, he looked out the rear porthole and saw the cops at the bank of the canal. He watched them board the raft and paddle toward the barge. Now, they were about four minutes away.

He gagged Maccabee and placed his Glock against her temple.

"One sound, you die."

He led her upstairs and looked through the small window at the captain's back. The old man's head was drooping, suggesting he was nodding off.

Stahl watched a helicopter fly overhead. Using the chopper roar, foghorns and barge engine noise as cover, Stahl opened the door and led Maccabee onto the deck opposite the approaching police raft. The old captain didn't move.

Stahl tied her wrist to his and led her to a ladder draped over the other side of the barge. They climbed down, eased into the cold water, swam to the rear hull and paused. He peered around the hull, saw Donovan's raft approach and then disappear around the other side, probably heading toward the rope ladder he'd seen earlier.

Stahl waited until he heard men climb the ladder and go up on deck. When they began talking to the captain, he pulled Maccabee around to the police raft: a Minuteman, like one he'd used in the Persian Gulf. He reached up and released the seal lid on the inflation tube. Air began to seep out. To speed things along, he took out his suppressed Glock and thumped an insurance bullet into the polyester belly of the raft. Air bubbles raced to the surface.

Then he pushed Maccabee's head under water and watched her air bubbles race to the surface.

* * *

De Waha flashed his badge at the surprised captain and handed him Stahl's photo. "Is this man on your barge?"

The old captain squinted at the photo a few seconds. "Don't think so, but if he is, he looks real different. My passenger's got black hair. Plus, he's got hisself a beard. But them eyes... well now... maybe."

"Is an attractive dark-haired woman with him?" Donovan asked.

"Yes indeed!"

"Where are they?"

"Where else... down below." He pointed to the door.

Weapons drawn, Donovan and the others positioned themselves at the door to the living quarters.

On a three count, they burst inside. Donovan and de Waha cleared the main rooms as the others checked the smaller rooms.

Within seconds, Donovan realized Stahl and Maccabee were gone.

He and de Waha ran back up to the captain.

"They're not on board!" de Waha said.

The captain's eyes shot wide open. "But I just seen him go down there ten minutes ago!"

"Did you see her then?"

"No."

"When's the last time you saw her?"

The captain paused. "Couple hours ago."

Donovan's stomach tightened.

Then he heard something on shore. The click of a car door. He turned and saw a tall man getting into the driver's side of the police car.

"That's *STAHL!*" he said, pointing at the car as it sped away. *Where was Maccabee?*

"Bastard!" de Waha shouted.

Panicked, they ran back over and looked down at their raft.

It was a foot underwater.

FORTY NINE

As Donovan started to swim to shore, the old captain grabbed his arm and pointed. Donovan spun around and saw a rowboat on the deck.

Quickly, they dropped the rowboat in the canal, jumped in and paddled like Olympic rowers for shore.

Donovan's heart pounded. He'd only seen a man Stahl's height get in the car. Had to be *Stahl!* But the captain hadn't seen Maccabee in over two hours. And she wasn't on the barge. Had Stahl disposed of her earlier?

Donovan searched the dark water, afraid of what he might see.

On shore, Donovan and the others hurried along the canal bank, searching for her shoeprints. He checked the grassy area around a concrete dock, then along some hedges. No prints. He ran down the canal bank a few yards. Still nothing. Much of the bank was covered with thick grass and pea gravel that made footprints nearly impossible to see, especially in the dark.

"Over here!" an officer shouted.

Donovan raced over to a patch of dirt. He looked down at a woman's heel-and-toe prints. Fresh prints. Next to them, Stahl's large prints.

She's with him! Donovan realized, as every muscle in his body melted.

"He's using her as a hostage," de Waha said.

"For now... "

The footprints led them over to where the police car had been parked.

Seconds later, another police car pulled up and they got in. De Waha grabbed its phone.

"This is de Waha. I repeat – Stahl is driving a stolen police car – license BE8-789. Track its GPS before Stahl disables it! He'll switch cars soon. Check out all stolen cars in the area. And remember - he holds Maccabee Singh hostage. Do *not* try to arrest him alone, unless her life is threatened. Call when you have anything." He hung up.

Donovan stared at the police radio, begging it to blast on immediately with good news, even though he didn't expect it. Part of him feared terrible news. After all, there was blood on Maccabee's scarf in the forest. She was injured. Perhaps badly!

Guilt suddenly overwhelmed him, the guilt of Sohan Singh's death, the guilt of bringing his daughter Maccabee to Europe... the guilt of bringing her to the Congo Museum. He knew the museum was Stahl's last chance, knew it would be dangerous, knew an explosion was possible, even likely. Yet, instead of asking a security team to take her back to the Amigo Hotel, he'd brought her to the museum. And then, like an idiot, he asked her to wait *outside* the door - where Stahl grabbed her. One huge mistake after another...

Donovan's rage was red hot. He wanted Stahl *now!* Wanted the bastard *dead!* And frankly, he wanted the honor of making him dead. But he couldn't budge until they had some idea of where Stahl drove.

"Stahl needs her," de Waha said, gnawing nervously on his pipe stem.

"He needs to ditch her."

"We'll find the police car first!"

"You'll find it ditched too!"

The car phone rang and de Waha punched the speaker button. "Director... ?"

"Yes?"

"Bad news, sir. Stahl disabled the police car's GPS."

"What about the computer and radio-phone?"

"Those too."

De Waha's face went crimson. "Find that goddammed car anyway!"

"Yes, sir."

Donovan looked down at the canal water, black as Stahl's eyes, and made a promise.

If she dies Stahl, you die.

* * *

Maccabee shivered even though the car heater blasted hot air onto her cold wet clothes.

Stahl drove the police car north at the speed limit. For the last few miles, he seemed to be searching for something alongside the road. He'd slowed a couple of times, looked into the forest, then sped up again.

Now, he seemed to find what he was looking for. He braked and turned into a small rest area surrounded by a thick evergreen forest.

Why here?

Then she knew. *The perfect kill zone!*

But if she ran into the forest, he'd shoot her. Still, running might be her only chance.

The car headlight beams slid across the fender of an SUV, the only other vehicle in the rest area. Stahl parked and spun a suppressor onto his gun.

She put her fingers on the door handle and got ready to bolt from the car.

"The gun is not for you."

Not yet, maybe.

"Relax!"

She did not relax.

Stahl opened the glove compartment, took out some flex-cuffs, fixed them around her wrists, then bound her to the steering wheel. He grabbed the keys and got out.

She watched him walk over to the SUV, a Volvo. He looked inside, then stuck the gun through the open driver's window at the middle-aged man and woman inside.

"Get out!"

They stared at him.

"OUT!"

Slowly, they stepped from the car.

"Walk over to those restrooms."

They turned to walk. One step later, Stahl raised his gun and shot them both in the back of the head. They slumped against each other as they fell to the ground, their blood splattering onto the driver's side door.

Maccabee couldn't believe what she'd seen. He'd killed the couple in cold blood. Tears spilled down her cheeks as Stahl removed the couples' IDs, then dragged their bodies like bags of trash into the forest. He came back and wiped most blood off the Volvo door. His face remained dead calm, his eyes like black ice, revealing no emotion.

He un-cuffed Maccabee, led her over to the Volvo, placed her in the driver's seat, then got in the passenger seat. He placed the key in the ignition and aimed his gun at her.

"Drive!"

Why does he want me to drive? she wondered.

Trembling, she drove out of the rest area. Traffic was light, a few cars, trucks, some campers, a police car going the other way, flasher off.

Minutes later, she saw a sign indicating the Dutch border was a kilometer ahead. She assumed it would be a drive-through, non-stop border crossing, like crossing from state to state in America. But maybe tonight, she hoped, border guards will be stopping cars, searching for Stahl.

"Slow down, turn in there and park under those trees."

She turned onto the street and parked under the trees.

Stahl reached into his backpack and pulled out a large cosmetic kit. He opened it and took out a blonde wig.

"Put this on."

She placed the wig on her head. In the mirror, she saw the long blonde hair completely hid her short dark hair.

"We're going to cross this border. I'll be right behind you, beneath all these clothing bags and suitcases. But you will feel my gun stuck in your left side. If you signal the inspector in any way, I will know, and I will shoot you. You will die or be paralyzed for life. I will also shoot the inspector. Do you believe me?"

She swallowed a chalk-dry throat.

"DO YOU?"

"Yes."

"If he asks why you're entering Holland, just say you're touring Holland, Belgium and Luxembourg."

"But my passport is at the hotel."

"Just tell him the hotel concierge said you could you could drive into Holland without stopping. A Schengen crossing. Your passport would not be required. So you didn't bring it."

"What if he asks my name?"

"Tell him your name is... Ann Smith."

"But if he asks for my driver's license - "

"Say you forgot your wallet with your passport at the hotel."

She paused. "He might ask me to get out of the car."

"If he does... those will be the last words he ever speaks."

Stahl crawled over the seat, and hid beneath the large hanger bags of clothes and suitcases. She couldn't see him - but felt his gun's suppressor digging into her left side.

She drove to the border crossing and pulled into line behind two cars. The other lines also had a few cars backed up. On the right side of the road, she saw armed soldiers checking only those vehicles with men.

One soldier looked over at her, but quickly turned to the car behind her with a man driver and a woman passenger.

One car ahead now. A grey-haired couple. The inspector, a short man, who seemed swollen with authority, questioned the old couple. He walked to their trunk and peered into the rear window, then walked back and waved them into Holland.

Then he signaled Maccabee forward.

She looked at him, hoping he saw the fear in her eyes. He didn't seem to.

"Nationality?"

"American."

"Passport, please."

"It's at my hotel back in Liege. The concierge told me I could just drive into Holland without stopping."

He stared at her for several moments. "Normally, that is the case. But tonight is different. What is the purpose of your visit to Holland?"

"I'm touring Holland, Belgium and Luxembourg." *Does he hear the quiver in my voice?* Again, he didn't seem to.

The officer looked at her, then looked in back at the large clothing bags and suitcases and raised his eyebrows. He walked alongside the SUV, peering inside for several seconds, shading his eyes with his hand.

He walked back to her. "Lot of suitcases and clothing bags for one person."

She nodded.

"All clothes?"

She had no idea what was in the suitcases and bags. "Well, yes, mostly clothes."

The guard walked back and looked in again for several seconds. He strolled around the other side of the vehicle, peered in, then came back, stared at her for a moment and shook his head.

"If I were to open all those suitcases, are you sure I would find mostly clothes?"

She panicked, paused, then shrugged. "Well, yes… "

"American women! Clothes-clothes-clothes! So many clothes!" he said, laughing. "You may proceed into Holland."

She froze. Should she alert him? Bolt out the door?

Would bullets rip into her? Kill her? Kill him?

"Is there a problem?" the guard asked as he started to walk away.

Stahl's gun jabbed her side.

"No problem… "

"Good. Proceed, please."

She drove slowly into Holland.

A mile further, Stahl climbed into the front passenger seat. He pushed the gun barrel into her face. He looked angry.

"You hesitated back there," he said.

She said nothing.

"It almost cost you your life. The next time, it will."

FIFTY

Maccabee drove north in Holland. She shivered more from Valek Stahl's stare than her wet clothes. His gaze felt like insects creeping over her skin.

Earlier, Stahl had yanked the Garmin GPS from the dashboard and tossed it out the window... eliminating any chance the police could track the Volvo. Chances were, they wouldn't even *know* about the Volvo since Stahl had removed all ID from the middle-aged couple he killed for the car.

He turned away from her and looked at his map, apparently planning his final escape route, an escape that she sensed would not include her.

Which meant she had to escape first.

"Why are you involved in the G8?" he demanded.

She was afraid to tell him she translated the Sumerian messages. "I'm a friend of Donovan Rourke."

"What's your job?"

She hesitated. "A professor."

"Of foreign languages, right?"

He knows.

"Yes."

"Liker du driv?"

She understood Norwegian. *"Yes, I like driving."*

"Du er veldig attraktivt," he said in Finnish. *You are very attractive.*

She grew concerned. *"Kiitos." Thanks.*

In Arabic, he asked, *"Kaifa I-Haal?" How are you doing?*

"Ana tamaaam." I'm okay.

"You lie easily," he said.

She said nothing.

"You also translate ancient Sumerian, don't you?"

He found the pictographs in my purse.

"Don't you?"

"A bit."

"Which has caused me problems."

She drove around a vegetable truck and thought about signaling the driver, but the man didn't look her way.

"The Sumerians, you know, had a very humane way of killing their enemies."

She said nothing.

"Simple and quick."

She waited.

"They drove a spike into their head."

She blinked and tried to focus on the road ahead.

"Death was fast. Too fast for my enemies."

She said nothing.

"Enemies like your friends, Rourke and de Waha. And, of course, you, the translator!"

Her pulse pounded and she took a deep breath of air.

She passed a truckload of sheep and looked into their eyes. They looked as frightened as she felt. *Are we both being led to the slaughter?*

Stahl turned his attention back to the map. As she drove, she saw road signs indicating the German border was just a few kilometers to the east. Donovan had mentioned that they believed Stahl lived in Germany. Would he try to cross the German border and head home? Would he take her with him?

By now the police would have found the Opel in the forest near the Congo museum, and maybe even the stolen red BMW by the canal. But linking Stahl to this Volvo might take hours or days.

The further she drove, the more desperate she felt. Her neck still ached where he'd knocked her unconscious. Her jaw throbbed where he hit her after learning that the G8 leaders survived the explosion.

Ahead she saw the lights of a Shell station. The fuel needle was touching *E*.

"We're low on gas," she said. "There's a stat – "

"Pull in at the full service pump. Say nothing."

She turned in and stopped at the full service pump. The station was attached to a restaurant filled with what looked like families, regular customers, and truck drivers. An attendant hurried out to the car. She had to signal him.

Stahl waved him over. "Fill it up."

The young, skinny attendant nodded, then walked back and began pumping gas.

The station phone started ringing.

The police calling maybe! Maccabee thought.

Go answer it!

The attendant turned and hurried toward the phone. But someone else picked up and the attendant strolled back to the car and began cleaning the windshield on Stahl's side.

Somehow, she had to signal the attendant.

Stahl was focused on his map. She reached into her coat pocket, felt a hairpin, a rubber band and an eyebrow pencil. She raised the eyebrow pencil up to her neck and pretending to straighten her necklace, she wrote… *H U L P*, the Dutch word for *HELP* below her neck between the open collars of her blouse.

The attendant strolled around and began cleaning her side of the windshield. As he wiped, he nodded and smiled at Maccabee, but didn't appear to see *H U L P*. She leaned toward him.

Still no reaction.

Glancing down, she saw why. Everything above her breasts was in dark shadows. Maybe if she slid down into the light…

She checked Stahl again. Still buried in his map.

She inched down until the station lights hit *H U L P* and looked up.

The attendant was gone, back at the pump, replacing the gas nozzle.

She watched him take Stahl's money and walk back to the station.

"Drive!" Stahl said.

"I need to use the restroom."

"Drive!"

* * *

The police car radio came alive and Donovan's stomach tightened.

"We've found the stolen police car," an officer said.

"Where?" de Waha asked.

"Roadside rest area south of Maastricht."

"Anything else?"

"Two bodies."

Donovan closed his eyes.

"Man and woman in their fifties."

Donovan was relieved, but outraged that Stahl murdered two more innocent people.

"No wallets, but we found a crumpled VISA receipt in the woman's back pocket. She's Mari Ange Battens, 402 Rue St. Laurent from Liege. We're running her through *Motorvoertuig Registreert,* our Motor Vehicle Records Division. We should have her vehicle any - hang on!"

Donovan heard background voices.

"The Battens have a Volvo V70. Dark blue, license BCD 4286."

"BOLO the Volvo to all police groups fast!" de Waha said. "Belgium, Holland and Germany. Make it Euro-wide." `

Donovan's hope rekindled. They had a vehicle to track. With every police officer in Europe looking for the Volvo, they might find it before Stahl did something to Maccabee… or switched vehicles again.

"Let's go!" de Waha said to the driver. The police car spun out of its parking spot, dinging gravel off the Kanne Bridge and into the Albert Canal below. Within seconds, the car was traveling at one hundred fifty kilometers an hour.

"He's heading home," de Waha said. "Back to Germany."

"Probably. It's only minutes away."

"But he knows border guards are looking for him and Maccabee."

"So he'll avoid the border guards and probably *walk* over."

De Waha nodded.

"After… " Donovan whispered.

"After what?"

"After he dumps her body."

"No! He *needs* her," de Waha said. "And don't forget the Stockholm syndrome. The longer a hostage and a captor are together, the stronger their relationship and the less likely the captor will kill the hostage. That's what happens normally."

"You forget something, Jean."

"What?"

"There's nothing normal about Stahl."

FIFTY ONE

Stahl knew the police would track him into Holland. They would discover the abandoned police car and the bodies of the middle-aged couple from the Volvo. They might even find something that linked the couple to the Volvo. Then they'd see video of the Volvo crossing the border into Holland.

By now they could be closing in on him. Which is why he would keep Maccabee close by for now. With her at his side, the police wouldn't risk a full-blown assault or sniper shot.

And soon, he'd be where a sniper shot couldn't reach him.

* * *

Maccabee knew she couldn't wait for a chance to escape – she had to create it, maybe even while she was driving.

But how? She was running out of time.

Ahead she saw a thick fencepost next to the road. What if she reached over, unbuckled his seatbelt, then slammed his side of the car into the fencepost? It might incapacitate him long enough for her to escape. The fencepost was coming up fast.

She had to decide!

Then she noticed he had a side-air bag. It would protect him enough to come after her.

She checked his gun in his left hand. He seemed to be holding it less tightly than earlier. Could she reach over and yank it from his hand? She visualized how she would grab it and aim it at his head.

She took her right hand off the wheel and placed it at her side.

Then, as though reading her mind, Stahl switched the gun to his right hand.

Frustrated, she drove ahead.

Maybe she could say she was very sick, about to vomit, then slow the car to a stop, open the door and bolt into a forest. She thought about that a moment, then knew she'd feel bullets enter her back before she got ten feet. Or he'd catch her and beat her again.

She'd have to wait for the right opportunity. One with a better chance of success.

She drove past the Dutch city of Maastricht and continued running parallel to the German border, a few kilometers to the east. Many roads led to the border, but Stahl gave no hint of his plan.

She knew she had to stay calm. She'd tried to not give him any reason to hit her again. She did exactly what he said, drove as he'd directed, at the speed he demanded.

She kept reminding herself that she was sitting next to a stone-cold psychopath. When he'd shot the couple in the Volvo and dragged their bodies into the forest, his expression, and probably his blood pressure, hadn't changed.

She was his hostage for now… and his next victim the moment he no longer needed her. And she saw no reason he needed her now.

Deep down, she knew that unless she did something first, it was only a matter of time before he killed her…

* * *

Donovan flinched when the police radio beeped, shattering the car's silence.

"Van Kampen here, sir!"

"What's up?" de Waha said.

"A customs inspector at the Dutch border south of Maastricht saw a dark blue Volvo V70 pass through a while ago. Woman driver. No man in the car. But lots of big suitcases and clothing bags in back."

"Enough for a man to hide under?"

"Yes."

"Was she American?" Donovan asked.

"Yes."

"Did she look part Indian?"

"Well, maybe, but... "

"But what?"

"He said her hair was blonde."

"Not Maccabee," de Waha said.

Donovan's hope sank. No one spoke for several moments.

"Hang on a second, sir," Van Kampen grew excited.

Donovan heard him speaking rapid-fire Dutch to someone.

"We got a match, sir!"

"A match... ?"

"The border DVD video just matched the Volvo license plate to the stolen Volvo!"

"But how could it be *Maccabee?*" de Waha asked.

"She's wearing one of Stahl's wigs," Donovan said, probably with a gun in her side."

"What road are they on?" Donovan said.

"E-25, heading north."

"When did they cross the border into Holland?"

"About... twenty-five minutes ago."

"Alert all police in the area," de Waha said. "We are now in pursuit."

The driver mashed the gas pedal down and Donovan watched the Porsche Turbo speedometer climb to one hundred seventy kilometers per hour in seconds. At this speed, they'd soon reach the beltway around Maastricht.

The problem was *which* beltway exit did Stahl take? The exits were as numerous as the spokes on a Schwinn tire. One road led to Germany, one into Holland, one toward the Atlantic coast, one back toward Belgium. And several led into Maastricht, a city of one hundred twenty-five thousand... perfect for Stahl to disappear in.

Donovan studied the map. He ran his finger along the E-25 Motorway toward Roermond, then up to the larger city of Venlo, then along the N-278 toward the German border city of Aachen.

Several roads led over to the German border, some only a mile long. But Stahl knew the border officers were on hyper alert for him and an attractive, half-Indian woman. Still, with Maccabee wearing a blonde wig, and Stahl wearing another new disguise, he *might* risk driving into Germany at a border crossing.

Or safer yet, he might *walk* into Germany.

Another loud beep from the police car radio.

"Van Kampen, sir. A gas station attendant on the A-73 near Swalmen says he saw a Volvo like the one we're tracking. A woman fitting Maccabee's description was driving – *and* a male passenger that fits Stahl's description. Lots of suitcases and clothing bags in back."

"Did she have blonde hair?"

"Yes."

"Does the gas station video confirm it's the same Volvo?"

"Their camera isn't working."

"Anything else?" de Waha said.

"Nope."

"How long ago?"

"Sixteen minutes ago."

"Where's Swalmen?" de Waha asked.

"Here!" Donovan pointed to the map. About thirty kilometers ahead."

"Did they head north on the A-73?"

"Yes."

"It's them," de Waha said.

Donovan nodded. "So he's still running north beside the German border."

"Right. Concentrate your men on A-73 north of the service station. Set up a roadblock just south of Venlo. Reinforce all German border crossings. Have choppers hugging the border. We're heading up 73 now."

Donovan calculated that Stahl was only twenty minutes ahead.

The driver hit the gas again and in seconds, the Porsche's 530 horse-power pushed the car up to two hundred kilometers an hour. Donovan couldn't believe the car's speed. They'd close the gap fast, assuming Stahl ordered Maccabee to drive at the speed limit.

And assuming Stahl remained on the A-73.

And assuming he stayed in the Volvo.

Donovan hated assuming.

FIFTY TWO

"Exit here onto Polderweg Road!" Stahl said.

Maccabee exited and saw a sign for the small Dutch town of Belfeld.

Minutes later, he said, "Park alongside that row of trees."

She saw the row of trees, but no houses, no buildings, no other vehicles, no signs of life. Just empty fields of tall grass leading up to a sprawling forest in the distance.

A perfect place to dump my corpse, she thought.

Trembling, she steered onto the road's gravel shoulder and crunched to a stop beside the row of evergreens.

She had to escape now… run away in this field, even though her chances of getting away were dismal.

Stahl grabbed the keys, came around and opened her door.

"GET OUT!"

She stepped from the car and took a deep breath. The cold night air felt like shards of glass piercing her lungs. Exactly how the bullets would feel.

She heard the rhythmic thump of a distant helicopter. Turning, she saw its searchlights bleaching the ground white. The chopper raced along the German border a mile to the east.

Stahl glanced at the chopper, then pushed her into the field of tall grass, heading toward Germany. A few feet later, he stopped and stared at her. Slowly, he reached toward her neck.

She took a step back and got ready to kick him in the groin and run - when suddenly he yanked her necklace off.

Then his eyes seemed to focus on something *below* her neck... something she thought she'd rubbed off.

He was staring at the remnant smudges of *H U L P.*

Anger flashed in his eyes.

He hit her hard. She stumbled back and steadied herself against a tree. Her jaw felt like he'd driven a nail into it. Had he broken it? She opened her mouth and it worked, but with pain.

He grabbed her arm and yanked her down a narrow path that led into the field. A few feet later, he stopped and positioned her necklace atop a small mound of dirt.

Then he turned the necklace so the moonlight reflected off it.

What's he doing? He wants them to see the necklace! Why?

Stahl pushed her farther into the soggy field toward the German border, stopping every few feet to check their footprints. He seemed pleased that their wet prints were easy to track.

They came to a narrow road, crossed it and continued into the next field, leaving more fresh prints. She looked ahead and saw the German forest was not far.

Stahl led her up to the forest, then inside several yards where he stopped and stared at her. His gaze slid from her neck... to her wrist.

"Give me your watch!"

She handed it to him. He placed it on a small clump of leaves next to her footprint. Then he positioned the watch so the moonlight glinted off the crystal face. The police couldn't miss it.

He still wants the police to follow us! Why?

A hundred feet farther into the forest, Stahl bent down and examined where they'd just walked. When he saw *no* footprints on the leaves and pine needles, he seemed quite pleased.

What's going on? First he *wants* them to follow us - now he doesn't?

Is he setting them up for something? Leading them into a trap? An ambush? How can one man hope to ambush a squad of armed police?

What's he really up to?

* * *

As the police car sped past Roermond, Donovan feared Stahl had already switched vehicles again and escaped deep into his home turf - Germany. There he would have numerous places to hide himself... *and* Maccabee's body.

Donovan saw three Dutch police choppers sweeping along the border, their spotlights bleaching the forest white below. He worried that the forest was so dense the pilots probably couldn't see anyone beneath, especially anyone wearing dark clothes and trying to hide, like Stahl and Maccabee.

The car phone blared to life – "We found the Volvo!"

"Where?" de Waha said.

"Near Belfeld. Off A-73, alongside Poldersweg Road. No signs of Stahl or Maccabee!"

"Any evidence they switched cars or were picked up?"

"No, sir."

"Footprints?"

"Still looking."

"We're four kilometers away," de Waha said, signaling the driver to hit the gas.

Minutes later, their Police Porsche screeched to a stop beside the Volvo and two Dutch police cars. Donovan jumped out and hurried over to the officers by the Volvo. When he saw some blood splatter on Maccabee's driver side window, he had to steady himself against the fender.

Did Stahl shoot her? Or is this blood from the couple he shot to steal the Volvo?

"Over here," shouted a young officer in the field.

The group ran over to him and looked down. Donovan saw the same heel and toe marks he'd seen in the mud beside the Albert Canal.

"Maccabee's footprints!" Donovan said, relieved she was at least walking.

"Look at this!" an officer shouted deeper in the field as he pointed at something.

Donovan and de Waha ran up to him and looked down at a necklace with a silver butterfly.

"That's *Maccabee's!*" Donovan said.

"She put the necklace here so we'd follow," a policeman said.

"Up here," shouted a tall officer farther in the field.

"What?" de Waha shouted.

"More footprints."

"He's heading toward the German border," de Waha said.

"He might have crossed it by now," Donovan said, as two officers ran up and aimed 400-lumen Torch flashlights on the prints. The blinding white lights turned the ground to high noon. The prints were easy to follow.

Several hundred yards farther, the group came to the narrow paved road. Donovan saw no footprints and no clues on the pavement. They crossed the road and within a few feet found the footprints again and continued tracking them east toward the dark wall of trees on the border.

Minutes later, the footprints led them into the German forest.

An officer shouted, "Over here!"

Donovan and de Waha hurried over. Donovan bent down and saw a silver wristwatch with a grey leather band.

"Maccabee's!"

"They're continuing through this forest," de Waha said. "Let's hope she's wearing more jewelry."

"She is," Donovan said, remembering her bracelets, ring and earrings.

He soon noticed they were walking on a thick carpet of pine needles and leaves. The footprints disappeared. And soon, he realized so
had her jewelry clues. Stahl and Maccabee could be walking in any
direction.

But something about the clues was bothering Donovan, something
that didn't feel right and he wasn't sure what it was.

Soon, they came to a treeless clearing the size of a football field.
Donovan's shoes sank into the soft ground and he sensed they'd pick
up the footprints here. The team and police spread out seven abreast
and methodically combed through the clearing. Flashlights swept the
ground as they walked in ten-yard sections. After several minutes and
several sweeps, Donovan realized there were no fresh footprints and no
more jewelry in the clearing.

"Stahl changed direction *before* this clearing," Donovan said."

De Waha nodded and looked at his map. "If they circled the
clearing and went straight ahead, they'd reach the German town of
Kalderkirchen. If they turned left, they're going along the border. If
they turned right, they're walking through several kilometers of forest.
The town of Kalderkirchen – straight ahead makes sense."

"Or... ." Donovan said, suddenly realizing what was bothering
him about the jewelry clues.

"Or what?"

"Or... straight back!"

De Waha looked at him like he'd lost his mind.

"I've had an uneasy feeling about Maccabee's jewelry."

"Why?"

Donovan turned and looked back from where they'd come. "Stahl
would make her walk in front of him, or at least beside him, right?"

De Waha nodded.

"Yet, we find large sparkling pieces of her jewelry... perched up
like Tiffany's displays along the path. Stahl's smart. He doesn't miss
things. He would have seen the jewelry if he was behind her or even
beside her."

"Maybe he was busy, looking at a map."

"Maybe. But those clues looked *positioned,* carefully placed, not simply dropped. We spotted them easily from a distance."

De Waha said nothing.

"Then suddenly in the forest, we see no more jewelry, no more clues. Why? Maccabee was also wearing some bracelets, a gold pin, a silver ring and earrings. She could have easily dropped another clue here in the forest. Again, why didn't she?"

De Waha stared at him. "You're saying *Stahl* positioned the jewelry?"

Donovan nodded.

"But why?"

"So we'd think he's continuing into Germany... "

De Waha closed his eyes for several moments. "While the bastard doubled back into *Holland!*"

Donovan nodded.

De Waha looked back toward Holland. "If you're right, he could be back near Polderweg Road by now."

"Or farther."

De Waha punched a button on his phone. "Look for Stahl back near Polderweg Road. Donovan and I are heading back there now. The rest of our team will continue through the forest to Kalderkirchen."

"If you're right," de Waha said, "we might get lucky and pick up their footprints heading back as we exit the forest."

And if I'm wrong, Donovan thought, I *may have signed Maccabee's death warrant.*

FIFTY THREE

Maccabee noticed the fog was thicker as Stahl pushed her through the grassy fields back in Holland. She couldn't keep this pace much longer thanks to her bruised knee. Stahl had slammed it against a tree a few minutes ago when she tried to escape while he studied his map.

Pain now radiated from her knee to her ankle. And her jaw still throbbed where Stahl had hit it.

She felt more desperate with each step and knew her chances of survival were not good.

Her only hope, slim and unrealistic, was that the border inspector or the gas station attendant might have somehow recognized her even though she was wearing the blonde wig. In other words, her only hope was a miracle.

Like the police arriving. Where were they? she wondered. Eventually, they would find the stolen Volvo. They'd track their footsteps, see her jewelry on the path, and find her wristwatch in the forest. But when they found no more footprints and jewelry they'd assume Stahl continued through the forest into Germany.

By the time they finally figured out that Stahl had set them up and doubled back into Holland, someone would be writing her obituary.

She had to escape - despite the gun constantly pointed at her.

Her thoughts turned to Donovan. He'd been right. She should have listened to him in New York. He'd warned her how dangerous this was. Tried to keep her out of it. But she'd insisted he let her help, pushed him. Pushing people, hard sometimes, maybe too hard, was one of the things she didn't like about herself. If she really wanted to do something, she would cajole, schmooze, manipulate and occasionally browbeat someone to get it. *My will be done!* Now she felt guilty for pushing Donovan. Very guilty.

Still, if she hadn't pushed, she wouldn't have come, and if she hadn't come, she and Donovan would not have had these last two miraculous days together. Days that had uncovered long-buried emotions in her, reawakened something she'd feared she'd lost forever when Andrew died.

With Donovan, she'd found the courage to love again. Whatever happened to her now, the last two beautiful days had changed her forever, even if forever was down to minutes.

But she wanted more than minutes. She wanted years and years with Donovan...

Stahl pulled her behind a tall hedge. Through its branches, she saw Polderweg Road. A half-mile down, red and blue flashers swept over the Volvo and several police cars.

Stahl grabbed her arm and led her through the fog to the other side of Polderweg Road. They continued walking until they came to a large river that she knew was the Maas. Checking his map, Stahl led her along the riverbank for several minutes. The cool river wind felt good against her aching jaw.

Ahead, she saw a sign for the *Serraris Jachthaven-Marina*. Yachts and sailboats lined three docks that jutted out into the river. The tiny guardhouse had a faint light on. They walked up and looked inside. No one.

She heard footsteps behind her.

"*Goii navent.*"

She spun around, hoping for a policeman. Instead she saw an elderly uniformed guard walking toward them. He held a palm-sized television tuned to a soccer game.

Sensing they were tourists, he tired English. "Good evening, folks."

"Oh, good evening," Stahl said. "We're looking for our good friends. They have a Hatteras here."

The old guard smiled with pride. "We have three!"

"Really?"

"Yep! End of the dock. Look!" He pointed.

The soccer crowd roared, then an announcer cut in, "We interrupt the game for this important message. Police are looking for… "

The guard squinted at the television screen. "Well, I'll be damned?"

"What?" Stahl asked.

"This guy on TV… he kinda looks a little like you!"

"Me? You're kidding… let's see!"

The smiling guard walked over and showed him the screen. "See, this fella's eyes are sorta like yours!"

Before she knew what was happening, Stahl's stiletto had slit open the guard's neck. The old man's eyes shot wide open as red arterial blood pumped through his fingers. He slumped to the ground, his gaze never leaving Stahl.

Maccabee felt ill. She had no time to warn the poor man. She slumped against the guardhouse and forced bile back down her throat.

Stahl shoved and kicked the guard's body down into the canal, where it drifted beneath the dock. Then he took Maccabee inside the guardhouse where he pried open a locked cabinet on the wall. In the cabinet keys hung on numbered hooks. He glanced at the yachts, then grabbed the keys for Number 17.

He led her down the dock toward a large white Hatteras at the end. Her heels clicked on the wood planks and she prayed someone in the yacht with a dim light on heard them.

Further down the dock, she took off an earring, and when Stahl wasn't looking, tossed it against the hull of a sailboat. It clicked and splashed into the river.

Stahl spun around and stared at her.

"I kicked a pebble."

He stared at her for several seconds, obviously not buying her explanation, then yanked her toward the big Hatteras.

As they started to step aboard the yacht, she bent down and placed her other earring on the dock.

On board, she looked for something to use as a weapon, but saw nothing. Stahl grabbed some rope and tied her to the deck railing.

He studied the instrument panel a moment then prepared to launch the vessel. He went back and checked out the yacht's Detroit Diesel engines for a few moments, then came back and inserted the key in the ignition.

He turned the key. The engines sputtered... stopped.

He turned the key again. Sputtered... stopped.

She prayed it was out of gas.

He tried again.

The big engines sputtered... coughed... stopped again...

then they roared to life.

Stahl walked over and unlooped the tether ropes from the dock poles and climbed up to the bridge. He took a small crowbar and a screwdriver from the tool compartment and pried off the dashboard screen displaying the yacht's GPS location. Then he pulled out some wires and cut them with his stiletto, disabling the system. The GPS screen went black.

Then he eased the large yacht out into the fog-shrouded river and turned north.

He cruised slowly up the river a hundred yards, and accelerated. Maccabee saw no other river traffic. She looked back and saw the lights of the marina fading fast.

Like her chance of survival.

FIFTY FOUR

Driving along the Maas River, Officer Wim Lenaerts checked himself in the rearview mirror and frowned. Once again, his comb-over had flopped over like the flue flap on his chimney. And his Rogaine? Forget it! Guacamole could grow more hair!

His police radio clicked on.

"Wim… ?" It was Daan, his captain.

"Yes, sir?"

"Stahl might be back here in Holland."

"But they tracked him to *Germany!*"

"Yeah, but we think he doubled back. Watch for him and the woman. And don't mess with this psycho! Call for backup!"

"Count on it, sir."

They hung up.

Moments later, Lenaerts drove by the stolen Volvo on Polderweg Road and nodded to his fellow officers and some CSI techie pals. He continued driving north. Everything looked like it looked an hour ago, normal.

A kilometer later, it didn't. The *Serraris Jachthaven Yacht Marina* was lit up like a Hollywood film premier. Thirty minutes earlier only the small guardhouse light was on. And weeknight parties were rare at the marina. What was going on? He better check it out.

He parked, got out and walked toward the guardhouse. He saw two old men in their pajamas hurrying down the dock toward him, waving their arms.

"Is there a problem?" Lenaerts shouted.

"Big problem, officer!" said an elderly guy with stalks of grey sleep hair sticking up like a punk rocker. Beside him stood an old bald guy in red wool pajamas.

"What's going on?"

"Well, I was sleepin'," Sleep Hair said.

"Me, too," Red Pajamas said.

"Yep, we was sleepin' when you wouldn't believe it!"

"What?"

"Old Henri Dumon's yacht cranks up and pulls right out."

"Henri like night cruises?"

"Henri's in Paris."

"Musta drove up."

"Drove up? Henri can't sit up. Man's in a coma. Celeste, that's his wife, she says it doesn't look good."

"Maybe he let someone use it."

"No damn way. Nobody goes on Henri's boat, less'n he's with 'em. He'd sooner drink rat piss, right Jan?"

"That's right," Jan said, buttoning his red pajamas.

"I'm tellin' you, officer, that yacht was just *stolen!* And old Dirk's missing, too!"

"Dirk, the security guard?"

"Yep."

Officer Lenearts grew more concerned. Dirk was always patrolling the dock, or watching sports on his small television in the guardhouse.

"Think Dirk took it?"

"No way. Dirk's afraid of the river. Doesn't even like boats, right Jan?"

"That's right."

"Did you see anything strange before the yacht took off?"

"Nope, but I *heard* something strange."

"What?"

"Clicks."

"Clicks?"

"Yeah. You know, like a woman's high heels hitting the dock clicks. High heels ain't too normal on docks or boats."

Lenearts agreed, growing more interested.

"After I heard that, the yacht engine cranks right up and cruises into the river."

Gotta be Stahl and the woman! Lenearts realized, his pulse pounding. "Which way did the yacht go?"

"Toward Nijmegen."

"Can you describe the yacht?"

"Hatteras. A beauty, right Jan?"

"That's right!" Jan said.

"Cuts water like silk. Double cabin. Fifty-four footer." Van Zant's love of boats turned his parchment cheeks pink. "Twin V8 diesel engines. All the fancy electronics."

"White?"

"Yep."

"Does it have a… you know, a top… ?"

"A bridge. Yep, and a good size rear deck."

"Any other distinguishing features?"

"Its name - *L'étoile d'Uzes* - in big black letters right across the back. French flag right above 'em."

Lenearts wrote down the name.

"How long ago did it leave?"

The old man looked at his watch. "Maybe… thirty-five minutes ago."

"Have Dirk call me the second he gets back." He handed the old man his card.

"I will, but… "

"But what?

"Well, it just ain't like old Dirk to go off and disappear, right Jan?"

"That's right."

Lenearts checked around the guardhouse and saw the key storage box had been pried open. He started walking back toward his car radio, then stopped cold. He saw something on the dock.

Spots.

Make that *drops,* wet dark drops… the color of blood.

Using his flashlight, he followed them down to the riverbank… where the beam hit a hand-sized television.

And then a human hand… and arm floating beneath the dock.

FIFTY FIVE

S tahl gazed down at the water, shimmering like black satin, as he
piloted the big Hatteras up river. The peaceful water calmed him
almost as much as the rows of white yachts the cops would have to
check along the shore.

He looked at the woman. She was shivering where he'd tied her to
a deck rail. She deserved to shiver. Her translations and her father's had
caused him trouble.

He checked his speed. One knot below the limit. River traffic was
light, and with 870 gallons of fuel, he could cruise all the way to the
Atlantic Ocean.

After disabling the GPS, he found a Maas River map. It showed
him water depth, tributaries, canals, marinas, even police locations.

The police would of course eventually figure out he'd doubled back
and stolen the yacht.

But by then, he would have ditched it.

And the woman.

* * *

Donovan was worried as he and Jean de Waha walked back into Holland. They had not found Maccabee's and Stahl's footprints heading back. Donovan feared he'd made a huge mistake thinking Stahl had doubled back. By now, Stahl could be deep in Germany.

As Donovan and de Waha stepped back onto Polderweg Road, a police car raced up and stopped beside them.

A young officer leaned out the window. "We think Stahl killed a security guard at the *Serraris Marina* just up the road. Then he stole a yacht!"

"Was Maccabee with him?" Donovan asked.

"We think so."

"Why?"

"A man heard what sounded like a woman's shoes on the dock just minutes before the yacht was stolen. And right where the yacht was moored, we found a silver earring."

"Shaped like a teardrop?"

"Yes."

Donovan melted with relief. "Maccabee's!"

The officer explained that the yacht was a big fifty-five-foot Hatteras with the name *L'étoile d'Uzès* on the rear deck beneath a red-white-blue French flag.

"Which direction did he go?"

"North from the marina."

Donovan looked up river. "He'll stay within the speed limits. So how far could he be now?"

The officer unfolded a river map and pointed. "Maybe around Kevelaer or Boxmeer."

Donovan heard a familiar *thump thump thump*. He spun around and saw the halogen spotlights of a helicopter speeding through the night toward them.

Two minutes later, he and Jean, were belted into the Dutch Police

Agusta-Bell AW 139 chopper as the fifteen-seater skimmed over the river like a pelican hunting dinner.

Two miles further, Donovan pointed at a big white yacht.

The pilot shook his head. "That's a Condor, 50-footer... "

Minutes later, near the town of Venlo, Donovan saw marinas with numerous white yachts moored side by side like piano keys. Most had their rear decks tucked tightly against the marina dock. Police would have to check each one.

But Donovan's gut told him Stahl had not docked, that the assassin was putting as much distance between himself and the police as possible. Eventually he'd ditch the yacht, steal another vehicle, and hide out in Amsterdam or Dusseldorf.

After ditching Maccabee.

The question was – alive or dead?

And dead was the smartest for Stahl.

Donovan was worried sick about her. The police found a lot of blood on her scarf and the Volvo's driver's side door. She was injured, in pain, and obviously terrified...

"White Hatteras!" the pilot shouted, pointing ahead.

Donovan looked down at a large white yacht, hidden beneath trees in a small inlet. The yacht seemed to be the right length, longer than fifty feet. And he saw a red white and blue French flag, hanging limp at the rear.

This is it!

He flipped the safety off his gun. The chopper swooped down to sixty feet above the yacht, flooding it in blinding white light. The rotor downwash unfurled the flag and Donovan's hope sank. The red-white-blue stripes were *horizontal,* not vertical. He was looking at a *Dutch* flag. Below it was a painting of a girl in a bikini and the yacht's name – *Amster-Dame.*

A terrified middle-aged couple peeked from the cabin window as the chopper swept up and away.

Four minutes later, Donovan saw two more white Hatteras yachts, one sixty-footer, another seventy-footer. Both flew Dutch flags.

"He can only be a few minutes ahead," de Waha said.

"Or miles away in Germany… or heading to the Atlantic Ocean."

* * *

Valek Stahl saw exactly what he was looking for. A perfect offshoot, a wide canal, just yards ahead. He turned into it, then steered around a commercial barge, the *Erik Willems, N.V.,* and some moored sailboats, then turned onto the waterway.

He continued for another half-kilometer, passing small pleasure boats and homes behind them. Soon, he saw a row of windmills, their blades churning in the night sky, and behind the mills, a large forest.

He searched for a place to conceal the big yacht, a cove with over-hanging trees, an empty boathouse, a shadowy inlet. He saw none. He cruised further down the channel.

Steering around a bend, he glimpsed the outline of an enormous windmill, its long blades groaning as they sliced through the thick fog. Next to the mill was a open, covered boathouse, large enough to hold several yachts. Large yachts had filled the first five slots and the seventh. The sixth slot was vacant.

He cut the engine to idle, drifted ahead, flicked the lights off and gently reversed the large craft into the open slot, tucking the rear deck tight against the dock so the cops couldn't read *L'étoile d'Uzès* from the water.

He turned the engine off and listened. He heard only the waves slapping against the dock and the windmill blades creaking in the darkness.

Stahl moored the boat to the dock poles and looked behind the boathouse. Through the fog he saw a thick forest and a three-story mansion a hundred yards up the bank on a hill. Dim lights were on downstairs. He'd stay on the yacht.

Fog was creeping from the forest toward the canal, shrouding the yacht even more. Everyone was looking for him now, scouring the highways and byways, so he'd lay low until he felt it was safe to leave.

Meanwhile, he had a beautiful woman below.
He'd be less than courteous if he didn't grant her one last wish.
The pleasure of his company.

FIFTY SIX

"*HOOGENBOEZEM! Where the hell are you?*"
Jerking awake, Officer Leo Hoogenboezem banged his knee hard on the steel frame of the police car radio from which Captain Ver Donk was screaming at him.

"Here sir!" Hoogenboezem said, rubbing his knee, trying to sound awake and shake off the knee pain and the pain from last night's party.

"Any sight of the Hatteras?"

"Not yet, sir."

"Re-check all yachts on the river and waterways up to three miles north of you."

"I just checked them."

"Check 'em again!"

"Right, sir."

They hung up.

Hoogenboezem yawned. He'd pulled two ten-hour shifts back-to-back, and gone to the party and drank too much. The party was a big bad mistake. He needed sleep.

Sometimes he wondered about the Captain. Smart guy, but anal as a tax accountant. Re-check this, re-check that, change that light bulb before it burns out. And the man demanded the impossible.

You forget, Captain, there's a shitload of boats along this stretch of the river!

Yeah, Stahl was top priority. And yes, Ver Donk was getting pressure from the heavy breathers in Amsterdam. Yes, Stahl damned near blew up eight world leaders. Yes, Stahl had killed innocent people for their cars. And yes, he was probably back in this part of Holland. But any moron with a room temperature IQ knew Stahl had dumped the yacht and stolen a car by now.

Hoogenboezem drove down the familiar narrow road that hugged the river. For two miles, he gazed at the same yachts, same homes, same cars and same windmills he'd gazed at earlier. Nothing had changed. Except the fog was thicker.

He yawned and felt the need for sleep creeping over him. He reached in the glove compartment, pulled out a *5-hour ENERGY* drink and chugged down the bottle. It should give him at least one hour of caffeine alertness, until he got off duty.

He drove down another offshoot of the Maas, rechecking the vessel names... *The My-tanic... Ray L.... Erna en Tony... Meuse Lambic.* He saw no Hatterases.

A kilometer later, he turned down another canal. Even though he'd checked the vessels docked along the canal earlier, he would turn his spotlight on them anyway. Check them out. Do what the brass says.

Forget that the brass probably got the yacht's brand and name wrong. And probably the length wrong. And probably which direction it took on the river. If he had fifty euros for each time those desk bozos were wrong, he'd be retired, sipping Margaritas with big-breasted ladies in the Caribbean.

He drove around the familiar big bend, crept past the smaller windmills, and then past the monster windmill. Through the fog, he saw the large, multi-berth open boathouse come into view. Behind it on the hills, he glimpsed the summer estates of business tycoons from Amsterdam.

He approached the boathouse and aimed his spotlight on the yachts. Yawning, he moved the light from one to the next.

He knew these yachts like the back of his hand, but read their names aloud to help stay awake.

"Maas Boss... NautiLust... Schiff's Skiff... De Amstel...

He noticed the sixth slot and froze.

The slot was *filled with a big white yacht!*

A Hatteras!

Forty-five minutes ago the slot was empty. But the Hatteras had backed into the berth, tucking its name against the dock. He needed to drive to the other side of the canal to read the name. As he started to turn back toward a nearby canal bridge, his headlights hit the left front bow of the yacht and what looked like small black script.

But he couldn't quite read it.

He crept a few inches closer, leaned forward and squinting through the fog, read - *"L'étoile d'Uzès!"*

"Jezus, THAT'S IT!" he said, banging his knee against metal radio frame again.

He doused his spotlight and whipped out his handgun as though Stahl was crawling through the window.

Hoogenboezem saw a very faint light behind a yellow curtain.

Stahl and the woman were inside!

Did he see my spotlight?

Hoogenboezem phoned Captain Ver Donk. "I found the Hatteras!"

"Where?"

Hoogenboezem gave him the location.

"Stahl inside?"

"I think so. There's a faint light on in the cabin. But the fog is getting thicker!"

"Did he see you?"

"My spotlight maybe." Hoogenboezem felt a drop of cold sweat slide down his neck.

"Stay on this line. *Any* changes, tell me. We're on the way!"

"Right, sir!"

Hoogenboezem shoved a full magazine into his Glock and watched the Hatteras.

* * *

In the yacht's master stateroom, Stahl sat in a plush leather chair and stared at Maccabee. A tiny nightlight illuminated her left leg and left wrist tied to the brass corners of the bed.

He sipped some Heineken and listened to a radio announcer report that police had established a global dragnet for him. He smiled. *You fools are dragneting for someone who won't exist in three days thanks to plastic surgery.*

He'd lie low for another thirty minutes, then leave alone – *after* he watched the woman's body sink to the bottom of the canal.

Then he'd head to a nearby farmhouse where he'd seen a grey Renault, hotwire it and drive to Amsterdam. From there, his colleague, Ali Bin Schothorst, would fly him to Iran.

Stahl took another long swig of the beer. Despite being Muslim, he'd started drinking alcohol years ago so he could move unnoticed among the infidels. Now, he liked alcohol. And other Western things.

Like their women.

He looked at Maccabee Singh's long, firm legs spread out... pointing toward all her good parts. A most bedable woman, he thought. Anglo-Indian. Half-breed. Like him. Hybrids were always more interesting.

He should probably feel some sympathy for what he was about to do to her, but he felt nothing. He didn't *feel* things like other people. By their standards, he knew, that wasn't normal. But then, what was normal? The answer was simple. Normal was a personal hallucination. And if in fact he'd once been *normal,* the Israelis ripped any semblance of it away from him when their bombs slaughtered his family. That crime, and many others against him, exempted him from following any rules but his own. Besides, rules were for morons.

He stood, walked to the window and peeked out through the curtain. Thick fog hovered over the water and forest. The more fog, the better. Praise Allah!

* * *

Through the police helicopter window, Donovan watched the rotors downwash ripple the canal water and flatten tall grass as the chopper touched down a kilometer from the Hatteras. He saw two police vans awaiting them.

He and de Waha deplaned and hurried over to a twelve-man Dutch anti-terrorist team standing beside a small raft. The team leader, Officer Koopman, made quick introductions, then showed Donovan and de Waha the Hatteras location on his iPad GPS.

De Waha and Donovan copied the yacht's GPS location on their phones.

De Waha turned to the men. "Seven of you take positions in the forest behind the yacht. Block him that way. The other five set up on the canal bank across from the yacht in case he decides to swim over. We've already blocked off both ends of the canal. We have him contained. Questions?"

There were none.

"Donovan and I saw Stahl today. We know what he looks like, what he's wearing. We've looked into his eyes. We'll take this raft to the yacht and board it. We'll enter the cabin and if you hear nothing, stay out. If you hear a problem, come in fast! If he tries to escape, apprehend him, and if necessary shoot to kill. But if Maccabee is with him, hold your fire, especially if her life appears at risk. Understood?"

Everyone nodded.

"There's a slight problem," Donovan said.

"What?" Officer Koopmans asked.

"We could use a bit more firepower."

Koopmans nodded, opened the cargo area of a van and said, "Take your pick!"

Donovan looked down at an arsenal of six Heckler and Koch G-3s, powerful battle rifles similar to G-3s he'd given to an anti-Al Qaeda tribe in Turkistan. He also saw several Glock 18s with 33-round extended magazines... and a large metal chest chocked full of eighty RGD-5 antipersonnel hand grenades, each containing 100 grams of TNT.

He was looking at enough explosive power to divert the flow of the canal.

Donovan and de Waha selected Glocks.

"How about a flash-bang grenade?"

Donovan shook his head. "It could injure or burn Maccabee. Maybe spook Stahl into shooting her!"

Donovan and de Waha put on Spectra bulletproof vests and helmets.

They stepped into the two-man Zodiac raft. De Waha started the silent electric fishing motor and Donovan sat in front. They whooshed off into the misty night. Donovan looked at his phone's GPS map and estimated they were four minutes from the yacht. Was that too long? Had Stahl heard the chopper and decided to leave the yacht?

He tried to calm himself by visualizing Maccabee as he rescued her.

But another visual kept pushing it away... a concrete block... tied to a rope... tied to Maccabee's body as she struggled to free herself at the bottom of the canal.

FIFTY SEVEN

S tahl's gaze felt like ice sliding between her breasts. He sipped his beer and stepped toward her, his eyes different now, hard, predatory, animal, lustful...

He was looking at her as a woman.

The thought of his hands touching her, the hands of a stone-cold murderer, nauseated her. He leaned close and she flinched, causing the gag around her mouth to dig in and unleash fresh blood into her throat.

Stahl sat down on the bed inches from her. He sipped more beer and patted her knee.

"Don't worry. It's almost over. You'll be free soon."

She didn't believe him.

"This friend of yours, Rourke, you must like him a lot."

She said nothing.

"Well, do you?"

She nodded.

"Do you *love* him?"

She saw no reason to tell Stahl and said nothing.

"Do you?"

She remained silent.

He grabbed her hair. *"DO YOU?"*

She nodded.

"And I'm sure he loves you, right?"

She shrugged and hoped he did.

"So he'd be sad, perhaps angry if you wanted to make love to an-other man. Say, an attractive man, right?"

Panic gripped her.

"Say a man like… me."

Her stomach clenched.

"Oh, don't worry, I would never take advantage of a woman who didn't want to make love to me. Never!"

She exhaled slowly.

"But it's so obvious you do. Your eyes follow me constantly, dare I say, lustfully even. Can't take your eyes off me as the old song goes. So a reasonable man can only conclude that you are highly attracted to me, that you like what you see, that you, well, let's just say it - that you *desire* me."

She said nothing.

"Most women do." He flexed his enormous bicep.

"But you're a 'Mushluhm!" she said through the gag, hoping reli-gion might stop him.

"Yes… and the Koran teaches us that a woman must be subservient to a man - in *all* things! Such a wise religion."

How can I stop him? she wondered. She saw nothing she could use as a weapon.

He moved closer and breathed out, reeking of sour beer breath.

She leaned away and realized her free hand was just inches from a heavy fishbowl on the bed table. If she could reach the fishbowl and slam it against his head, it might daze him long enough to untie her ropes and escape.

Or it might enrage him enough to kill her on the spot.

He unbuttoned his shirt, flexed his muscles and preened like a pro wrestler. "Nice, huh?"

She refused to look and leaned away, trying to inch her fingers toward the fishbowl without being noticed.

"Here, have some beer."

She turned her face away, but he twisted it back.

"Speaking of beer, the ancient Egyptians had a wise proverb. 'Never cease to drink beer or make love.'"

She said nothing.

"In that order. So, beer first."

He poured beer over her gag and into her mouth. She coughed when the icy beer hit her dry throat. Then, on purpose, he spilled much more onto her white blouse, drenching her.

"Now look what you've done!" he said.

She turned away. Again, he turned her head back and gazed down at her breasts and dark areolae pushing up through the thin wet silk.

She saw his gun on a table about ten feet away. If she could just daze him with the fishbowl and untie her hand, she might be able to reach the gun before he came to.

"Look at your blouse. I dare say Mr. Rourke would not like you wet and shivering, would he? You could catch your death. We should dry your blouse."

She leaned away... closer to the fishbowl. When he wasn't looking, she brushed its base with her fingers. But the rim was still too high to grab.

Slowly, Stahl undid the top button of her blouse. She tried to not feel his presence, not feel what he was about to do to her...

He guzzled more beer.

"By the way, forget the fishbowl. It's mounted to the table."

She felt all hope drain from her body.

He undid another button... and another.

She wanted to scream.

FIFTY EIGHT

Donovan squinted into the thick fog as de Waha navigated their raft down the pitch-black canal. Donovan feared the raft might hit unseen floating debris, maybe logs or a dock pole hidden in the murky mist.

Visibility was less than thirty feet.

"How far?" de Waha whispered.

Checking his GPS, Donovan said, "We're should be getting close. Maybe two hundred yards."

De Waha slowed the silent raft and phoned Officer Hoogenboezem who was still watching the Hatteras from across the canal.

"Any changes?" de Waha whispered.

"No," Hoogenboezem said. "Stahl and Maccabee have not left the yacht."

"Is the faint light still on inside?"

"Yes, sir."

"Let us know if anything changes."

"Right sir."

Donovan heard what sounded like the creaking of windmill blades.

Seconds later, the fog lifted a bit and he glimpsed a massive windmill along the left bank. Seconds later, he glimpsed the long open boathouse covering several yachts.

Soon, he saw the rear deck of the first yacht, then the rear decks of the next four. The sixth yacht, a Hatteras, was backed into its slot. He lifted his binoculars and saw some words on the bow slowly came into focus… *L'étoile d'Uzes.*

His heart pounded as he pointed the yacht out to de Waha.

De Waha cut the silent fishing motor and let the raft drift toward the boathouse dock.

Forty feet… thirty… ten…

Stretching his arms forward, Donovan cushioned the arrival at the dock. He then eased the raft's ropes over the docking poles. Weapons drawn, they stepped silently up onto the dock.

The Hatteras was inches away.

Donovan saw the faint cabin light behind a thick curtain. They'd have to enter the cabin blindly and overwhelm Stahl.

Donovan signaled he would board first. Slowly, he placed his foot on the yacht's deck and paused. He brought his other foot on the deck. He detected no change in the vessel's balance.

Very slowly, de Waha stepped aboard. Again Donovan felt no shift in the yacht's yaw.

They moved to the main door. He wasn't surprised to find it unlocked. More proof Stahl had the keys and was inside.

On Donovan's *three* count, they burst in, guns drawn.

They swept the main cabin and saw no one. They rushed to the master bedroom and bathroom. Empty. They checked two small bedrooms and closets. Empty.

Donovan turned and saw some flex-cuffs on a coffee table. Beside them was a handwritten note. He picked it up and read…

Rourke...

By the time you read this, I'll be in
Germany... or France... or who knows
where... But rest assured, one day soon you'll
pay for the trouble you've caused me today...
like your wife paid a while back... and like
your friend Maccabee is about to pay.

Seems like you have trouble protecting
your women!

V. Stahl

Donovan's rage exploded. He felt like barbed wire was being pulled
through his veins.

"Stahl left this yacht before Hoogenboezem got here," de Waha
said.

But did he leave with or without Maccabee? Donovan wondered as
he took a deep breath. They hurried back out on the dock.

*Did Stahl take her into the fog-shrouded forest? Down the dark road
beside the windmill? Down the road to steal a car?*

Or did he kill her and dump her in the canal?

De Waha pointed to a large home on a hill. A light was on downstairs. "Let's check it out."

They started up the dirt path leading to the home. The path was
lined with two-foot high brick walls on each side. The pitch-dark night
made it difficult to see. Donovan flicked on his phone's flashlight and
it helped him see the pathway better. But moments later, Donovan was
bothered by something he didn't see. He stopped.

"What's wrong?" de Waha asked.

"This is the only way to the mansion, right?"

"Right. So... ?"

"So the soil is very wet, but there are no footprints."

De Waha looked at the ground and nodded. "Bastard took her
somewhere else."

They turned around and headed back toward the dock. As they walked onto the dock, something flashed in Donovan's eye. He turned and saw it sparkle on the dock beneath the boathouse lights a hundred feet away. He pointed it out to de Waha and they walked down to it and paused.

Donovan aimed his flashlight - and saw Maccabee's gold ring.

Positioned on the walkway.

The walkway to a sixty-foot SeaRay.

Donovan pocketed the ring and flicked off his flashlight. He and de Waha studied the yacht. It was dark inside, except for what looked like the faint glow of a night-light behind a curtain. Donovan listened for any sound coming from inside the yacht, but heard nothing.

Then a human shadow moved behind the curtain.

FIFTY NINE

D onovan stepped aboard the SeaRay, slowly, one step at a time. He felt no shift in the yacht's equilibrium.

De Waha stepped aboard and paused. Again, no shift. He took another step and Donovan saw his shoe slide on the fog-slick deck. De Waha fell forward on his hand and knee... but without making any sound.

Donovan thought he felt a slight tilt, very slight, nothing more than the tilt a tiny wave would make.

De Waha nodded he was fine and got up slowly.

They inched toward the cabin door.

* * *

Valek Stahl slid his fingers down the smooth, silky skin of Maccabee's shoulder, then paused. He sensed something. Movement.

Not wave movement. More like a slight tilt to the left. He glanced

at the nearby fishbowl. The red castle had just dipped under the water
– *and remained under.*

Only one explanation.

Weight.

Human weight!

Added to the left side of the yacht.

Stahl grabbed his gun, untied Maccabee, pulled her into the front
cabin and listened at the door.

He sensed someone on the other side.

* * *

Donovan and de Waha, their weapons drawn, bolted through the
cabin door and swept the main room. Empty. Donovan hurried into
the master bedroom. Also empty.

He saw a messed-up bed, a piece of rope and a beer bottle beside a
fishbowl. The master bath and closet were also vacant. He looked at the
only room they hadn't checked. The door was closed. Donovan walked
over to it. Now or never.

He yanked it open.

Empty.

Behind them, he heard a latch click. He spun around and saw
Stahl, gun in hand, and Maccabee emerge from the huge storage bins
beneath the sofa cushions in the stateroom.

"Welcome aboard!" Valek Stahl said, jamming his gun against
Maccabee's temple. Her mouth had bled onto her blouse which was
unbuttoned. She looked terrified… but when she realized it was Donovan and de Waha, tears welled up in her eyes.

Donovan stared at Stahl, fighting the urge to empty his Glock between the man's eyes. "Maccabee. We're not alone!"

"Put your guns down!"

Donovan and de Waha hesitated.

"Do it or her brains paint the wall!"

Slowly, Donovan and de Waha placed their guns on the floor.

298

"Phones down too!"

Both men placed their phones on the floor.

Donovan couldn't take his eyes off Stahl. Finally, he was face to face with the psychopath who killed his wife Emma… and hundreds of innocent people… and almost killed the world's most powerful leaders…

… . and might kill Maccabee any second.

He saw the bloody gag around her mouth, a purple gash on her swollen cheek, her drenched blouse. Stahl had beaten her and worse. Donovan's anger rose like molten lava.

Please Lord, just a few minutes with this bastard!

"The police have this yacht surrounded, Stahl," Donovan said. "You have no chance."

"I assumed as much." His accent was American.

"Assume something else, Stahl!" Donovan fought to control his rage.

"And what is that, Mr. Rourke?"

"That you will die if you hurt her any more!"

Stahl smiled, but said nothing.

"And maybe even if you don't."

Stahl smiled again. "Brave talk, Mr. Rourke, for a man who couldn't even protect his own wife."

Donovan felt like he'd been kicked in the gut.

"Question for you Stahl… "

"Yeah?"

"How brave were you when you slit my wife's throat while she slept?"

Anger flashed in Stahl's eyes, but he said nothing. He looked hard at Donovan for several moments, staring at his shirt and pants. Staring too long for some reason. Donovan looked down and realized his clothes were the same colors as Stahl's.

He sensed what the man was planning.

Stahl pulled off his fake beard and tossed it behind a chair. "Throw your vest and helmet over here, Rourke! *Do it now!*"

Donovan stalled, searching for some way out of this.

"NOW!" He pushed the gun barrel into Maccabee's temple. She cringed.

Donovan took off his vest and helmet and tossed them over. Stahl slid the vest on and forced Maccabee to fasten its Velcro straps.

"Walk backward toward that storage room!"

Donovan and de Waha stepped back toward the small room.

"Get in the room and shut the door!"

They got in and shut the door.

Stahl locked it with a key, then it sounded like he wedged something under the handle.

"If you follow me, she dies."

"Stahl… ?" Donovan said through the door.

"Yeah?"

"You're a dead man."

* * *

Clutching Maccabee, Stahl peeked out the windows. He saw no cops in the fog, but knew they were there, probably hiding in the trees.

But now, he was Rourke. Same height and weight, same color pants and shirts, same bulletproof vest. The helmet would hide his hair, the fog and darkness would obscure his face, and the Glock would keep Maccabee nice and quiet.

He pulled off her gag. "We're going outside. Button your blouse. Act normal. If you warn them – I'll kill you and some of them. Understand?"

She nodded.

Stahl opened the door and led her outside onto the rear deck, then down to the fog-shrouded dock.

His face down, Stahl kept his hand around her shoulder as though comforting her. His other hand jammed the gun into her spine. He looked ahead into the dark, misty dock area and forest, still seeing no one, but knowing the police were out there.

"You need help, Agent Rourke?" a voice from the forest.

"No. We've got Stahl cuffed inside. De Waha wants to question him alone for a couple minutes."

He heard the officers start to walk toward them from the forest.

"Stand back! Don't crowd her. Maccabee needs some time alone. She's been through a lot."

"Okay… you need anything, Miss Singh?"

She said nothing.

Stahl nudged her with the gun.

She said nothing.

"Miss Singh… ?"

He nudged her hard.

"No."

Stahl led her along the misty canal bank. In the distance he saw the outline of the large windmill and beyond that some unattended police cars.

Wouldn't surprise him if the idiots had left the keys in them again. He also remembered some homes further up the canal. Cars were parked in the drives.

And then he remembered seeing a Renault Clio at the farmhouse just up the road. So many choices.

He'd be out of here in minutes.

SIXTY

"Stand back, Jean!" Donovan said, moving de Waha away from the locked door.

"Why?"

"This." He yanked a 9mm mini-Glock from his ankle holster and aimed at the doorknob.

Donovan fired and the bullet shattered the lock mechanism and broke off chunks of wood. They lunged against the door, but it gave only a half-inch. Stahl had wedged something against it.

On a three count, they kicked the door – but only gained an inch. They kicked harder, and then harder again, finally slamming the door open and knocking a chair away. They ran into the cabin and saw that Stahl had taken their handguns.

Rushing out onto the dock, Donovan saw Officer Koopmans and other officers running toward them, looking astonished.

"Donovan - we thought you – "

"Where'd Stahl take her?"

"That way - along the canal!"

"Are there police cars down there?"

"Yes."

"Did you hear a car start?"

"The choppers are too loud to hear anything down there!"

Donovan saw two Dutch Agusta-Bell Police helicopters sweeping over the forest, their spotlights bleaching the trees white.

"Tell them to search this area for Stahl and Maccabee. Stahl has dark clothes, but she's wearing a white blouse."

Koopmans gave the order into his phone.

"Any houses down there?" Donovan asked.

"Several."

"Check them and the cars out too."

Koopmans repeated the command into his shoulder mic.

"What about the forest?" de Waha asked.

"SWAT teams just started combing it, working their way toward us now."

Donovan hoped their net was cast earlier enough and wide enough.

"He took our guns," Donovan said.

Koopmans turned to an officer who quickly produced two 9mm Berettas and handed them to Donovan and de Waha.

Donovan looked around. Where was Stahl?

Logic suggested he was getting as far away as possible. But Stahl often used logic to deceive the cops. Maybe Stahl did not run and was hiding close by.

And maybe when he heard my gunshot in the yacht, he knew he had to hide fast – maybe in the forest or along the canal.

"Jean, let's you, Koopmans and I start with the big windmill first, then the canal and forest."

They nodded.

"Is the windmill door unlocked?" Donovan asked.

Koopmans shrugged that he didn't know.

Donovan studied the windmill. It was far larger and taller than any mill he'd ever seen. The blades, more than fifty feet in length, groaned in the wind. He heard a motor running inside and wondered if the mill was both power and wind driven? Its base was sixty feet wide and surrounded by white tulips and large decorative boulders. A wood railing and wood plank walkway also circled the mill. The roof swooped down like a Chinese pagoda.

As Donovan switched his Beretta's safety off, he thought he heard something near the mill. Not the blades whirring and groaning, and not a mechanical sound, but a sharp click. Like a shoe clicking on the wood walkway. A hard heel click?

The hair on his neck stiffened.

He signaled de Waha and Koopman that he would approach the windmill while they blocked the other sides. If Stahl bolted, he'd face cops, bullets, or canal water.

Donovan inched toward the windmill, reminding himself that he was *not* wearing his bulletproof vest or helmet.

Stahl was!

A few steps closer, Donovan paused and squinted into the fog. He saw the faint outline of something or someone backed up against the mill. He blinked to be sure. Then he was sure. He was looking at a tall man's profile.

Stahl!

Holding his gun!

His back against the mill.

But no Maccabee...

Donovan looked left, then right, then left again, but didn't see her. Then he looked back.

Stahl was gone!

Cursing himself for losing Stahl, Donovan moved to the left and seconds later managed to catch Stahl's profile – this time clutching Maccabee in front of him - his gun jammed against her head!

Donovan flattened himself on the ground, giving Stahl less to shoot at, and began creeping toward the man, keeping his eyes focused on Stahl's shoes forty feet away.

The shoes did not move. Nor did Maccabee's.

Only thirty feet now... twenty...

Then Donovan's hand came down on a fallen branch. It snapped loud as a bullwhip. He looked down at the damned branch, cursed silently – then looked back up.

Stahl and Maccabee were gone!

Donovan rolled left, fearing Stahl would shoot toward the sound. But Stahl did not fire. Instead, Donovan realized, he had to be backing up around the windmill.

If I go in the opposite direction, he should be backing up toward me.

Donovan heard noise in the forest.

Did Stahl just sneak past Koopmans and de Waha into the woods? Possible, but not likely. Something told him that Stahl was still at or near the windmill.

He crawled along the mill's wood-plank walkway in the opposite direction Stahl had taken. He paused and listened. Nothing.

As he crept forward, his finger slid between two wood planks. He pulled it out and felt a large sliver rip into it. It stung like hell, but he kept crawling, watching for Stahl's back to emerge from the fog.

But Stahl's back did not emerge.

Nor did any sound.

Donovan waited several seconds.

Still nothing.

Was Stahl waiting for him?

Donovan inched ahead. No sight of him. Did he take her *inside* the mill? Or along the canal? He couldn't possibly get past de Waha and Koopmans, could he?

Donovan listened hard, but heard only the huge blades, groaning and creaking.

Something was very wrong.

Where the hell was Stahl?

Then... Donovan *felt* something.

Behind him!

A wood plank had dipped down.

He spun around and saw Stahl pulling Maccabee backward, her high heels clicking across the planks.

Donovan raised his gun to shoot - but Stahl yanked Maccabee in front of him as a shield and aimed his gun at Donovan.

As Stahl squeezed the trigger, Maccabee hit his elbow.

One bullet grazed Donovan's shoulder, the other missed his head by inches.

Stahl pulled Maccabee back.

And that's when it happened - her heel suddenly lodged between the wood planks. As she fell, she grabbed Stahl's arm and pulled him down. Stahl jerked his arm free, straightened up, then aimed at Donovan again.

Too late.

Donovan's first bullet ripped into Stahl's shoulder. The second and third bullets ripped into his neck near the carotid artery.

Stahl seemed to freeze.

Maccabee pushed him. He tripped over her stuck shoe, then flipped backward over the railing, his legs flying up into the air.

And then incredibly... so was the rest of him!

Donovan couldn't believe his eyes... Stahl's body was being dragged *up into the foggy night sky!*

His leg had wedged itself into the grids of a huge windmill blade. Stahl struggled to free himself, but couldn't dislodge his leg.

Donovan wrapped Maccabee in his arms – and watched Stahl swing high above their heads, struggling to free his leg. If he managed to pull his leg out, he'd fall one hundred feet to the ground. But he couldn't free the leg. The shin and knee were *locked* too deeply in the blade's gridwork.

Stahl flailed like a wounded animal as his body swung over the apex and began descending – down toward the huge decorative white boulders, his head dangling well below the blade.

His eyes widened as he saw what awaited him below.

The blade swept down faster.

Donovan buried Maccabee's face in his chest as Stahl's skull *smashed* against the jagged boulders, crushing his jaw and eye socket. His skull scraped along the boulders a few feet and swung up again.

Donovan couldn't move. He stared at Stahl's misshapen, bleeding head, at his dislodged-jaw hanging open, at his limp ragdoll body sweeping up toward the top again.

He knew what he should do. Try to dislodge him. Stop the blades. The human thing to do. But he wasn't feeling human toward Stahl. And something in him wanted the bastard mutilated for mutilating Emma, and for mutilating hundreds of innocent men, women and children with his bombs over the years, and for what he'd done to Maccabee.

But then, some other part of him said – *no… don't play this sick bastard's game!*

As Stahl swung down toward the boulders again, Donovan eased Maccabee to the side and positioned himself to pull Stahl's leg from the grids.

As the body swung by, Donovan grabbed the leg – but the speeding blade nearly yanked his arm out of its socket.

Stahl's skull bashed against the big stones again, split open further, misshapen as a deflated football now, dripping blood on the white tulips. Then the body raced upward again.

"Jean, stop the damn blades!"

A sudden gust of wind pushed the blades faster as the body neared the apex again, crossed over, and swept downward.

He heard gunshots near the mill door. As the body raced toward the bricks. Donovan positioned himself to throw a shoulder into Stahl's body.

Then he heard screeching – metal on metal – as the huge blades ground to a halt. De Waha had thrown the mill's brake.

Stahl's body swung back and forth like a bloody carcass in a slaughterhouse.

De Waha ran out of the windmill and over to Donovan.

They stared at Stahl's hanging corpse, a grotesque pendulum.

"Bastard got off easy," de Waha said.

"Yeah."

"So what do we write down for cause of death?" de Waha said.

"How about death by hanging?"

"Works for me."

Donovan placed his arm around Maccabee, helped her to her feet and guided her from the carnage.

They strolled along the canal. Each step took them further from the madness. Further from the monster who'd destroyed their families and caused so much pain in their lives.

The irony, they both knew, was that this same monster had brought them to each other.

EPILOGUE

MANHATTAN

D onovan led Maccabee past lots of happy faces as the two of them stepped outside Manhattan's St. Patrick's Cathedral into a beautiful, steamy afternoon...

... and in hours, he hoped, an even steamier honeymoon...

He was overflowing with love for the woman beside him as they walked through smiling well-wishers... accurate rice-tossers... pushy camera-clickers... to leaping streamer throwers... and a friendly cop flashing his car lights.

Donovan helped Maccabee into the spacious back seat of a black limousine the length of a battleship.

"Gee - our family car!" she said, smiling.

"Dream on."

She laughed as the limo pulled away and headed up Madison Avenue. A few minutes later, they entered the Plaza Hotel's Grand Ballroom for their reception, an ethnic mixed salad. Donovan's Irish and Italian relatives partied with Maccabee's Indian and Irish cousins. The Micks crooned Hindu love ballads and danced the Kathak while the Indians danced the jig and sang *Danny Boy*. What the singers and dancers lacked in talent, they made up for in passion, thanks in large part to the booze.

Libations ruled the night! Irish Bushnells and Jameson, Italian Chiantis, and New Dehli Savignons flowed faster than the East River at high tide. The five-piece band played a mix of Clancy Brothers, Ravi Shankar, Mario Lanza and an occasional Hava Nagila.

His life and family felt reborn. Because they were.

Three hours later, Donovan and Maccabee, happy and tipsy, departed for the airport, leaving their happy tipsy friends to party on.

His beautiful daughter, Tish, the flower girl, danced every dance until she exhausted herself and collapsed on Gramma Anna's lap. Donovan was heartened by how Gramma Anna and Maccabee had bonded into a warm mother-daughter relationship over the last few months, clearly filling the huge voids in each other's lives. He was equally delighted and amazed by how quickly Tish and Maccabee had bonded and grown fond of each other.

As the limousine tunneled through Manhattan's concrete canyons, Donovan's cell phone rang. He saw Caller ID and punched the speakerphone.

"Congratulations again, folks," said National Intelligence Director Michael Madigan, calling from London.

"Thank you, sir."

"Though I'd update you two on the *Medusa* Plot before you escape into matrimonial and connubial bliss and refuse to answer your phones."

"Good thinking, sir."

"Maccabee, as a result of your translations of the newly uncovered Sumerian documents, we've learned the full dimensions of the *Medusa*. It was far more complex than we imagined. Its tentacles spread into every major financial institution in the world."

"Who was behind it?" Donovan asked.

"Karlottah Z. Wickstrom."

"The billionaire recluse in Curacao?"

"The very one."

"But she supports a lot of charities."

"For good reason. Most of them funnel money right back into her offshore dummy corporations."

Incredible, Donovan thought. He'd only read positive PR and media about the famous businesswoman. Which proves that media image and social media rule. Pay enough people to say nice things about you – and voila - you are nice. Except that you might be evil.

"Anyway, this morning the Curacao police armed with search warrants and working with our Special Ops team, made several requests to enter her estate. All requests were refused. When her security guards opened fire, we shot back, killing seven of them. One of our guys was wounded, but he'll recover."

"Was Wickstrom there?" Donovan asked.

"Yes."

"She talk?"

"Nope."

"She lawyer-up?"

"Nope. She bottom-upped. She's dead. Ate a cyanide capsule minutes before we got to her."

"So… finding out who else she was involved with will take time."

"We *know* who else."

"You cracked her computer files?"

"Didn't need to. Woman didn't trust computers. Amazingly, she kept a handwritten notebook in a secret drawer beneath her office safe. Contains all the names. Who did what. The notebook is a prosecutor's treasure trove. *Medusa* is enormous."

"Global?"

"Oh yeah. USA, France, Germany, China, Britain, Russia, Italy, Japan, Belgium to name a few. The *Medusa* was a select group of greedy bastards who used shell corporations to buy what looks like thousands of futures contracts and options, calls and puts. All designed to make huge profits based on an unnamed catastrophic event early in June."

"Did they know the event was the assassination of the G8 leaders?"

"No. They were led to believe the event might be the dissolution of the Euro… or a major re-evaluation of the Chinese yuan. Some thought it would be the collapse of the European Union. All they knew was that the event would make them very rich. Which is all these kinds of people need to know."

"So how many *knew* the event was the assassinations of the G8 leaders?"

"At this point, we know of three people. Karlottah Wickstrom, a man named Simon Bennett and, of course, the extremely deceased assassin by the name of Valek Stahl."

"And Wickstrom was behind all this?"

"Yeah. But Bennett set it up and managed everything for her."

"Where's Bennett?"

"In the slammer! We grabbed him trying to board a JFK flight to Venezuela last night. He'll do life without possibility of parole."

"So it was all about big money?"

"Billions big."

"As they say, follow the money… "

"Yeah. We estimate Wickstrom's slice could have personally netted her nearly three billion dollars."

"Jesus… !" Donovan was stunned by the numbers.

"And that three billion added to the billions she already had, might well have made her the richest person in the world. That was her goal according to Simon Bennett. And she wanted to achieve it fast. She was dying of cancer and had months to live. She wanted to go out on top. Money drove the woman."

"Stahl, too?"

"No. Vengeance drove that bastard. He was repaying Israel, Europe and America for killing his family. He wanted revenge."

"So did I," Donovan admitted.

"That's why I wanted you in Brussels."

"I figured as much. One question, boss."

"Sure."

"Why didn't we detect Stahl's explosives in the Elephant Gallery?"

Director Madigan paused as though considering whether he should explain.

"The explosive rocks that Valek Stahl buried in the sandy soil beneath the elephant were covered with Herr Rutten's secret sealant. It uses ozone and nanobot technology that masks the scent of the PETN explosives. Even the most sophisticated sniffers can't detect them."

"Please tell me Herr Rutten's secret sealant formula died with him."

"Wish I could. But I can't. We're searching for his formula in his underground laboratory or in the antique shop. Haven't found it yet. Problem is he may have kept it in his head. In which case it did die with him."

"So what's the answer?"

Director Madigan paused. "Better detection, better sniffers."

"Any technology in the works?"

"Some new high-tech prototypes down at Aberdeen and Fort Detrick are proving successful."

"Sounds promising."

"Yeah, by the way, Maccabee, the president would like to honor your father and Mossad's Benny Ahrens for uncovering *Medusa,* and you for your translation efforts at a private White House ceremony when you return."

"Thank you, Director."

"You're welcome."

They hung up.

An hour later, Donovan and Maccabee boarded an Air Singapore 747. It would fly them to the South Pacific for a two-week honeymoon in Bali.

But Donovan would need to sit and chat with Director Michael Madigan when he returned. The Director's famed CIA Intelligence resources had failed to learn one critical piece of intelligence. Donovan would not be returning to them.

Thanks to a suggestion from the President, Donovan had been offered, and accepted, a position as special advisor to the President, along with a part-time professorship at Georgetown University's School of Foreign Service.

Somewhere over the Pacific Ocean Maccabee whispered in Donovan's ear.

"You worried about changing careers?"

"No, I'm worried about something else."

"What?"

"Changing diapers."

Know anyone who might enjoy reading

G8

If so, just phone AtlasBooks at 1 800 247 6553?
Or log on to AtlasBooks.com
And Order … **G8**

ISBN: 978-0-9846173-0-2
Visa, MasterCard, American Express accepted.

OR

order from MikeBroganBooks.com

Also by Mike Brogan

MADISON'S AVENUE

First, she gets the frightening phone call from her father. Hours later, he'd dead. The police say it's suicide. But Madison McKean suspects murder – because her father, CEO of a large Manhattan ad agency, refused a takeover bid by a ruthless agency conglomerate. Madison inherits his agency – and his enemies. When she and her new friend Kevin zero in on the executive behind her father's death, they soon discover an ex-CIA hitman is zeroing in on them.

MADISON'S AVENUE takes you inside the boardrooms of today's cut-throat, billion dollar corporations – to the white sand beaches of the Caribbean – to the high hopes and low cleavage of the Cannes Ad Festival … a world where some people take the phrase 'bury the competition' literally.

Also by Mike Brogan

DEAD AIR

Dr. Hallie Mara, an attractive young MD, and her friend, Reed Kincaid, learn that someone has singled out many men, women and children to die in ten cities across the U.S. in just a few days.

But because Hallie has no hard proof, the police refuse to investigate.

When Hallie and Reed try to find proof, they unearth something far beyond their worst fears. And as they zero in on the man behind everything, the man zeros in on them. Barely escaping with their lives, they finally convince the police and Federal authorities that a horrific disaster is imminent. But by then there's a big problem: it may be too late.

Midwest Book Review calls DEAD AIR, "a Lord of the Rings of thrillers. One can't turn the pages fast enough."

Available at Amazon.com
ISBN 1-4137-4700-0

Also by Mike Brogan

BUSINESS TO KILL FOR

Business is war. And Luke Tanner is about to be its latest casualty. He's overheard men conspiring to gain control of a billion dollar business using a unique strategy – murder the two CEO's who control the business. The conspirators discover Luke has overheard them and kidnap his girlfriend. He tries to free her, but gets captured himself.

Finally they escape, only to discover that the $1 billion business is his company … and that it may be too late to save his mentor, the CEO. The story takes you from the backstabbing backrooms of a major ad agency to the life-threatening jungles of Mexico's Yucatan.

Writer's Digest gave BUSINESS TO KILL FOR a major award, calling it, "the equal of any thriller read in recent years…"

Available at Amazon.com
or MikeBroganBooks.com
ISBN 0-615-11570-5

About the Author

MIKE BROGAN is the *Writers Digest* award-winning author of BUSINESS TO KILL FOR, a suspense thriller that *WD* called, "… the equal of any thriller read in recent years." He writes about the international world he lived and worked in for many years. His years stationed in Europe gave him a unique perspective on global conflicts. He witnessed hostile terrorist activities first hand and twice escaped bombs that went off within one hundred yards of him and his family. He brings this global experience to his latest novel, *G8*.

Brogan lives in Michigan where he's completing his next novel.

To learn more, visit MikeBroganBooks.com